BEYOND PLUTO

By
JOHN SCOTT CAMPBELL

ARMCHAIR FICTION
PO Box 4369, Medford, Oregon 97504

For more information about Armchair Books and products, visit our website at…

www.armchairfiction.com

Or email us at…

armchairfiction@yahoo.com

WHISKED AWAY TO ANOTHER WORLD!

David Lawrence and his companions set out to find an ancient lost city hidden in the wilds of southern Egypt. After days of trekking through the wildest country imaginable, they discovered a fantastic, miles-long ridge of unbelievable proportions. But what lay beyond that mammoth blockade of earth and stone was far more than just the ruins of an ancient city. What they discovered was a futuristic civilization so advanced that travel between the stars was commonplace. And before they knew it, Lawrence and his fellow explorers found themselves catapulted through the deepest reaches of outer space and dropped into the middle of a massive interplanetary war!

This memorable science fiction classic is a must-read, combining the best of steamy deep-jungle adventure and the nail-biting thrills of interstellar combat.

FOR A COMPLETE SECOND NOVEL, TURN TO PAGE 139

CAST OF CHARACTERS

DAVID LAWRENCE
When this geologist embarked on an expedition to find a lost city, little did he know he would end up a prisoner on a far-off planet.

LORD HANAVAN
A famed archaeologist and a bigwig in London society. He found out how primitive the culture of modern man really was.

PROFESSOR MILROY
His mastery of foreign languages was the one thing that kept an interplanetary war from becoming an interplanetary disaster.

DR. CUMMINGS
He was a geologist by trade, but the lure of an archaeological expedition up the Nile proved to be too great a temptation.

PROFESSOR PFEIFFLER
Though kind and generous by nature, this bespectacled German professor was mistaken for a gun-wielding assassin.

EL ZOIA
As the supreme ruler of Zongainia, he knew all outsiders to his country must be exiled—but to a planet in a distant star system?

VER VERA NADJI
She was the seasoned commander of a Zongainian spaceship— and the lives of six Earth exiles lay in her hands.

CHAPTER ONE
Vacation Interrupted

WHEN Dr. Cummings and I came down the coast from Rasel Milah we were thoroughly ready for a vacation. With the last page of the manuscript, our work, which had kept us over eight months in the highly mineralized and little known mountains of Cyrenaica, was concluded. Cummings, on our first night in Cairo's famous hotel, *The Shepherd*, relaxed comfortably with the remark: "Just think, Lawrence, another fortnight and we will be in London proofreading our text. *Recent Investigations on the Metaphoric Rock Deposits of North Africa*, by G. A. Cummings, F. R. S., M. A., and D. W. Lawrence, M. A. How does that sound?"

The two days spent in Cairo disposing of our equipment and packing specimens passed quickly, and on the third we were ready to leave. Then Fate intervened.

I was in the cigar stand at the hotel when my attention was attracted by two men at the next counter. The taller I at once recognized as Lord Mitchell Hanavan, well known to the archaeological world as the discoverer of the key to the Cretan sherds. His companion, a scholarly and rather preoccupied appearing person, I mentally classified as Prof. Sheridan Milroy, Britain's dean of dead-language scholars.

From the deep brown of their skin they had evidently been up river, engaged in one of their rather dangerous and decidedly dirty excavating expeditions in some royal graveyard. Inwardly congratulating myself upon having chosen the safe and sane profession of geologist, I started toward the lobby when I was halted by hurrying footsteps and Prof. Milroy's voice.

"I say, pardon me, but aren't you the Mr. Lawrence who was working in Cyrenaica?"

I admitted the charge, adding that Dr. Cummings was the senior member of our party. Prof. Milroy seemed delighted. "Excellent, sir, and most fortunate—our meeting here, I mean... And did you visit those ruins on the coast west of El Milah? Remarkable structures, resemble the Scottish dolmens, but Phoenician, undoubtedly Phoenician. I have read that there are

BEYOND PLUTO

By John Scott Campbell

(Illustration by Paul)

Down came the big switch and at the same instant a crackling roar, a curtain of flaming electricity descended before us. We shrank back.

burial vaults that have been sealed since the Third Dynasty. The author I refer to claims that he visited the spot in the Twelfth Century B.C. and that..."

At this instant Lord Hanavan arrived. "My apologies, sir, but Prof. Milroy seems to have taken you by storm." Then to the other, "Wait, my dear Sheridan, give the gentleman a chance to recover himself... Why, there have been no introductions yet."

This vital ceremony over, Hanavan explained that they had both been interested in the coastal regions on the Cyrenaican peninsula for some time, in fact ever since Prof. Milroy had accidentally run onto a travelogue on papyrus in the Louvre.

Of course I had to disappoint them. Our budget was altogether too slim to allow side trips, even in search of worthwhile geological specimens. As I was explaining this and suggesting that they talk to Dr. Cummings, that person himself appeared at the door. Introductions were performed again. After hearing a repetition of our financial excuse, Lord Hanavan remarked: "You know we are geologists ourselves, in a way. Specialize in man-made stones, though. Run up against things lots of times that I fancy you don't find in sedimentary deposits."

"Well," laughed Dr. Cummings, "we find plenty of the bizarre, too, and human relics that were dust before your mummies' great-grandfathers were born. By the way, where have you been excavating? At the Valley of Kings?"

"No, farther up," answered Hanavan, "near Assuan, directly opposite the Island of Philae, in fact. We've been at it some time on a rumor of another temple buried in sediment and sand that rivals Philae itself for size. And, you know, we found things there that Philae doesn't have, I'll wager. But I say, can't you come up to our rooms this evening for a smoke? I can tell you all about it then. Sort of get it off my chest."

As may be guessed, we accepted the invitation with alacrity. Taking Prof. Milroy's arm in a paternal sort of way, Hanavan led the way to the street door, while Cummings and I went on into the lobby.

Dr. Cummings and I were delighted with the opportunity of getting acquainted with the pair. Lord Hanavan was internationally famous among archaeologists for his work in Egypt and

Mesopotamia. His paper on Cretan hieroglyphics is universally regarded as the final word; while the collections of relics he has brought back from his numerous expeditions are unsurpassed.

Prof. Milroy, his colleague, while of the second magnitude when compared to Hanavan, was a first-class anthropologist himself, numbering among his accomplishments a splendid knowledge of dead languages including Greek, Egyptian, Sanskrit, Ancient Persian and Hittite, as well as most of the tongues and dialects of the Orient in use today. His ability at learning foreign languages was uncanny; he seemed to grasp their complications by a kind of instinct, and nothing delighted him more than to study some intricate native *patois*, inventing phonetic spelling and classifying grammar as he went along.

WITH the coming of evening and its attendant calling of the *Muzzeims* from their slender mosque towers, Dr. Cummings and I ascended to Lord Hanavan's and Prof. Milroy's rooms on the floor above. It overlooked, across a narrow garden, the native quarter of the city. One could, in fact, see into the windows of the nearer mud brick buildings.

Sitting down to our iced tea and cigars, Dr. Cummings and I listened with rapt interest to Lord Hanavan's story.

"You see," he began, "all my life I have had a desire to explore the unusual, the mysterious. I suppose that is why I am an archaeologist. In any case, when I heard peculiar native legends concerning a certain spot near the river at Philae, I hastened there at once. Ordinary excavating through sand is bad enough, but water seepage made our pit all but untenable, in spite of the fact that we had pumps working twenty-four hours a day. And then, no sooner did we get started than the natives living nearby became hostile. They tried to set fire to timbers in the shaft and one night we caught two devils with a maul about to wreck the pump housing. After that episode a good watch was kept; either Dr. Milroy or myself sitting up nights in addition to a couple of native sentries.

"At first the job was rather discouraging, what with river seepage and interference by man; but as time went on a number of very interesting things came to light. After having descended about nineteen feet we came upon a layer of flat stones, which turned out later to be the roof of a building. The entire structure was packed full of fine silt which probably helped preserve the contents by stopping oxidation.

"Well, after digging through about eight feet of this, we came upon a layer of rotten wood, crisscrossed by what had once been iron bands but were now only layers of rust. Side digging disclosed that it was a big chest. Inside, mixed with the river mud, we found remnants of papyri rotted beyond all possibility of reading, and a quantity of square platinum coins, stamped with strange characters. The oddest thing—they were milled around the edges like a gold sovereign. You may imagine how excited we were by this time, but as night was coming we decided to wait the morrow before continuing. Just before we climbed out for the day, one of the diggers stumbled against something under the foot of water and mud that covered the floor. Picking it out we discovered it to be a well-preserved baked clay tablet, like the Egyptians used for writing, completely covered with fine hieroglyphics.

"That night there was no sleep for anyone. First we went after the papyri, but they were hopeless—the ink had faded and the sheets of the roll were melted together into a solid cylinder. The coins were better preserved—here..." he dug in his pocket, "are some of them." He handed one to Dr. Cummings and to me and then continued.

"The inscriptions upon them were quite unintelligible even to Dr. Milroy, a thing which caused him much chagrin—eh, Sheridan?" He nudged his companion who looked anything but pleased.

"However, the strangest thing about these coins is their neat modern appearance. Most old coins are a sort of rough oval with the very rudest of characters stamped on their faces. But these were exactly square and bore a finely engraved design, one side of which looked like a bas-relief of the moon, while the other side was covered with very complicated characters unrelated to any known inscriptions. There is no sign of a 'picture writing' influence, for nowhere can we find even the remotest resemblance to natural objects. You can see for yourself how different these are from Egyptian or Phoenician money. And then they are made of platinum—a metal hardly ever used in the ancient world. But enough for the coins. The clay tablet was easier. In fact, Milroy translated at sight, so disgusted was he with the money. Later he made a written translation."

Here Lord Hanavan interrupted his narrative again and handed Dr. Cummings a sheet of paper. He read it aloud:

"Isis speaks and the words of Isis go as a thunderbolt across the world. Though the power of the Roman presses sorely upon the neck of Egypt, and our former greatness is as dust, the Gods of Egypt are not gone—they live and in battle they turn the lightnings upon the legions of their enemies and slay.

"For has it not been said by Has-id, the Priest, who went with our oppressors to the end of the Great River and beyond, until the hands of Horus and Ra stopped them? Did he not return with the news that our Gods and the Kas of our ancestors have returned to the Earth and that far to the South they do repulse the might of Rome and slay her armies even as the desert lion rends the hyena who ventures too near?

"And has Has-id not returned from the South with a great treasure of the white metal that is rarer even than gold, that the impoverished of Egypt may have food? Aye, such is so, and even now, we, the faithful remnant of desecrated Philae, prepare to go up the River to join our Gods. Beware! O might of Rome! And beware, O ye who would venture to the promised land! For the temper of Isis is short and her lightnings smite quickly."

"WELL," exclaimed Cummings as he finished, "this is interesting. What else did you find?"

"Nothing," replied Lord Hanavan. "We didn't go to bed until after one and, of course, forgot all about setting a guard. Next morning we found the pumps smashed and the pit filled with water and half full of mud that had slipped from the sides. That was the last straw. We could not re-dig that shaft for weeks and, as the rainy season was coming, we simply had to give the job up for the year.

"Well, we swore about a bit and then started to pack up, when up the river shore came one of the natives. He was a particularly ugly old fellow named Achmed, who owned a little farm nearby and seemed rather well supplied with money, in contrast to the other poor wretches. After the usual courtesies this person asked us why we were leaving. I knew right away that he was responsible for our damaged pumps. But, you know, there was no evidence, so I controlled my desire for revenge and told him that we had found everything we wanted—including a most important tablet.

"I had expected this would disturb his smug contentment but, by Jove! I never anticipated such a demonstration. He simply went up in smoke and demanded to see the tablet on pain of some terrible doom. But we only laughed and told him he would land in jail if he kept that up. At that he calmed down and said he would bide his time, but when we left we knew there was at least one Egyptian who did not bear us any love.

"Well, we packed up and came down to Cairo—that was three days ago—and now we are resting on our oars, as it were, until we can make further plans. We are going to visit the library here and see if we can locate any other records bearing on that Roman expedition. They have, you know, many papyri which escaped the fire at the Alexandria Library."

Dr. Cummings fingered one of the coins. "You seem to have run right into a real oriental mystery here. I wonder what there is up the river? I suppose—"

At that instant his words were cut short by the crack of a rifle and the splintering of the windowpane. Lord Hanavan jumped to his feet and switched off the light while Prof. Milroy, belying his pacific appearance, drew a wicked-looking automatic and leaped to the window. Outside there was utter silence. No light showed in any of the windows across the court from whence the shot had come. Apparently the noise had passed unnoticed.

There was a moment of silence in the room. Then Lord Hanavan whispered: "Achmed! It must be. To think he would go to such extremes…"

As he said this, Dr. Cummings, who was standing near the door, stepped quickly over to Lord Hanavan and whispered to him…

"Someone breathing…outside the door…waiting for you to come out…"

The other nodded. "That's good." He paused and added, "Rotten way to treat you—like this—when you are my guests, but—"

I felt his smile through the darkness. Stepping over to where Cummings and I stood, Hanavan whispered his plan to us.

"I will wrap my coat about a pillow and push it out the door. Then, when whoever is there shows himself, we will both fire." This to Milroy, who nodded silently.

"Then," continued the archeologist, "we will rush him. Have either of you a gun?" Cummings and I shook our heads.

Hanavan went to a drawer. Coming back in a moment he pressed something cold into my hand. "Ancient Nubian dagger," he whispered, "very efficient." He gave something similar to Dr. Cummings.

A moment later he had folded his overcoat about the pillow, placed a hat upon the top and was slowly opening the door.

The hall was faintly lighted from the window at one end. It seemed quite unoccupied when suddenly a bare human arm with a wicked curved knife gripped in the hand, shot down and into the coat. At the same instant Lord Hanavan and Dr. Milroy's guns spoke. Together we leaped into the hall. Halfway down toward the farther end ran a man crouched low and holding one arm against his body. Lord Hanavan shouted at him: "Stop, or we fire!" But the fugitive paid no attention. Then, just as he was at the fire-escape window, Prof. Milroy shot. With a cry of pain the man went down and lay kicking on the floor. We rushed to him where we found that, beyond a shattered wrist and a flesh wound in the calf, he was unhurt.

As we bent over him there came a commotion from behind; the night clerk, a native policeman and a number of guests of the hotel surrounded us. Lord Hanavan explained tersely what had happened. The would-be assassin was taken to the room while an ambulance was sent for. Here Lord Hanavan proceeded to question him.

At first the wretched native would only moan and cry that he was dying. But finally, under Hanavan's insistent quizzing he burst out, "Yes, I will tell. I will speak truth. As Allah is my witness! Here I am dying for that dog Achmed, who is not even a true believer. He was to pay me two pounds to stab whoever came from the door first, after he had shot one of you. But he missed and now I am to pay for it with my life! *Allah! Il' Allah!* Allah is the only God and Mohammed is…"

The ambulance patrol sounded outside. Lord Hanavan shook the native. "Why did Achmed wish to kill us?"

"Because you have that Tablet," cried the man on the bed. "I myself do not know what it means, but it is priceless to him. He is…" He paused and glanced about.

Sensing his thoughts, Hanavan said, "You are beyond his power now. Speak while you can."

Writhing with the pain of his wounds and the fear of the hereafter he replied:

"He is the High Priest. He seeks to receive messages from the Old Gods who walked the Nile Valley many years ago—he is the Priest of Isis."

At this instant the policemen entered the room and shortly afterward they carried the native out on a stretcher, cursing the name of Achmed and crying to Allah for mercy.

CHAPTER TWO
Up the River

I DO not think any of us slept the rest of that night. We sat in Hanavan's room until near dawn, consuming innumerable cigars and trying to figure out just what it was all about. Hanavan, who was most experienced in Oriental ways of thinking, was of the opinion that we had simply crossed with some obscure religious sect. But the peculiar tablets, and the still more peculiar coins hinted at something deeper.

Finally, after many hours of fruitless discussion, Dr. Cummings and I returned downstairs to our own rooms, where we spent the rest of the night talking to each other and thinking to ourselves.

About ten the next morning we received a note from Lord Hanavan stating that he was going to the library and wished our company. Rather glad to continue with this mystery we sent word that we would be down at once. Ten minutes later in a cab, we were *en route.*

Conversation languished until we had arrived at our destination. There was really nothing to say until we had more definite information.

At the library Lord Hanavan's name was sufficient to gain us entrance to the innermost vault. And, as it turned out, it was just the place that we wanted to go. The Curator escorted us through the reading rooms, then down into the binding rooms in the basement, past rows of dust-laden mummy cases and unopened papyri, and then down again into the little-used sub-basement where the Alexandrian papyri were stored. It was a musty place, fairly exuding the odor of centuries. The Curator left his lamp and returned to the upper floors. We were alone with the past.

Prof. Milroy was in his element. Passing down the long shelves of cylindrical papyrus cases, he dusted off and read the name on each. At last he stopped with an exclamation of pleasure, and opened a crinkly roll. It was inscribed in Latin, which Prof. Milroy read as easily as English. After a moment he replaced it in its receptacle saying, "The expense account of one of the Roman Satraps' hunting parties in Nubia... Ah, this looks interesting, 'Report of the Expedition under Julius Marcus to the land of Punt.'"

After reading several pages he replaced the roll. "Nothing here." He scanned the next roll and similarly replaced it. Then his eyes lighted upon something of interest. Unrolling the crackling paper he read silently; then his face lit up.

"This is it—as I live and breathe, we have before us the very thing..."

Holding it before the lamp he read:

"After ascending to the headwaters of the River Soaht from the Nile we entered into a country of many people, including Egyptians who have fled from Roman justice. Living with them was a strange race believed to be immortal. But this was not so, for we killed many in battle. But, by the grace of an evil god who prevailed against us in this far land, we were driven back and attacked by a wondrous sort of Greek fire, which shattered all near it as a thunderbolt. And so failing to receive aid from the noble Satrap, we retired down the Soaht unto the Nile and thence into Egypt. It is recommended that a stronger force be sent to this land to conquer it for they are rich in gold and jewels and the rare white metal from the North..."

He paused. "This is the very thing, Mitchell. We have it!" This to Lord Hanavan. "Soaht...Soaht... What river is that, I wonder? I seem to have heard of it before..." He folded up the roll; his brows puckered in thought. Then:

"Ah! I have it. It means the Sobat River...a tributary of the Nile that enters well below the tenth degree, as far south as Addis Ababa if I am not mistaken. Well, Mitchell, here is our little mystery all solved. A camp of Egyptians fled from 'Roman justice.' I'll wager there'll be something there for an archaeologist." He rubbed his hands together. Lord Hanavan, taking the roll, replaced it. "Yes, that explains everything," he said, "except the writing on the coins. It is not Egyptian."

We made our way up from the sub-basement in silence. As we passed through the relic-filled stack room, Prof. Milroy stopped a moment to examine a particularly ghastly mummy, when Lord Hanavan seized his arm and pointed down a long aisle where the shadows were darkest. "Something...moved...there," he whispered.

Prof. Milroy drew his ever-present automatic. Leaving the lamp on the table we slunk into the shadow and waited. After a moment there came down the dark aisle between the book stacks a muffled shuffling sound. For an eternity, it seemed that sound approached, and presently I thought I detected a faint breathing. I felt the hair rising on my head and a weird tingling go up my spine. The others waited...breathless... Dr. Cummings was holding a white club-like object he had seized from the table as he passed. Second by second the shuffling came nearer. It was evidently in the next aisle from us. Stooping, Lord Hanavan peered between the rows of books on a shelf, but evidently he saw nothing. Finally the footsteps were opposite us; then they stopped. Silence, which was both tangible and horrible, set in. The beating of my heart seemed like a pile driver in the place. Not the faintest echo came from the streets above. I saw that Lord Hanavan was edging toward the end of the case where he could look down the next aisle. Dr. Cummings, Milroy and I followed, and now I observed, with a sort of horrible fascination, that the geologist grasped a human thighbone in his hand.

FINALLY Hanavan reached the end of the bookcase where he slowly extended himself around. Milroy waited, his fingers becoming white as he grasped the gun. Then, like lightning, Hanavan swung his own gun up and shouted, "Throw up your hands—I have you covered!" I commenced to run toward him, when from the next aisle there came a clatter of falling objects and a voice.

"*Was ist das?* Don't shood mit dot! Id might go off!"

Hanavan lowered his gun in amazement, and the next instant a stout, bespectacled gentleman in swallowtail coat and bowler hat appeared.

He at once produced a vast white handkerchief with which he mopped his forehead copiously. "Vot kind uf blace is dis ven beeple come around like highwaymans mit guns?"

The reaction after those few tense moments was great. Milroy, Cummings and I leaned against the shelf, while Hanavan interrogated the newcomer.

"Sorry, old man, really. But we were attacked by an assassin only last night so, of course, hearing steps in what we thought a deserted cellar..."

"Ach vell, den id's all right. Bud you did giff me vun scare. I thoud sure dot I vas going to be killed." He hesitated. "My name is Professor Ludwig Pfeiffler, University of Heidelberg. Und whom have I the pleasure uf meeting?"

Lord Hanavan introduced us all and then suggested that we ascend to the street. While doing this, Prof. Pfeiffler explained his presence in the library.

"In the University," said he, "I hold der chair uf Biology und Physiology. Dis trib is mein first vacation in five years. I travel through France, Italy, Turkey, Palestine, und I haf been spending the last few days here in Cairo before I return home. In der library I am collecting literature on ancient locust plagues. Effen ven I am on a vacation der University oxbects me to do some vork. Und I haff not de heart to disabboint dem. Vell, gendlemens, if I do not seem too curious may I ask aboud yourselves? Und esbecially aboud dot assassin of last night."

By this time we had passed out of the library where Hanavan, after finding that Prof. Pfeiffler had no engagement, suggested that we all return to the hotel for lunch. In the cab he explained all that we knew concerning the mysterious coins and tablet, Achmed's hostility, and the papyrus that we had recently found in the library.

"Vell," said Prof. Pfeiffler when Hanavan had finished, "dot is inderesding, I must say. I subbose you are going to go op de rifer und dry und locade dis blace. My, I vish somding like dot vould habben to me so I could haff a goot reason for extending mein vacation. All mein life I vant to haff at leasd one goot adventure, but so far de most exciting thing I haff done is shoot at katz in de night."

For some time we rode in silence. I noticed that Lord Hanavan was looking at Prof. Pfeiffler as though sizing him up. However, he said nothing at the time, and in a few moments we arrived at our destination. Here Lord Hanavan's first act was to bring from his room a large map of Africa. While we were awaiting our lunch he traced the path of the ancient Roman expedition up the river until he came to the end of the known, the place where the map was a blank, with a single dotted line running across—the surmised course of the upper Sobat. Here he paused, his finger resting on the blank. A space roughly four hundred miles through dense forests to the rolling plains. A place untraveled, avoided by explorers and shunned by the natives.

"It seems odd," mused Hanavan, "that the Egyptians should have gone there when no one else did…"

At this moment the luncheon arrived and for a time conversation ceased. Afterwards, over the ever-present iced tea and cigars, we talked. Prof. Pfeiffler listened. Indeed for some reason we already regarded him as one of us. Lord Hanavan was speaking:

"You know," he began, "this idea of a lost city in the jungles rather intrigues me. It has so many possibilities. I have always wanted to find such a thing. Now, there seems a chance, and a good one, of making a really valuable archeological discovery and at the same time having a little adventure of our own. I am in favor of going up the Nile, on to the headwaters of the Sobat, and then finding out just what is up there. Milroy and I can be the archeologists; Dr. Cummings and Mr. Lawrence will attend to the geology of the region, and…" he hesitated, "Prof. Pfeiffler, if you can, we will be glad to include an expert biologist to note the flora and fauna. What do I hear, gentlemen? Is it agreed?"

The answering chorus was enough. Once our minds were made up, there was no backtracking. Our conversation turned immediately to planning. What had, but a few moments before, been a group of chance acquaintances was now a united party, all working toward the common goal. Thus strangely does the mind of man rush him into bargains whose results he cannot hope to foresee.

Well, it was done. For better or for worse we must see it through.

ONE who has never had a hand in planning an expedition of exploration cannot conceive of the amount of thought necessary to get even a modest party like ours under way. In the first place, its drain upon the exchequer was tremendous; money seemed to melt into nothing at every meeting, yet we knew that compared to some exploring parties we were very economical. To begin with, it was necessary to buy an almost complete new outfit, for the equipment Lord Hanavan had used at Philae was too heavy to carry on a long trek. Then we had to have food, arms and ammunition, clothing, a portable radio sender and receiver, and a thousand other accessories, small in themselves, but still mounting in the aggregate to many hundreds of pounds.

Lord Hanavan, however, met the financial situation with the same *sang froid* with which he faced other dangers. And so, near the end of the rainy season when the muddy flood of the Nile was beginning to subside, we were ready to start.

Passage for five persons and three tons of equipment was secured on the steamer. Hanavan telegraphed Assuan, the end of the steamer schedule, for a smaller boat to be chartered. Then we were off.

The voyage up the Nile remains in my memory as a period of peace and tranquility between the bustle of preparation and the work and worry of the long trip on the White Nile. Egypt dropped behind us league by league. The broad fertile belt near the Nile Delta narrowed into two parallel strips of irrigated farms, squeezed between the river and the bleak desert hills. On either side bluffs of red or gray rock arose, parched and hot in the day and silvery and mysterious at night. We sat out upon the deck for hours each evening, watching the moonrise and the land slip astern like a procession of ghosts wrapped in a dim mantle of mist.

At last the journey ended. The river was cut off from farther navigation by the long low bulk of the Assuan dam. Here we must push forward on our own.

The boat for which Lord Hanavan had telegraphed awaited us at the quay above the dam. It was a native craft, some twenty-eight feet in length, powered with sails and a somewhat erratic gas engine, and manned by five muscular and sullen Arabs.

Our luggage was immediately transferred to the boat from the steamer and then we disembarked. Lord Hanavan had some business of his own to attend to—getting letters of introduction to the resident Governor at Khartoum in the Sudan; so the four of us after seeing our baggage safely stowed away, proceeded to see the sights.

Assuan is not a particularly interesting place. It is too far up the river to receive any great bulk of tourist traffic, so here was revealed the squalor of the Orient rather than its showy side. The bazaars were filled with unsavory-looking food and crude clothing and brassware, instead of the finely wrought trinkets on display in Cairo. Mingling with the Egyptians and Arabs were many black men—from Ethiopia and the tropic jungles far South. It was as though the first cataract of the Nile marked the boundary, between civilization and savagery. Here our real voyage was to begin.

That night we all slept on the boat; that being the only sure way of knowing that our baggage would not disappear. Ali, the "captain," and his four odorous companions said their prayers and huddled together in the bow. We made ourselves as comfortable as possible in the tiny cabin aft.

Next morning we arose before sunrise, while the mists were still upon the river and the nighttime chill kept the boatmen in huddled torpidity under their blankets. Prodding them into consciousness we all ate a little breakfast and then, starting the engine with two Arabs rowing and Ali at the stern sweep, we pushed off.

The voyage up the Nile to Khartoum was long and uninteresting. There were five rapids to portage over; a task that necessitated the complete unloading of the equipment each time. There were stretches where the current was so swift that the four Arabs had to go ashore with the rope and haul the craft. But Ali, the captain, knew the river. So at last the low mud buildings of Khartoum appeared.

Here Ali was paid off and his boat went shooting down stream to accomplish the return journey in a fifth of the time taken to ascend.

Once ashore, Lord Hanavan and Prof. Milroy went to the Governor's residence with their letter while Cummings, Pfeiffler and I remained with the baggage. The waterfront of Khartoum was as different from that of Assuan as that city was from Cairo. Here the Arabs were in the minority, their place being taken by negroes from the lands to the South. The substantial mud houses of lower Egypt were partly replaced by the characteristic rush-dwellings of the equatorial regions. At Khartoum the Nile forked; its two great tributaries, the Bahr-el-Azrak, or Blue Nile, turning East, while the Bahr-el-Abiad, the White Nile, continued Southwest. It was on this latter stream that our course lay.

CHAPTER THREE
Into the Unknown

WE had been waiting at the quay for perhaps half an hour when Prof. Pfeiffler spoke to me.

"Look over there. Behind close barrels. Vot an awful oxbression!"

I peered where he indicated just in time to see a dark Egyptian face, twisted into an expression of mingled horror and rage, vanish behind a heap of goods. Dr. Cummings, who had seen the apparition too, smiled.

"He doesn't appear to bear us any love, does he? I wonder who he is?"

At this instant Lord Hanavan and Prof. Milroy returned, accompanied by a man whom they introduced as the Governor himself.

The Governor of Khartoum has left the most pleasant impression in my memory. He was so tanned from residence in the tropics that, were if not for his clothing, one might mistake him for an Arab instead of an Englishman. He was much interested in our expedition and contributed some information about our objective.

"When you speak of it, I do seem to recall something about a lost colony of Egyptians. A sort of legend passed around among the blacks here. They talk of a country of enchantment and evil spirits in the South. They placed it rather definitely in the region northwest of Lake Rudolph: a place, by the way, quite unexplored and, from what I hear, a wild mountainous waste where even the savages cannot exist.

"You know, I have heard some of the oddest yarns about the district. When an army plane came up from Assuan some time ago, a lot of the blacks came running to me crying that one of the evil spirits from the South was after them. They speak about moving stars on cloudy nights, and of parties of hunters that ventured over the cliffs that surround the place and never returned."

Lord Hanavan seemed impressed. "I wonder," he asked, "why no white men have gone to find just what basis these rumors have?"

"Oh, there have been expeditions like that," replied the Governor, his face clouding. "Two. Both came through Khartoum. The first was in the summer of '14 a surveying party of eight—they never came back. In 1915 a search party was sent out; they carried a wireless set and we received from them for several weeks, then the messages stopped—we have never heard another word of them. In 1916 the excitement of the war prevented another search party, and after that everyone seems to have just forgotten."

This was rather ominous news, but after our weeks of anticipation all it did was to send a thrill of excitement through us. Lord Hanavan assured the Governor that our radio would send messages each night and if we were overtaken by some unknown danger the outside world would at least know what to prepare for.

Final preparations consisted in procuring three long native canoes, each with four rowers. The Governor's assistance greatly facilitated matters here, with the result that two days later we were being propelled swiftly upstream by twelve muscular and taciturn Ethiopians.

As we continued south, the rocky barren bluffs of the river gave way to tree-covered hills, while far to the southeast the bluish mountains of Ethiopia appeared. Dr. Cummings mentioned the face we had seen at Khartoum to Lord Hanavan. The latter seemed rather perturbed and ordered that two of our rowers should stand guard every night. We proceeded onward thus for some days, when one evening one of the negroes anchoring a canoe some distance downstream to fish, discerned about eight miles below and around a point of land, a campfire. He said it lasted only about twenty minutes, as though whoever was camping did not wish to be conspicuous longer than necessary to cook a meal. As the fire was on the same side of the river that we were, Lord Hanavan ordered an immediate transfer to the other bank. Next morning before proceeding on we returned to our former encampment and found it was well that we had moved. The soft mud was covered with the tracks of sandaled feet.

That night we stayed on an island and Prof. Milroy, a rifle on his knee, sat all night on a mass of brush jutting into the stream. However, he saw nothing but crocodiles.

Four days later we tied up at the little station of Kodok. Sixty miles farther was the mouth of the Sobat River.

Three days after leaving Kodok our sturdy oarsmen turned the prows of the three canoes into the current of the Sobat River. Now indeed we were entering the unknown. White men had been up and down this stream, but upon either bank the jungle was haunted only by savage beasts and the no less savage blacks. We camped on islands whenever we could, and at other times at the extremity of a bar where the boatmen drove herds of crocodiles away to make room for us. Our pursuers did not show themselves, and after one of the canoes had drifted some seven miles down stream with Lord Hanavan watching the shore through his night glasses, we decided that they had given up the chase.

DURING the days we sat under improvised awnings, rifles across our knees, watching the dark jungle slip by. Occasionally we glimpsed forms regarding us from the trees. "Gorillas," said Lord Hanavan.

One hundred and twenty miles up the Sobat was the village of Nasser, where swarming dogs gave us a magnificent ovation from the moment we came into sight. There were no white men in the town, but we were told that at Akobo Post, forty miles up the Pibor River, a tributary of the Sobat, we might find one.

At first there was some argument about deserting the Sobat. Finally, one of the old natives said he remembered that several white men had journeyed up the Sobat many moons ago and that they had turned at the Pibor. That decided us. Two days later we arrived at Akobo Post.

The lone Englishman who resided there remembered the two expeditions distinctly. Their radio was the first he had seen, and he had arranged to keep their heavier equipment until they returned. He had it yet. The Englishmen, he told us, had turned off the Pibor River into a small unnamed stream, which led due south for an unknown distance.

Asked about the peculiar moving stars by Lord Hanavan, the man replied that though he had never seen such he had heard many tales from the natives. Some, he said, swore that they had seen the moonlight reflected from something shiny in the air, like "a big fish."

Well, we rested at Akobo for four days—the guests of the Englishman. Our canoes were given a thorough going-over and the rowers feasted heavily. Then, early in the morning, we started out.

The stream into which the canoes turned was so narrow that the towering trees touched together overhead, making a sort of green tunnel. The banks were, in places, less than thirty feet apart, while through the coffee-colored water we could see crocodiles and many strange and ferocious-appearing fish.

On the first night after leaving Akobo, Prof. Pfeiffler commenced to function as a biologist. We had stopped early, so Pfeiffler—fashioning himself a net of mosquito netting—went down a jungle trail in search of insect life. He had not been gone ten minutes when we were startled on hearing his voice calling lustily for help. Seizing rifles we all rushed down the trail, fully expecting to find our poor friend's mangled remains in the clutches of a lion. However, when we at last came in sight of him, what should we see but the Professor rolling about in the grass, his arms fast around a tiny furry brown creature which had torn his coat to ribbons in its efforts to escape. We pounced upon the animal and tied it, while Prof. Pfeiffler was recovering his feet and breath.

"What is it?" we asked.

"*Ursidae*—a dwarf bear—a most rare specimen..."

Two days later the stream became so shallow that the rowers had to spend half their time overboard. The current had increased considerably and the more open character of the forests warned us that we were nearing the mountains. Finally, around a bend we herd the roar of water, and a few moments later we found the way blocked by a beautiful cascade.

At a word from Lord Hanavan the boats were drawn to shore and we all disembarked. Hanavan, Cummings and two natives climbed at once to the top of the cliffs over which the stream poured. After a half hour they returned with the news that beyond, the land sloped upwards through open woods and grassy glades, and that the river became a mere babbling brook. We had reached the limit of water travel. That night we completely unloaded the canoes and pitched the tent inside a *boma* of thorn bushes. We cooked and ate our supper in silence, and were about to retire when the leader of the blacks appeared from the place where they had been sitting. Saluting, he spoke to Lord Hanavan:

"We," indicating the group around the fire behind him, "want to know what you going to do. Our women are waiting for us in Khartoum."

Hanavan, sensing that there might be some difficulty, replied:

"We are going on south, but we do not ask you to go, if you don't wish to. You can camp here with our supplies and the canoes while we go.

"We will go for five days march and then come back. You wait here fifteen days and then if we do not return, go back and tell the Governor at Khartoum to send aid. Understand?"

The native nodded and bowed again. As he turned to leave us, there suddenly resounded a cry of fright from the other fire. One of the rowers was pointing upward through a rift in the trees and crying in his tongue: "Flying devil! Flying devil!"

Springing to our feet we rushed to where we could see, and there in the sky above we clearly saw a speck of light, like a brilliant star moving swiftly and silently across the heavens.

Lord Hanavan at once seized his glasses and peered at the strange object until it was out of sight. But he discovered nothing. Dr. Cummings suggested it might be a meteor, but it left no luminous trail, and it was going *upwards*.

THE visitation left the blacks in a pitiable state, and it was with great difficulty that Hanavan persuaded them to promise to stay the fifteen days. A little later we set the radio up and around ten p.m. got in touch with Khartoum. Lord Hanavan sent a message for the Governor, telling our location, the character of the land ahead and of the strange sight we had just witnessed. We conversed in code with the operator at Khartoum for some time, and promised to send another message as soon as we returned—ten days hence.

Then, accompanied by the roars and howls of the myriad forms of jungle life about us, we made our beds.

The first glimmering of dawn found the five of us up and packing. We could carry only the most necessary things—rifles, ammunition, blankets, food and cooking utensils, compass and field glasses, a first aid kit and a Sept camera made up our total equipment. Ours was to be a survey trip a dash over the mountains and back to determine further action. At about seven a.m., we tramped away, rifles slung on our backs, leaving the boatmen eating their breakfast of fish and monkey meat over a smudgy fire.

During the course of the day we ascended steadily through a park-like forest of majestic trees. Twice we sighted small deer; a sure sign that we had left the swampy jungle definitely behind. The air became cooler and in the little open prairies We felt breezes. In the evening we camped at the foot of a gigantic tree in whose hollow bole we all huddled. Lord Hanavan's barometer indicated 3,100 feet elevation.

About noon the next day the forest suddenly ended and we found ourselves on the edge of a narrow rocky plain whose other side was bounded by a towering rampart of rock. East and west as far as the eye could reach, this imposing cliff extended; trees occasionally waving over its top, and little cascades spurting out from its surface at intervals. Not a rift, not a crevice could be seen. Dr. Cummings, the geologist, expressed his amazement at such a formation. "It is either a remarkable fault or an immense sill," cried he. "Wait a minute while I photograph it."

Whatever the cliff was geologically, it nevertheless presented to us an impassable barrier. Unless we could find a way of scaling it, the lands to the south would have to remain unexplored. As we had some three and a half days left of our five, Lord Hanavan suggested that we search along its base for a break. Prof. Milroy flipped a coin to decide the way, and then we all turned and marched due west.

All during that day the precipice presented no break. Its base was piled high with great chunks of rock broken off from the top; while the bleached skeletons of animals attested the presence of life above. Lord Hanavan estimated that nowhere was the cliff lower than 800 feet while in many places the crest was a good 1500 feet above us.

As the fourth day drew to a close we had about decided that our quest was hopeless, when Prof. Pfeiffler, with the glasses, discerned a dark streak running up the facade of the rampart.

We hurried on, half expecting to find only an outcropping of dark rock, but arriving abreast of it we found a crevasse scarcely four feet wide extending up and back through the solid rock for an unknown distance. It sloped at an angle of some sixty degrees and led right to the summit. Boulders wedged here and there would make easy the task of climbing. At last, after weeks of delay, fortune favored us. That night, camp was made at the foot of the crack, up which a draft of cold air continually poured, and at daybreak on the fifth day we began the ascent.

Climbing proved much more arduous than we had thought, for the rock, a smooth basalt, made necessary the use of ropes at times. We stopped near noon atop a giant boulder wedged between the walls and ate some lunch. Prof. Pfeiffler at that time discovered a small orange-colored snake in a crevice and almost slid down the shaft in an endeavor to catch it.

We were upon the balcony peering off into space. We were overlooking an enormous amphitheater, miles long and wide.

At one p.m. we started again and at four, exhausted by the labor, we hauled each other out on the top of the cliff.

From our position over a thousand feet above the forest, a wonderful view could be had of the trail northward. Through the evening mists one could make out the silvery ribbon of the Sobat River—more than sixty miles away—winding out of sight. We could see no sign of the boatmen's camp because of the haze and dense foliage.

After a few moments' rest at the top of the "chimney." the five of us turned our faces south again and started on upwards. In the three and a half hours of day that remained, we ascended more than three thousand feet. At last, near sunset, the slope leveled off, and pressing on through the last ranks of trees we came upon the top of the ridge. There we stopped in sheer amazement at the wonder of what was spread before us.

Directly beneath our feet the mountain descended, possibly a thousand feet, to a wide plain covered with mist. And on the other side of this—some forty-five miles from where we were—there reared up the most impressive mountain I have ever seen. A wide base of blue forest-covered foothills pyramided themselves upward through banks of clouds made scarlet by the sun, until the whole mass culminated in a single summit, shimmering white in the sunset, arising majestically to a perfect cone in the still air. After our hot struggles during the day and the weeks of viewing only hemmed-in jungle flats, the sheer beauty of the peak held us spellbound. Dr. Cummings' camera lay unnoticed in its case and even Prof. Pfeiffler was silent. Then, even as we watched, the vast clouds massed themselves together and in a whirl of colored vapors covered the mountain from our sight, leaving only a towering cumulus cloud.

For some minutes we said nothing; then we all distinctly saw a strange thing. At the very foot of the mountain in the midst of the evening mists, there suddenly appeared a number of brilliant specks of light, like sunlight reflected from windows. They shone for a moment and then one by one vanished.

Five minutes later the sun's enlarged disk disappeared behind the western hills and the tropic night set in without warning, blotting all from view.

CHAPTER FOUR
Prisoners!

IN spite of the fact that we were going over our time limit, Lord Hanavan determined to push on to the base of the mountain. In the first dim rays of dawn, when the valley was still covered by a thin blanket of fog, we ate our cold breakfast and started down the mountain. Within a half hour we found a dry creek bed whose bare rocks presented a much better road than the tangled thickets on either side. Once off the mountain summit the more distant view became invisible; indeed, we caught no glimpse of the great peak until we were well into the valley.

For some hours we proceeded down the little canyon without seeming to near the valley. Then, utterly without warning, we came upon the amazing, the unbelievable. The trees that had hemmed in the gulch suddenly ended and a cleared space perhaps a hundred yards wide cut across the creek. But it was not this break in the trees, not even the fact that they were cleanly sawed, that we noticed. It was what was evidently a steel railroad trestle spanning the canyon.

I think we all stopped dead for an instant at the sight. Then Lord Hanavan ran forward to the nearer pier, we following. The column of steel rested upon a massive block of concrete. Beams and braces radiated from it; their joints welded together. The column was triangular and apparently hollow for it resounded when struck.

Lord Hanavan was the first to recover his voice. "A bridge of this sort—here! It can mean only one thing—white men—civilization! A railroad…"

Prof. Pfeiffler interrupted, pointing upwards: "Look! There iss only one rail."

Dr. Cummings pounded on the column, "Look at its construction; those beams would require a foundry to make, and the welds… I never heard of such a thing!"

"Those lights!" cried Prof. Milroy suddenly, "Those moving lights…what connection have they? An airship?"

But at this instant our conversation was cut short by a metallic rumble from above. Turning in common apprehension, we raced for the shelter of the trees and then waited. In a moment it came, the car that ran on the strange track. A long, low steel structure with a pointed prow and many round windows. Underneath were two metal shoes upon which it slid. A cogwheel between the runners revolved rapidly, carrying the machine forward. I caught a glimpse of two men in the front, through the windows, and then it was gone.

For fully five minutes we remained under the trees, too stunned to say a word.

"What kind of a country is this?" gasped Prof. Milroy, "a train...on runners...airships...such a mountain... Are we dreaming?"

Lord Hanavan cut him short. "We are not dreaming. This unknown mountain is easily explained by its perpetual covering of clouds...the airships are only hypothetical. The train...well, let's go on and see what it means."

After listening for the possible return of the car, we scurried across the clearing like scared rabbits, and started down the creek bed.

We had proceeded perhaps three miles when wonder number two presented itself to our eyes. It was in the form of a huge mass of twisted, rusty metal, overgrown by creepers and evidently very old. Roughly it resembled the car we had just seen, for in some of the side plates there were round windows. But there was no track or bridge near, and closer observation showed that it had no sliders underneath, or indeed any sign of traction device. Prof. Milroy said he thought it had fallen from the skies as the trees above showed old scars. The top of the car was neatly cut open as with an acetylene torch, and evidently much had been taken out from inside. But where the contents had been carried, or how, there was not a sign. Up and downstream huge rocks made even foot travel difficult; while the steep, brush-tangled canyon walls were quite impassable.

We did not tarry long at this mysterious wreck, but hurried down towards the valley, which somehow we all felt held the key to the whole situation.

I don't suppose the dry creek bed was more than ten or twelve miles in length at the most, but to us it seemed endless. We proceeded with great caution—a needless thing, as the dense woods were screen enough, but our imaginations were running wide open by this time and every tree was a potential abode for some monster.

About noon the ridges on either side dropped away, and the rocky stream lost itself in an open forest of semitropical trees. We made our way through this more carefully for perhaps an hour and a half, when the forest abruptly ended. Beyond lay broad cultivated fields, roads, buildings, the monorail track, while southward the towering white buildings of a city shone in the sun. We all stopped; but somehow we were not very surprised. The steel trestle had prepared us for such a sight.

Lord Hanavan looked long with his binoculars and then passed them to the rest of us. We each had a look. The city, through the lenses, could be seen quite plainly—a dark mass of residences measuring a good fifteen miles wide lay in the foreground, while beyond arose a series of flat-roofed structures, some with tall spires, which appeared to be of immense height. A slight haze hung over the buildings, and the faint echo of human life reached us.

AFTER some moments we brought our attention to the present again. Lord Hanavan was speaking:

"By Jove!" he exclaimed, "but won't the people back home at the Academy be surprised when they find a place like this in British territory. A forgotten colony of exiled Egyptians, building up a city in the wilderness, unknown to anyone! And, I suppose, forgetting that there is an outside world. What a story! Milroy, old boy, you will have to brush up on your Latin and Greek if we are to talk to them. What a tale we will have to tell when we go back..."

Prof. Milroy interrupted him: "*If* we go back. What became of those other expeditions that came down here years ago and never returned? These people may not be so willing to be discovered."

After some consultation we decided to remain within the forest until nightfall and then make a rush for what appeared to be an orchard some ten miles closer to the city. During the rest of the day we cleaned our rifles, Prof. Milroy wrote in his diary and Cummings, with the camera, climbed to the top of a tree and took several pictures.

After the seemingly endless afternoon was at last over, and the sunset colors were fading from the snowy pinnacle beyond the city, we shouldered our equipment and started across the fields. A half-mile out was a flat-roofed house, which we avoided. Whatever crop was grown in the fields had not yet sprouted, so we soon found ourselves absolutely without shelter. The roads, one of which we crossed, were of some kind of bluish concrete, with gutters at either side and not the slightest trace of the roadside weeds so common in Europe and America. Everywhere we saw signs of the most intense cultivation. Whatever kind of people lived here were evidently cultured. About one a.m. we reached the grove that was our destination. The moon was dark and the presence of occasional clouds made the terrain almost invisible. The city shone with a blaze of light, which could mean only one thing—electricity. Far to the southwest low-hanging clouds glowed as though another city lay in that direction.

Our excitement, which had been growing all the time, was now near a "bursting point." As I pressed close to Dr. Cummings for a moment I felt him shivering, and doubtless I was in the same nervous state. Lord Hanavan was more calm. After examining the trees for a moment he said, "We are in some kind of an orchard."

"Grapefruit," furnished Prof. Pfeiffler, a leaf in his hand. "A grapefruit grove, which is evidently part of a farm. If ve are here ven daylight comes some one will be sure to discofer us. Den…remember the expedition uf 1914. De only vay iss, I tink, to go to de nearest house und either secrede ourselves vere ve can see und overhear de inhabitants, or seize a building und make ids beobles prisoners."

Hanavan nodded and added, "Action in any case is imperative."

Prof. Milroy stared about through the glasses. "I think we might try that building." He pointed.

Picking up our rifles and packs the five of us left the grove and proceeded at a brisk walk toward the city. None spoke. We crossed another smoothly surfaced road and then the outlines of the house loomed before us. It was low and flat-roofed and with what appeared to be an oval dome of glass in the center. The windows, small and high up on the wall, were all dark.

With infinite caution we approached the wall, stepping over the ornamental shrubbery in the front and treading softly on the cement-like walk that led to the door. The modern appearance of everything struck me oddly. Somehow we seemed more like five burglars on a lawn in the United States than a party of explorers stalking the dwelling of a bloodthirsty savage in Africa.

But now Lord Hanavan was at the door. A solid panel of blue color without knob or keyhole. Hanavan's hands slipped over it an instant and then discovered a small countersunk ring. He tugged but the door held. Quitting the porch we essayed a window. Climbing upon Hanavan's back Prof. Milroy poked and pulled, then he signaled to be lowered. "No good. Absolutely burglar proof. Let us try the back." We turned past the front door toward the rear of the house when, without warning, the panel swung open and a blaze of light fell upon us.

A tall man wearing a blue tunic-like garment stepped off the porch, peering at us. He carried a curious little metal instrument in his right hand. Walking toward him, hand on holster, Milroy spoke in Latin.

"We are weary travelers from a far land seeking the hospitality..."

The man appeared suddenly galvanized. He raised the metal device toward us and poured out a torrent of words in some strange language. Lord Hanavan approached him, but the man moved his hand toward him and spoke one or two words in a threatening tone. Hanavan stopped. "He has some kind of a weapon. A gun, maybe." He paused. "Cummings, see if you can get behind him and grab his arm..."

Prof. Milroy now stepped into the circle of radiance beside Lord Hanavan and began to address the man in the blue robe in Egyptian. At the same time Dr. Cummings began to fade out into the shadows. Pfeiffler and I stood motionless, at a loss as to what to do. Several tense moments passed, while Milroy ran on with his conversation. The other appeared nervous and impatient. His attention wandered and twice he started to speak, only to be cut short by Milroy. Then out of the corner of my eye I detected Dr.

Cummings gliding among the shrubs behind the man. Step by step he advanced. With a sort of fascination I noted him gather himself together and then silently rush forward. One hand seized the man's right arm, jerking it downward, while the other closed about his throat stifling any outcry. In a second they were rolling about the lawn, and then Cumming's opponent went limp. The geologist regained his feet. "Is he hurt?" demanded Lord Hanavan.

"No, hasn't any strength at all. He just caved in."

SUDDENLY we became conscious of an imminent danger from the light. Dragging the senseless man after us we entered the house, Hanavan closing the door. There seemed to be no switch to extinguish the floodlights outside.

The interior was dimly lit with a blue-green radiance, which seemed to emanate from the upper part of the building. With Hanavan and Milroy carrying their burden, we entered a large room—the one under the glass dome. It was plainly furnished, the space under the high windows being filled with built-in benches, desks and shelves. The floor was of a soft, yielding substance, like a thick sheet of rubber, and of a dark blue color.

But we had no time to examine details. No sooner had we entered than our prisoner recovered consciousness. We expected a struggle, but the man in the blue robe made none. Prof. Milroy covered him with an automatic and motioned him to arise. Then Lord Hanavan again addressed him in Latin. The man replied—apparently intelligently. Afterwards Hanavan told us what the conversation was about. He had asked the man if he was an Egyptian.

"No...Zongainian," the man in the blue robe had replied.

"How many people live here?"

"Many. You are from Europe?"

"Yes." Hanavan replied, trying to conceal his amazement. "We have come to deliver an important message to your king."

At this the one in the blue robe laughed. And then, apparently overcome by a dizziness caused by Hanavan's attack, staggered, barely catching himself upon the wall. He remained there for a moment, leaning upon one of the panels, and then walked toward us. Addressing Lord Hanavan, he spoke in a clear loud voice:

"People from Europe, explorers from the outer world who have made me a prisoner, listen to Ver Vilot. It has been many years since any of your race has penetrated through the jungles over the great barrier cliffs to Zongainia. They who enter Zongainia cannot leave, for if they did the whole outer world would enter our happy land. The curious, the dishonest, the diseased—and soon our cities would be desolate, our culture destroyed and our beautiful country as wretched as Europe itself.

"For twenty centuries we have lived isolated and happy, protected by the barriers of nature and our own vigilance. Once we did have commerce with your people. Persians, Egyptians, and Phoenicians rubbed shoulders in our cities. But they brought vice and corruption and El Zoia forbade their coming anymore. So the highways to the sea were permanently closed; a river was diverted to turn the only route to Zongainia into a swamp, and the men of the outer world remembered it only as a legend called—I think in Europe—Ophir."

He paused and appeared to listen. Then he broke out afresh in a very loud voice. "Men of the outer world, you have penetrated beyond the forbidden barriers. You have passed the point where you may return. You have made me prisoner." Again he hesitated. "But soon it will be different and you will be..."

He stopped, and at that instant the door burst open and a dozen men attired in short robes and carrying the little metal weapons rushed into the room. We grabbed at our guns but there was no chance. In a moment they had surrounded us and with a surprising thoroughness stripped us of guns and knives.

The man who had, but a moment before, been in our power addressed a few words to the leader of the newcomers, who nodded in answer. We looked to Prof. Milroy for a translation, but he only shook his head. Then the one called Ver Vilot walked to the door while our captors indicated that we should do likewise. Outside were perhaps a score more men, standing in front of a large boat-like metallic structure, which had not been there before. Sounds of conversation stopped as we appeared; they crowded forward to view us. Near the door we paused for a moment while "Blue Robe" and the leader of the new party conversed a moment.

When Lord Hanavan called "Ver Vilot," that person instantly turned toward him.

"What are they going to do with us?"

"You are going…to Andorks."

"Then…"

"You will find out." He turned away.

"One thing more," Hanavan called after him, "how did you summon these people?"

The other paused, and then stumbling on the unusual use of the ancient Latin tongue said, "The long-distance talk-by-lightning device on the wall. I turned it on when I seemed to be faint…"

The next instant our captors shoved us toward the metal car where a doorway gaped. All of us—including our captors—marched into it. Ver Vilot disappeared among the other figures, and then with a sickening rush the cylinder shot up into the night sky and the earth dropped out of sight below.

CHAPTER FIVE
At Andorks

THE disappearance of the earth as our captors' strange airship arose into the midnight sky, marked a dividing point in our adventures. Heretofore we had made our way forward against natural obstacles, progressing through our own efforts. But now we were in the hands of Fate, as it were, and our actions were almost altogether directed by others. But I digress.

For perhaps fifteen minutes the airship—I continue to call it that, although subsequent experiences showed it to be utterly different from what we ordinarily consider such—shot dizzily through the sky at a high velocity. Our captors, who numbered about twenty, spoke no word to us. They sat in seats around the sides of the cabin and talked among themselves. We stood, or rather huddled in one corner, not even daring to look out the portholes. The cabin was quite dark, save for a dim glow over what were evidently navigating instruments.

After a quarter of an hour or thereabouts the ship began to drop earthward like a plummet. There was no gliding about it. Our bodies literally arose from the floor as the car fell from under us. I seized Prof. Pfeiffler desperately and then the machine came to a stop. Tumbling in a heap on the floor we lay for some moments afraid to move lest we find all our limbs shattered. However, the Zongainians did not seem inconvenienced, for they arose and, helping my companions and myself to our feet quite kindly, filed out of the now open door. We followed.

The airship rested upon a series of metal rods and rollers, on what appeared to be a large paved field. A pair of floodlights at some distance threw everything into sharp relief, making long grotesque shadows. A pulsating rumble like a vast buried machine was faintly audible.

Still surrounded by the Zongainians, we were marched across the illuminated area under the lights and along one side of a wall. From the other side of this came an odd confusion of sounds, thumpings, musical gong-like tones and a prolonged hissing, not unlike the noise made by certain kinds of automobile tires on a wet pavement.

Suddenly we came to a stairs. Feeling clumsily in the dark we ascended to the top of the wall. Involuntarily I looked over and then recoiled. We were on the roof of a gigantic building, of which the "wall" was but the cornice. Down, down the eye dropped into a canyon-like street whose bottom was lost in a maze of moving lights and a confusion of strange shapes. On the other side loomed the facade of another building, its thousands of windows glowing with a pearly light.

I looked downward again and then the guard behind gave me a shove and I was forced to stumble down another stairs. My head whirling with the brief glimpse into that glowing immensity I walked mechanically down a ramp underneath the roof level and shortly after entered a lighted hallway. It was bare of carpet or other ornamentation. The illumination of a soft bluish-white color emanated from behind the moldings. I heard Lord Hanavan murmur something about "a Geissler tube."

Fifty feet down the hall we were halted. In one wall was a round opening some four feet across and about a yard from the floor. On a rack to one side hung a number of metal objects, somewhat like overgrown plasterers' trowels. Taking one of these, the leader of the party fitted its blade into a groove in the bottom of the hole and leaping lightly astride of it, vanished. Without a word the other did the same. I stepped nearer, peering. It was like one of those package chutes used in department stores; highly polished, egg-shaped in cross-section and dropping down at an angle of 70 degrees. A narrow groove lay in its bottom. Involuntarily I drew back, when one of the Zongainians grabbed my arm and putting one of the "trowels" in my hand shoved me towards the orifice. I struggled. "No," I cried, "No, no…I can't!"

The man seemed surprised and started to explain. Shoving the blade of the thing into the slot, with the aid of another, he forced me to sit on the lip of the chute, feet pointing downward, and grasping the handle between my legs. Making a gesture illustrative of hanging on, the Zongainian gave a push and off I went.

For ten seconds I experienced as real a terror as I ever hope to feel in this life. Down I shot at an incredible velocity, clinging desperately to the handle of the guide. All was black, and the wind whistled past effectively preventing any outcry. I rocked dizzily back and forth and finally turned completely around and rushed down headfirst.

Then suddenly I shot out of the tube, near the ceiling of a vast lighted room…dropped down a long trough and, as the guider began to slow down because of some automatic braking force, I let go completely and slid across a flat table into the arms of a dozen Zongainians. Not even bothering to pick me up, they hauled me from the slide. They were not a moment too soon, for the next instant Prof. Pfeiffler came out of the hole in the ceiling, down the chute and squarely into the "reception committee," which he knocked to the floor with the violence of his impact. Twenty feet behind came the handle of the guider. Pitching my poor friend out of the danger zone they gathered themselves for the next arrival. It was Lord Hanavan, who, with drawn and pallid features, clung manfully to the handle of the guide and consequently decelerated smoothly within fifteen feet of the end of the slide. Cummings and Prof. Milroy came next, both sliding freely many feet in advance of the guide.

AS soon as they were safely picked up by the "reception committee," who suffered many black and blue spots, the remainder of our party descended, gripping the guides easily, and stopping with an enviable grace. It was our first experience with the Zongainian chutes that, so we found, were used universally for descending in the big buildings.

The chamber in which the chute ended was roughly sixty feet square and half as high. Perhaps twenty doors opened onto it from all four sides and, in and out of these, people were constantly passing. By the side of each door was a shiny black panel, covered with rows of lettering in white—a lettering, which I quickly recognized to be similar to that of the platinum coins.

The floor was of the same dark blue yielding substance that we had found in the house. Walls and ceilings were of polished metal plates, inlaid with black enamel in a remarkably beautiful geometric design.

We had, however, little time to examine the architectural beauties of the place, for our captors hurriedly escorted us through one of the doors and down a long passage. Once or twice we passed people—tall, slender men and women, dressed alike in a short tunic, and wearing flexible sandals. Many of them turned and stared at us, but at a word from one of our party, they laughed and went on their way. Prof. Milroy listened intently to everything that was said and he told us that he caught many words related to Latin, Persian and Egyptian.

"But the grammar," he confided in a whisper, "the grammar is beyond me—absolutely beyond me."

During this time we were conducted along a series of passages more or less filled with people, until finally we arrived at a place very suggestive of the booking office of a prison. A man, dressed in a blue tunic with a light orange cape over his shoulders, sat behind a counter made of what appeared to be a hard, blue granite-type substance. Several complicated instruments were arranged before him to which he gave much attention.

Upon our arrival, however, he arose to his feet and addressed the leader of the party in an excited voice. That person responded at some length making frequent gestures toward us and using the words, "Europe, England, Deutschland." When he was done the other addressed us in Latin.

"I am sorry that you made the mistake of coming here. We of Zongainia wish to remain unknown, so it becomes necessary—unfortunately necessary—to confine by force all who cross our borders. You will not be ill treated, but for the best interests of the country you will not be allowed to return. Have you anything you wish to say?"

The last phrase sounded unpleasantly like the words spoken to a condemned man before sentence is passed. Lord Hanavan now took our case as spokesman.

"Yes, I have a great deal to say. We are a scientific expedition, exploring for the interests of civilization. We cannot understand your desire for seclusion, your country would be benefitted immensely by commerce with the civilized countries of the world. You must still imagine that Roman legions hold mankind in subjection. The world has changed a great deal since that day. People outside of Zongainia fly through the air, they have conquered the oceans, the poles..."

The man in the cape interrupted him. "A list of the virtues of your race is unnecessary. If you wish to say anything relative to your confinement here..."

"Well," replied Lord Hanavan with dignity, "all I can do is to protest against the uncivilized manner in which we have been seized and imprisoned for no offense save that of unwittingly entering your country."

"I wonder," said the other musingly, "what punishment your country metes out to housebreakers? If you feel disposed to argue the case you will have ample opportunity to do so when El Zoia sees you, as he doubtless will. As for now..."

He relapsed into his native tongue, evidently giving some sort of instructions. A few moments later we were escorted out by another door, up a ramp and into a small room where we were bidden goodnight.

The instant the door had closed we all began to search for some way out, but the place was foolproof against us. Save for the door the walls were unbroken by any aperture. Their surfaces of a bronze sheet metal sounded solid when pounded. A number of built-in benches, upholstered with a thick rubbery mat of dark blue, constituted the furniture. Illumination came from a single, long, glowing glass tube in a groove above the molding. After much wall tapping, Prof. Pfeiffler located a stream of warm air entering from a number of small openings hidden in a design near the floor. At least we would not suffocate. But there our search ended. Sitting in a dejected group on the benches in the corner, we eyed one another.

"Well, here is the end of this expedition," remarked Prof. Milroy finally. "Tomorrow our bearers may start back with the same old story, 'walked off into the jungle and never came back.' Just like the expedition of 1914... I wonder where they are?"

"EITHER here...or dead," replied Hanavan. "I suppose they will send out a search party."

"Maybe. But if they do find the crevasse up the cliff, they will be captured as soon as they arrive. It is against human nature to turn back after only a sight of a land like this."

"But," interposed Lord Hanavan in a more cheerful tone, "don't you think it is worth the little inconvenience to find a country like this Zongainia? It is the archaeological find of the age! Even if we never escape we will finish our lives in such a place as man never dreamed existed. Did you see that street and the airship? I believe they are ahead of us in some respects."

"I neffer saw buildings like dot oudside of Noo York," added Pfeiffler, "und dot slide!" He shuddered. "I wonder how long dis coundry hass been here?"

"Since Roman times at least, two thousand years—maybe three...can't tell," murmured Hanavan. "I say," he yawned, "did you notice if that airship had wings? Folded up...perhaps..."

There was a pause. I felt very drowsy. Somehow our conversation seemed to run out although there was plenty to talk about. I observed with a sort of mild surprise that Prof. Pfeiffler was slumped backward, snoring.

"Who is this 'El Zoia' they were talking about? A king or something?" I yawned... "Feeling sleepy..."

"I wonder what the population is..." started Dr. Cummings, and then I slipped backward onto the couch. For an instant my eyes remained open; I glimpsed Hanavan rubbing his eyes hard and

Milroy leaning heavily on Prof. Pfeiffler, and then the world went black. I sank into a deep and dreamless slumber.

Consciousness returned to me through the violent shaking of my person by Dr. Cummings.

"Wake up!" he cried, "It's morning."

"Is it?" I replied sleepily, looking about. The room was exactly as it had been before, the soft glow of the Geissler tubes filling it.

"It is eight-thirty, if our watches are correct," added Lord Hanavan. "We must have been drugged last night through the ventilator."

Milroy commenced to speak when, without warning, the door opened and three men entered. Two carried covered dishes.

"Be ready to leave within one-fourth of an hour," said one of them. Leaving the dishes they departed.

"Breakfast," announced Cummings, looking into a covered platter.

The meal consisted of a sort of jelly tasting somewhat like bouillon, and a cold liquid with an invigorating effect whose flavor resembled that of sauerkraut juice. However odd the food was, we fell to and by the time the quarter-hour was up were ready for whatever was to come.

At precisely the fifteenth minute the door opened and we were bidden to march. We were escorted through the office where we had been the night before, into an elevator, which ascended a great distance, and finally out onto the roof again.

By day the city was an imposing sight. Great flat-roofed buildings covering many acres each and rising sixty stories from the ground, stretched miles in every direction. Tall trees grew on the roofs, and we could see people walking about on shaded lawns.

On top of our building there were no roof gardens. The space was taken by a number of great steel cradles like the ways of a shipyard. In one of these rested the airship of last night; by daylight we could examine it more closely.

Imagine a submarine without the conning tower, some eighty feet long. Imagine it lined with portholes and with big square windows in front—of a light grayish color and with stout runners underneath—and you have a picture of a Zongainian airship or *prolo*, as they are called there. Of wings or propellers we saw not a sign; their method of propulsion is based upon an entirely different principle, that of the little known action of high frequency current upon certain kinds of crystals.

Later we were to learn much more about these wonderful *prolos*, but just now time pressed—at least it pressed our conductors for they hustled us into the open door of the craft at once, followed us in and made it fast.

One took his place in a seat at the front windows, made a number of adjustments with dials and levers, and the next instant we silently left the steel ways and sailed into the morning air.

If the city had been impressive from the ground it was marvelous from above. Through the crystal-clear atmosphere we could see its streets extending mile after mile, up to the very foot of the mountain now hidden in mist. To the north the range we had crossed yesterday blocked the view, but southwest another wonder was unfolding itself.

As we arose I glimpsed over a buttress of the mountain, a wide expanse of blue water, a lake, and on its west edge directly opposite the peak another city.

But such a city! Seen through the haze of some seventy miles we did not at first grasp its full immensity. We could not realize that that dark mass of buildings extended thirty miles along the lake. Even more amazing were the buildings in the center of the city—how could we know that their spires soared a half mile into the sky!

CHAPTER SIX
An Astonishing Fact

NUDGING one of the crew I pointed in mute questioning at the vast scene now lying eight thousand feet below. His eyes lighted with something like pride and he replied, "Imperium."

For some twenty minutes the flying machine steadily approached the city. It did not descend at all until almost directly above the first ranks of tall buildings. Then with a hair-raising swoop the car shot vertically downward. Our destination seemed to be an immense tower rising far above the other roofs into the air.

For miles in every direction the ground was covered with giant buildings, separated by long glass roofs like a green house. Under these, as we learned later, lay the streets. Beyond the "business section," straight avenues radiated in all directions, lined with smaller houses whose individual construction could not be discerned. In the aggregate they suggested a green plain strewn with colored pebbles.

But now our descent brought the tower and its surroundings to the center of attention. It was situated on a wide half-circle of park, possibly a half-mile across and about two miles from the lake. The tower was of an almost pure white stone, artificial we found, whose top ended in a series of green rounded domes and roofs.

To the very tip of this structure went the *prolo*. What appeared to be the end of a spire turned out to be a roof space, roughly a hundred feet square and partly occupied by another of the landing ways. The airship landed without a thump and the next instant we were all piling out. A dozen or so people hurried out from the enclosed upper end of a ramp to greet us, or rather to greet our captors. Much conversation ensued, plainly about us, for many looks and gestures were made in our direction. Prof. Milroy listened intently and in the pause before we were taken down into the building gave a report on what he understood.

"I could almost believe," said he, "that they speak two languages. Part of the time I can follow quite well, and then they will break into a patois, which has not a familiar word. But here is what they just said: Our escort wants to know 'Is El Zoia here.' Answer, 'Yes.' 'He has been told?' About us, I suppose. 'Yes.' And he will do something to us this afternoon. Used a verb I couldn't get. All the rest was a curious mixture of Latin and other tongues. Then our escort wanted to know where we were to be kept. 'Here until they have seen El Zoia—then take them to the Kont-se-el-Heligz,' whatever that may be, 'until further orders.' So unless the Kont-se-el-Heligz is the morgue we seem to have no cause for worry."

At this juncture further conversation was stopped by the Zongainians who, by various gestures and words in their tongue, indicated that we were to go below.

The interior of the immense tower was quite similar to the various apartments and halls we had been through. I looked forward with a quaking sensation to another chute, and resolved to die rather than descend the immense distance to the earth.

However, though we passed a number of these ominous round apertures in the walls, nothing more dangerous occurred than the descent of about four floors by gently sloping ramps.*

At the bottom of the last incline we were led under a wide arch, and through a sort of reception hall to another high-ceilinged room. Here a man behind a dark blue counter was addressed, whereupon he turned to an instrument and spoke at some length. Prof. Milroy listened but appeared, by his general expression, to comprehend little.

Our guide listened respectfully and then ordered us to the sidewall, where a low bench lay beneath the windows. Seating ourselves we waited. Milroy, without being asked, translated for us.

"He—the one who brought us—wants to know if somebody called 'Ver Menisto' is occupied. The gentleman at the desk, who, so I gather, is a kind of secretary, telephones
in that other dialect and then tells our friend to some length of time. He said 'a deck'—whatever that may be."

Lord Hanavan occupied himself in staring out of a window. We had a marvelous view towards the east of the lake. Some forty-five miles away the mountain uprose on its farther shore. Through rifts in the clouds I could make out buildings of no mean size upon their flanks. The near view was obstructed by the wide sill of the window. Down by the lakeshore the ranks of skyscrapers made a solid cliff overlooking a long park.

Dr. Cummings, glancing nervously about, unslung his camera that he had been allowed to keep after the search for weapons.

"I wonder," he murmured, "if they would object..." He started to sight through the finder when we were startled a deep melodious voice speaking *English!*

"Don't waste films on that, I will give you a photograph."

* As we afterwards discovered, the stairway is hardly ever found in Zongainia.

BEYOND PLUTO

BY JOHN SCOTT CAMPBELL

And such creatures they were. Looking at them one had a sensation of flabby bonelessness.

Illustrated by
Frank R. Paul

TURNING toward the voice, we beheld, standing in the now open door to the inner room, a tall dark-haired man in a brilliant blue cape. Amazed as we were by his command of English, I could not fail to note a peculiar distinction, a sort of nobility of appearance that set him apart at once from every other person we had seen. His smooth-shaven face had the stamp of character upon it that cannot be described in terms of features. His eyes, of a steely gray, bore the command of an imperator and the understanding of a philosopher. Instinctively I knew that he was

46

the ruler of the country, the El Zoia we had heard mentioned so often. Lord Hanavan and the others must have realized this also, for we all arose to our feet with one accord. For an instant we stood thus. Then our conductor, much embarrassed, addressed himself to the man at the door.

El Zoia listened and then dismissed him. Addressing himself to us he spoke: "Come into the other room." We did so; the door closed of its own accord behind Prof. Pfeiffler, who was last. The other seated himself behind one of the desks and indicated that we do likewise. Then he began:

"May I ask your names, gentlemen?"

He listened quietly to the introductions, saying after they were done, "I have your paper on the Cretan inscriptions, Lord Hanavan. You are to be congratulated upon its accuracy." Then, "Well, gentlemen, you are, I suppose, searching for a trace of the Lloyd-Turnbull Expedition of 1914?"

His manner was so casual, so utterly unbecoming to our position and the adventures we had been through, that it was difficult to think we were not back in some club room in London.

Lord Hanavan, as the spokesman of our party, entered into a detailed account of his discoveries at Philae, the manuscript we had found in Cairo, and the journey up the river. He left out, of course, any mention of the returning bearers.

The man in the blue cape, somehow the title "king" seemed too plebeian for him, listened with great interest until our friend was through. Then he spoke:

"Isn't it too bad that people have such a curiosity complex? If you had written another paper on those coins instead of coming up the river, you might now be back receiving honors at the Royal Society. But, well, you English live on adventure, so perhaps it is well." He paused, leaning back in his chair.

"I suppose you have had something told you about this country—Zongainia. And of course you have drawn plenty of conclusions. I won't enter into our history or anything else concerning the land now save to say that Zongainia has existed here in the state more or less as you see it now, for almost two thousand years. Since that Roman expedition you read about, not a rumor of our country has reached the rest of the world. Natural barriers augmented by our own construction have for eighteen centuries prevented traders and explorers from carrying tales. We keep track of things outside. Of course," he paused, "one of the most fashionable men-about-London is our Ambassador to England. He sends newspapers weekly. All the most interesting books, magazines and music. Everything to keep me up with the world. I…" he smiled, "have been in London several times."

Lord Hanavan put in a question. "We have been told," said he. "that we are not to be allowed to return. Is this true?"

El Zoia shook his head sympathetically. "Unfortunately, it is. Once you enter Zongainia the policy of our country demands that you never leave. The expedition of 1914 and its relief party are both living and well, but they shall never go back. We have one old man, a French explorer who entered Zongainia from the west forty years ago; I talked with him in this room. Another, a Spaniard, who died a decade ago, came up from Lake Rudolph through the swamps in 1868. A well-educated young man, he taught me a great deal of Spanish."

The ruler appeared so genuinely sorry that Lord Hanavan seemed to see some ray of hope. Arising to his feet he cried:

"But why do you want to keep this seclusion? Why must this country remain hidden? These cities inactive? When you could, by a word, have the commerce of all the planet pouring in? You could become a world power! You could share your scientific achievements with the other nations instead of selfishly concealing them. Why do your people hide in this little valley when the whole wide earth would welcome them…"

The man in the blue cape interrupted. He appeared bored, as though reciting an oft-repeated formula.

"Zongainia could not exist that way. If we made ourselves known, Imperium would soon swarm with tourists, with criminals, with sick people. We would become involved in diplomatic squabbles; wars—you forget, Lord Hanavan, that Zongainia lies mostly on 'British soil.' Our money standard is platinum. The cheapness of gold here would precipitate a financial disaster. Our people are not the same as yours. Our food is utterly different. A banquet such as you would sit down to with enjoyment would kill me. Your vice and corruption would seem to us like the filth and squalor of a Bushman family. We have abolished pests; stamped out disease. If your world were turned loose in Zongainia plagues would sweep the land and the city of Imperium would become but a place of mourning." Pausing for an instant he stepped to the window and threw it open.

"You speak of commerce, Lord Hanavan, you speak of the wide horizons of world trade. You deplore our isolation—*look!*"

Crowding forward, we peered skyward to where he pointed. For a moment I was blinded. Then I made out, high in the blue, the shape of a flying machine. At first it seemed tiny but as it dropped I saw rows upon rows of windows, windows whose smallness brought out the craft's huge proportions. Lower it swept, now it paused above the rooftops. Hanavan gave a gasp of awe. "It's—it's a half-mile long!" Gently the immense bulk of the vessel vanished behind the buildings. When it was gone, El Zoia turned to us and said, "That is the *Alf-Nueri*—it is bringing twenty thousand passengers from the star you call Alpha Centauri. You see, we are not very confined."

CHAPTER SEVEN
Exiled!

EVENTS have a habit of coming so fast that one cannot react fully to them until hours later. After our interview with the ruler—his title, so we learned, was "Presonio," meaning first judge—the five of us were conducted to the Kont-se-el-Heligz. It was located, so I believe, in a building removed a mile or so from the great tower. We were conducted thither by an underground pneumatic tube at a great velocity.

I recall an ascent of some length in an elevator and a walk down a long hall, terminating in another living chamber. Our guide said something in Zongainian, closed the door, and we were once again alone. Then our pent-up feelings burst out like a flood.

For fifteen minutes we fired wild unanswered questions at each other. We were completely carried away upon a spate of new ideas and new conceptions. We had come prepared to find a semi-civilized race of exiles living in ignorant isolation. We found—

"It seems," cried Lord Hanavan, "that *we* are the isolated ones! Man, they've solved the problem of interstellar travel—Alpha Centauri! Why they must be having commerce with the whole universe! They are a part of a cosmic league while we are still limited to our own little earthly horizons! To think of finding this in the twentieth century!"

"How long have they been doing it?" interrupted Milroy. "The Romans said nothing about flying ships or moving stars..."

"And the size of this city...Imperium, do they call it? There must be millions living here...scores of millions!" added Cummings.

"Dey have exterminated insects...disease...dey must be subermens," put in Prof. Pfeiffler.

Now our conversation swung to the subject of the man we had so recently talked with. Somehow he seemed to be the center of everything here. The network of streets radiating from his tower; the easily comprehended title El Zoia, apparently unofficial for he was not addressed thus, all pointed to him as the commanding genius at the controls. His personality would have impressed us anywhere, but here it was actually awe-inspiring. Prof. Milroy who had conversed somewhat with our guide on the way, explained that his real name was Ver Zanaos Menisto.

"The 'Ver' part," he added, "seems a sort of title like Esquire or Mister—I was trying to associate it with some Egyptian name roots, but I can't place it at all. I don't believe he is of Egyptian descent even. His frame appears decidedly Nordic, and his gray eyes aren't Roman or Egyptian..." He rambled off as was his habit when against a blank wall. Conversation dragged, repeated itself. Oddly enough no one thought of escaping. I believe that if the walls had been cleft for us to walk out free, we would have remained. Our "curiosity complex" was too strong.

Well, we passed the night and a good part of the next day in the little room. Two meals were brought—of gelatine, a sort of salad made of fruit chopped fine, and the bitter yellow drink. Then along toward night, according to our watches, the door opened to admit two men bearing between them a complicated-looking machine. Another Zongainian, a woman, followed them and proceeded to make some adjustments upon the machine. Then the first two left and the woman addressed us in English.

"I have been sent from the Bureau of Instruction to give you a general plan of our country, its history, and of the universe that surrounds us."

Turning again to the apparatus she started a small motor, put out the lights of the room, and the next instant upon a panel in front of the device a picture, colorful, moving, and stereoscopic, appeared. The lady proceeded to explain in a matter-of-fact voice as the pictures changed, while we five representatives of the outer world sat hunched in the dark and listened like little children.

It is impossible to go into that history in detail for much of it has slipped my mind and it has little bearing upon our subsequent adventures. Little talk was necessary from our instructor. The moving pictures, some of them twelve thousand years old, told the story better than any words.

Many years ago—thousands of years—the moon, satellite of the Earth, had had an atmosphere, seas and rivers, life, people. Its chemical composition, explained the lady, being identical with that of the Earth, produced the same forms of life, while their environment influenced by the same sun and atmosphere, directed the long processes of evolution, even as they were being directed a quarter-million miles away upon the Earth. A great race of men grew upon the moon who called themselves Metyrs.

Their cities of massive stone housed untold millions of people. For centuries they lived in peace and security, enjoying the fruits of a hundred-thousand-year-old culture. But then came disaster. It struck first fifteen thousand years ago in the form of a great swarm of meteors, which pierced the moon's thin atmosphere easily. One entire hemisphere of Metyr was laid waste and nine-tenths of her people killed.

As time passed the survivors gradually built up another civilization—this time on the other side of the planet. But in the year 65 B.C. the moon was shaken by frightful earthquakes. Immense underground caverns containing a partial vacuum were opened and into these the atmosphere commenced to pour. The doomed Metyrs made desperate attempts to save themselves, and in a year managed to send a hundred and twenty thousand people to the Earth in a huge, winged rocket ship, which glided to a safe landing when it touched the Earth's atmosphere.

TWELVE ships left the moon and then fresh earthquakes took the last vestige of air, leaving the planet what it is now, frigid by night and torrid by day.

On the Earth the refugees gathered at a lake in Central Africa where the altitude thinned the air to an amount bearable to their lungs, and there they built up again the culture of their fathers and kept alive the ancient ideals of the Metyrs.

At first the other peoples of the world were courted, but their crudity and barbarism soon turned the cultured Metyrs against them. In the year 50 A.D., a battle was fought in which the Metyrs drove back the legions of Persia and Rome and destroyed the highway to the sea. A river was diverted that its waters might turn the route into an impassable swamp. In the year 91 A.D., a last attempt was made by the Romans to conquer Zongainia, but the use of explosives drove the enemy back.

The Metyrs now set about the immense task of civilizing I the six million Egyptians, Romans and Phoenicians in their midst. It was a task for generations, but the superior culture of the Metyrs ultimately won. The centuries passed; gradually Zongainia grew and gradually the need for commerce with other nations increased. It was then, in the year 1200 A.D., that the first electric flying machines were made, and by their magical agency a market vaster than a thousand worlds was opened up—the Universe.

"And since," concluded our teacher, "you see the results."

We were given opportunity to ask questions after this, and through them we learned a number of other rather astounding facts that our lady had taken so much for granted as to forget. Prof. Milroy's suspicion of a second tongue was confirmed.

"You see," she said, "the Metyrs had a tongue of their own but it was much too complicated for the savage peoples of the Earth, and as a result a second simple language was developed partly from the Metyr, but mostly from Latin and Egyptian. It is this language which has puzzled you so much by its use of familiar words."

In answering a question of Dr. Cummings, she casually mentioned that in the year 1230 (our calendar) El Zoia landed the first spaceship upon the planet Venus.

"What's that?" cried Lord Hanavan. "What do you mean?"

"Why, El Zoia—Ver Zanaos Menisto, of course. You saw him yesterday."

"But 1230—that's over seven hundred years ago—how could…"

Suddenly a light seemed to dawn upon her. She laughed and then explained. "El Zoia is not a Voyian—an Earthman. He is a pureblood Metyr. The life span of a Metyr is much greater than that of one of you. They sometimes live as long as 2500 years—I am four hundred and sixty years old now. We think it was caused by the lesser gravity of the moon, or the admittance of some ray that Voya's—pardon me, the Earth's—atmosphere is too thick to pass. There are many people alive now who were born long before your Christian era began. It is that longevity that has enabled them to assimilate the vast horde of barbarians that was thrown upon them."

"How old," said Lord Hanavan, "is El Zoia?"

"He was two thousand and thirty-three years old on—" she paused as though making some mental computation, "on the first of July—he was born, you see," she added, "in one hundred and two B.C."

After answering a few more questions the young lady, who was four hundred and sixty years old, packed up her machine and went, leaving us to cogitate upon all that we had seen and heard.

With the coming of the next day we were all escorted from our rooms into the presence of a business-like person who spoke English with a peculiar accent—more like an Irish brogue than anything else, and who handled us as impersonally as though we were pieces of freight.

"You are," he informed us, "to be sent to Dunsaan immediately. You will find comforts and fellow-countrymen there. You will leave this evening. In the meantime, you may go to the roof gardens if you wish."

Guards stepped up and before we could put in a word we were in an elevator bound upward. Well, it was a relief to know that we were to see the sunshine again.

The afternoon was spent in a tropical garden with the great city spread about on three sides and the magnificent panorama of lake and mountain on the other. A mile to the north, the white shaft of the tower shot skyward. We attempted to count its floors, but as we all got different results we soon gave it up.

Then we fell to discussing our case and wondering where we were going. For lack of a better explanation, we concluded that Dunsaan must be another city or a prison. We leaned toward the former supposition, mainly because of a repugnance to finishing our days in the latter. We wondered if they had prisons in Zongainia; it seemed so Utopian, so like dreams of the future of our own civilization. Lord Hanavan became reminiscent and compared the splendor of Imperium to London. He seemed much impressed by the absence of smoke or dust...

UPON a suggestion from Cummings, we climbed over the edge of the garden to where the glass roof of the street curved fifty feet upwards. There we spent a fascinated hour watching the traffic, a thousand feet below. With Hanavan's glasses we could make out multitudes of enclosed three-wheeled vehicles, their drivers sitting where the engine is found in autos, whirring along like big distorted insects. Prof. Pfeiffler conducted a careful examination of the cultivated palms and grasses of the garden, furtively pocketing numerous specimens when he thought we were unobserved...

Early in the afternoon we were brought food and drink by an attendant who refused to say a word. We ate in silence... Lord Hanavan and Milroy went off together later to seek a way out, but were soon sent back. Cummings took pictures...

And then, before we knew it, it was sunset. The vapors about the snowy peak parted for a brief fifteen minutes while the perpetual heaps of cumulus turned blood red. It was so like the first sunset we had seen on the mountain... And then with tropical suddenness, it was night. From the glass cover of the avenue there streamed a white luminescence, throwing odd black shadows athwart the garden. Lights glowed here and there upon the mountain's flank, while the white tower, like a condensed constellation, reared into the evening mists.

We were given only a short time to view Imperium by night, however. Attendants came immediately and we were gently but firmly impelled below. Our guides then tried to make us enter another chute, but the frenzied protests of Prof. Pfeiffler, whom they had singled out to go first, deterred them. We descended by an elevator to the pneumatic tube. The guide said nothing, even when Prof. Milroy tried out his version of their tongue. He gave up his efforts when the car stopped and we were conducted to another elevator.

Up again and out onto a long blue-floored corridor.

I had lost all sense of direction by then. The hall along which we walked ended in a wide balcony, which from our brightly lighted position seemed to look out over a black infinity. As we neared it, metallic sounds of clanking and thumping became audible. The next instant we were upon the balcony, peering off into space.

As our eyes became accustomed to the obscurity, we realized what lay before us. We were overlooking an enormous amphitheater, miles long and wide. The floor lay some three hundred feet below, lighted at intervals by flood-lamps, which only served to accentuate the weirdness of the place. On the floor were immense steel frames upon several of which the black forms of resting airships lay. Across, I caught a vague glimpse of derricks working over something. Overhead the stars twinkled brightly; while occasionally passing clouds shone with reflected light from the city.

The next second we were prodded into activity and hurried along the gallery. "Dockyards for their spaceships," murmured Lord Hanavan, "what a place!" From behind I heard a muttered exclamation in German.

A few minutes' walk brought us alongside one of the quiescent monsters. A sort of gangway led to a door in its side, and up this we were escorted. Here it was that the first inkling of the truth flashed upon us. As we stepped into the ship Lord Hanavan seized the Zongainian by the shoulder and said, "Where are you taking us? Where does this ship go?"

"Dunsaan," replied the other, wincing.

"Where is Dunsaan?" cried Hanavan. "Is it—"

"Dunsaan is—planet of—you call Alpha Centauri—all Voyians sent there—please, release my shoulder—" Hanavan's hand dropped.

"We would like to see El Zoia—Ver Menisto." He spoke evenly, as though trying to control himself.

"Very sorry, but El Zoia cannot see you. He is gone to Palata; out of the city. Besides these are his orders."

The man started to descend the gangway. Lord Hanavan paused a moment and then hissed under his breath:

"If we don't make a break now, we never can—knock that one over, Milroy—now!" With this he seized the nearest man by the neck and sent him spinning down the gangplank. Then, with us close at his heels, he started racing toward the balcony. For an instant it seemed that our mad attempt might be successful, for the gallery appeared empty. But before Hanavan was halfway down, a score of men armed with their little guns raced out and pointing these toward us ordered us to halt. Hanavan's rage departed as suddenly as it had come. Stopping, he pivoted and marched stiffly back to the door. We followed in silence. We were defeated.

Once aboard the craft, things proceeded exactly as though nothing unwanted had occurred. We were escorted to a small windowless room and locked in. After a time we heard the faint sound of machinery, and a few moments later a series of gentle jerks. After that the ship might have been resting on solid granite for all the motion it gave; but we knew it was not. We were flying—perhaps already beyond the Earth's atmosphere toward Dunsaan, beyond the solar system.

CHAPTER EIGHT
En Route To Alpha Centauri

FOR more than two hours we remained in our little cell without receiving a word from outside. We listened, hearing nothing, but gradually an odd feeling became apparent. We seemed to be gaining weight. Lord Hanavan reasoned that this might be caused by extreme acceleration in an upward direction; that is to say, toward the roof of the car. We soon found that even sitting up was rather tiring—so we stretched full length upon the couches. At eleven p.m. by Milroy's watch the door to the room suddenly opened and an officer stepped in.

"You may come to the control room," said he in fair English. "Follow me."

Five minutes after, we ascended a short ramp into the "pilot house" of the great spaceship.

The room was of an oval shape with walls and roof of metal-ribbed glass panes. It measured some thirty by twenty feet. Upon the walls and the tables on the floor were dials, levers, and instruments. Outside—

It is beyond the power of man to describe the spectacle that lay beyond the windows. Above, to all sides below, a sky of velvety blackness, blazing with stars of every hue of the rainbow—millions of fiery points of light, hanging magically in a tenuous web-work of nebulae, invisible from Earth. We could fairly feel the immensity we were looking into. I was overcome by dizziness at the thought of the distances below. We appeared to be suspended motionless in the center of infinity. I became conscious that Hanavan was pointing to one side and speaking.

"Look! There... it's Mars!"

It was. Like a small full moon of a bright orange color faintly mottled with dark lines, the planet hung. Even as we watched, it dropped appreciably downward as the space flyer shot up from the sun.

Our conductor was at our elbow. "Soon," he said, "it will commence to show phases like the moon. We are still between it and the sun. Look," he pointed, "down there is Voya."

We peered, expecting to see the hypothetical blue-green disc, but only a thin crescent greeted the eye. We were already far beyond the Earth's orbit. The moon, which lay on the other side of our planet, was quite invisible.

Our guide then proceeded to explain something about the navigation of the ship itself. I fear none of us comprehended much at the time. Later we were to become familiar with these wonderful crafts, but in a much different way.

It seems that the navigation of Zongainian *prolos* across the voids of the Universe is a most complex process. A line is made between two stars, its exact length computed with extreme accuracy, and the ship is directed with a continuous acceleration for just half the distance. The craft is then turned around and after a short "glide" at peal velocity it begins to slow down reaching a speed of zero relative to the destination within a few thousand miles of it.

The amount of acceleration is determined by the distance and is limited by the extra strain it puts upon the human system. If a *prolo*, so we were informed, turned off its power while out in space, everything inside it would be weightless. This, we were told, produces excessive nausea and might result in the death of passengers. So the plan was adopted of letting the acceleration maintain a continual inertia force and consequently an artificial weight. On long trips this acceleration was much increased to save time. The officer said that we would cover the distance to Dunsaan in about eight weeks. "This is a very fast ship," he explained, "it is not a passenger craft, but what you would call a battleship—we have international difficulties here, too." He added, in answer to our questioning looks. "The *prolo* is carrying supplies to the Zongainian dockyards on Dunsaan—you are the only passengers."

"What is our velocity now?" asked Prof. Milroy.

"We have gone, roughly, fifty million miles from Voya," he explained. "This has taken three hours at a mean velocity of about 4,400 miles per second. Since our acceleration is constant the velocity relative to the Earth is now 8,800 miles per second. We are going very slowly now. As soon as Jupiter and the asteroids are passed, the acceleration rate will be great increased. For five or six days the ship will be traveling several times faster than light."

Dr. Cummings looked surprised and asked, "Our physicists have always held that it is impossible to travel faster than light—doesn't one experience some peculiar phenomena at 186,000 miles per second?"

"Possibly your physicists never experimented to prove their theories," replied the officer. "But we do see a number of interesting things. What your scientists called Doppler's effect causes all the stars ahead to become purple and ultimately vanish, while those behind redden into invisibility also. As the *prolo's* velocity from the oncoming light separates the waves, when the *prolo* reaches the speed of light it will be impossible to see anything save in a thin ring at right angles to the direction of light, because the light from in front has been changed to extreme ultra violet as we plunge into it, and the light from behind traveling at the same speed, goes along with the ship.

"Then, as the ship approaches twice the speed of light it begins to catch up on the light from behind and when we cut into it at the right velocity we see ahead of us what really lies behind. It is very like one of your ocean ships cutting into water waves from the windward when it is traveling at full speed. As the velocity increases, however, all light vanishes save for a ring-shaped rainbow around the ship, which becomes thinner as we race faster."

We listened to this explanation comprehending very little. I am not a scientist and so the best I can do is to leave it to some more highly trained mind to discover the reasons. Suffice it to say, however, in the ensuing weeks the very phenomena described by the officer occurred exactly as he had predicted.

The rest of the journey through the solar system was accomplished in some twenty hours. The great outer planets passed us one by one; but in general, after our first surprise, we were rather disappointed. Jupiter was only a tiny, colored disk but Saturn proved more interesting. For hours it loomed in the sky, softly pastel-shaded, surrounded by its delicately spun tracery of rings, which we could see extended much farther out than can be seen through the Earth's atmosphere. Then it dropped downward, changed to a crescent and disappeared. Now the *prolo's* velocity began to increase in earnest. Everyone reclined on padded couches; including the man doing the navigating. A bell rang stridently and then a giant hand seemed to press down upon us crushing our bodies suffocatingly into the cushions. I lifted my arm; it fell back as though made of lead. From his position on a near divan the officer spoke without raising his head.

"You weigh about eight times normal. As soon as it becomes uncomfortable we will slack up a little… Ships don't usually do this, but we are hurried."

We lay still for some twenty minutes, when the deadening weight of inertia was lifted—weighing but twice the normal weight—we were again able to walk about.

At four a.m. by our watches, the *prolo* passed the orbit of Neptune. The solar system now lay below; propelled by its mighty engines, the spaceship shot upward at an ever-increasing velocity.

The Doppler effect was now quite noticeable; the stars and nebulae above glowed violet while the sun, which we were so fast leaving behind, was only a small, ruddy, disk against a background of dim orange stars…

At five a.m. the signal bell announced the hour of sleep. Much fatigued by our increased weight we were led back to the room. The officer gave us all sleeping potions, explaining that as the *prolo* increased its acceleration greatly when everybody was reclining, we must have an artificial agent to sleep with the increased weight.

"We keep no watches," he explained. "At the rest time everyone sleeps—navigation is wholly automatic."

So we drank down our potions and spreading on the couches as directed by the officer, sank into a deep and dreamless slumber, while the spaceship raced across the universe at a hundred thousand miles a second.

Morning, which in the little world of the space flyer came at three p.m., found us far beyond the orbit of Neptune. From the control room where we gathered after breakfast, the sky appeared dead black. The velocity reading when translated into English units indicated a speed of two hundred and seventy thousand miles per second. Our guide, the officer, explained that in an hour or so we would be moving at twice the speed of light and that as we cut into the light from the sun we would behold ahead what the ship was leaving behind.

At lunchtime the navigating crew, numbering some fifteen men and women—the captain of the craft was a woman—computed the path of the flyer and corrected some slight error in direction. The change was exceedingly minute, less than a thousandths of a second of arc, but the lateral jerk caused by our immense forward velocity threw everyone sideways. Shortly after eight p.m. a little less than twenty-four hours after our start, the sky above glowed with the stars we were leaving behind. At first red, they slowly changed through the colors of the spectrum and at one a.m. the next "morning" vanished. For the rest of the trip—so we understood—the heavens would be a solid, intense black, unrelieved by a single star.

At five a.m. we were again put to sleep and the *prolo* increased its acceleration for another ten hours.

Slowly day followed day and week succeeded week. Our velocity gradually mounted into figures beyond all human conception. Each "forenoon," by some method we could not comprehend, the direction of the *prolo* was checked. Then we would eat the weak-flavored jelly and the bitter drink. Our officer friend—his name was Ver Vlygar Moti—would patiently teach us Zongainian. The simpler common language made up of Latin and Egyptian words was easy to understand; but the classic tongue of the ancient Metyrs presented great difficulties. In the first place a good speaking vocabulary required some six hundred thousand words at the least, while educated people had at their command as many as a million and a half. For once in his life Prof. Milroy was up against something. But that person, evidently realizing that the honor of the party was at stake, stuck manfully to the job and before the end of the trip had mastered the grammar and a good hundred and fifty thousand words.

As for the rest of us we did the best we could with the conversational tongue, acquiring by much practice with the crew a fair fluency in its eight thousand common words.

SOMETIMES when he was not on duty, Ver Moti would tell us stories of the universe and its countless worlds. Many of them, he said, were inhabited by weird forms of life utterly different from anything on the earth. He told tales of his marvelous experiences on a Zongainian stellar patrol cruiser; of battles with creatures of the metallic elements; of flights over intelligent animals weighing millions of tons; and of communication with civilized bacteria on great cold worlds of the outer nebulae.

Only on a few planets in all the known universe, he said, lived creatures whose form was generally human. Most were barbaric, but a dozen planets or more were inhabited by peoples with whom trade could be established. To these scattered worlds the far-flung fabric of the Zongainian *prolo* transport system reached.

Near the end of the fourth week the navigating crew announced that we had covered half of the distance to Dunsaan. Everyone became more interested at this and seemed to consider it a special occasion. Upon inquiry Ver Moti explained as follows:

When half a voyage is accomplished the motors are turned off and the *prolo*, turning about, presents its crystal propulsion plates forward. Then after a short time of free "gliding," the motors are turned on, this time slowing the ship. The deceleration takes as long as the acceleration. The period of free gliding, however, was what the crew looked forward to, as everything on board would lose weight. Different people, explained Ver Moti, were affected in various ways. Some become frightfully nauseated; others have fits; while many are wholly unaffected by their weightlessness. Crews are picked for immunity from "gravity-sickness," as *prolos*—by gliding at peak velocity—can cover much distance using a minimum of fuel. Usually our ship glided for an hour or so, when the crew put on a sort of acrobatic circus trying all kinds of tricks of floating.

Late that "afternoon" the captain announced that the motors would be stopped the next day at noon. No one was to breakfast—as a preventive measure.

Next morning, as may well be imagined, we five passengers shared the excitement of the crew for the forthcoming experience. Lord Hanavan, who had read the physiological aspects of the case, hoped that we would not be sickened. We counted the minutes until noon.

The navigating crew worked all morning over their incomprehensible mathematics, gave their verdict, and then the alarm bell rang. The crew stopped everything they were doing—and waited. "It's coming!" cried Ver Moti.

Suddenly I sensed my weight going. It felt like the lifting of burdens from my back...lighter...lighter. And then, without warning, we seemed to be falling. There was no motion of the *prolo* but over my body came that horrible feeling of dropping...down...down...illimitable distances. The nearest approach to it I know is the sudden swoop of a rollercoaster car. But this was continual.

I made a wild leap for a stanchion, when the cabin apparently began turning and twisting around me while I hung suspended in the center of the room. All my internal organs were rising upwards... Then I glimpsed the officer, upside down, his cape floating weirdly above, come drifting toward me. He bumped me with a slight shock and his momentum carried us to the farther wall. There I clung, my feet resting upon the ceiling while the crew, now all assembled in the control room, began going through the strangest performances.

Clothing, inanimate objects, round globules of liquid, all revolved and slipped and drifted back and forth, up and down through the room. After a few moments my brain cleared and, emboldened by Hanavan who was floundering about and having the time of his life, I pushed out.

Through all our subsequent adventures, that first swim without weight remained in my memory as one of the oddest of experiences. It is impossible to describe the sensation of turning head over heels in mid air, colliding with drifting chairs, pieces of clothing, balls of the sour drink made spherical by surface tension, and all of the time filled with that most terrible sense of falling.

We glided for about twenty minutes, then the ship's alarm bells—the ship having been turned about by some more sober member of the crew—sounded again, signaling that weight was about to he resumed. All floundered floorward hastily, and then without warning we became solid material beings again, and decidedly dizzy ones at that. Prof. Milroy and I led each other to the nearest couch where we rested. "Remarkable!...Remarkable!" he kept repeating, rubbing a bruised spot. Prof. Pfeiffler sat heavily across the room, blinking at us in a not wholly displeased manner. Finally he found his voice.

"*Gott im Himmel!* I schver, id's as goot as schnapps!"

CHAPTER NINE
On Dunsaan

HALF of our voyage was now finished; for another four and a half weeks the *prolo* would be slowing down as it raced toward its destination. In spite of the fact that it was likely to he our prison for the rest of our natural lives, we all began to feel a growing curiosity regarding the planet Dunsaan. Accordingly, one morning at four a.m. we gathered to the room of our friend, Ver Vlygar Moti. Here we gleaned considerable information regarding our future home.

Dunsaan, so Ver Moti explained, had a circumference a little short of forty thousand English miles. But its density being somewhat less than that of the Earth, its gravity was only slightly greater. The surface of the planet was going through a geologic age very like that of the earth's early Paleozoic—that is, it was mostly swamp and shallow seas, covered with a profusion of low orders of plant and animal life.

There was a transported population of thirty odd million from the neighboring planet of Duranko, a large sphere inhabited by a somewhat manlike race, and a few hundred Zongainians who maintained a dockyard for battle *prolos*. In addition there were about thirty exiles from Mother Earth, who had had the ill luck to stumble upon Zongainia.

The principal industry was mining under the beds of ooze for the partly decayed bodies of a species of small reptile, much prized by the people of Duranko.

Of course, we were much interested in our fellow prisoners but Ver Moti could offer little data in regard to them. "They are, I think," he said, "in the majority, prospectors, professional elephant hunters; Boers; some have been here thirty years. There are the two exploring expeditions, of course. The Lloyd-Turnbull party of 1914 and the relief expedition. They number, I believe, six...not sure though."

The four weeks passed like centuries. Every day was the same: data collected, corrections made, meals served. Then for us there was movie entertainment—Zongainian dramas of weird adventures. I don't believe we saw a single play that might be termed a love story. Suppers were followed with a half-hour for digestion, which we often spent patching our battered clothing. Then came bed and sleep powders. Every day it was the same thing all over again. Near the end of the time, Ver Moti finally prevailed upon us to throw away the old khakis and wear the loose tunics, the transparent composition sandals, and flowing capes of the crew. We found these surprisingly comfortable.

Well, all things end at last and so did our journey. Once again the stars appeared in the sky, changed color and then remained. But what a difference! The heavens blazed with unknown spheres, while directly below the *prolo* lay Alpha Centauri, a magnificent twin star of orange and green. With some difficulty Ver Moti pointed out a little yellow disk far below. "That," said he, "is Dunsaan." The two suns whose glare illuminated the whole heavens cast strange green and orange lights upon the wall, dimming the Geissler lamps. With a small telescope we could make out the faint markings on the fast approaching planet.

Then observations were suddenly stopped by the ringing of the alarm bell. We were going too fast; deceleration must be increased. I threw myself on the couch just as the iron hand of momentum pressed down. For a few moments my very breath was squeezed out and then the weight was released. This drastic measure secured the necessary result; in a few minutes the *prolo* was flying at the rate of only thirty miles per second just beyond Dunsaan's atmosphere. Prof. Pfeiffler peered down with our glasses, staunching a nosebleed at the same time.

Quite rapidly the surface of the new world slipped below, a wide flat expanse of morass interspersed with shallow lakes and seas. Over all lay a murky haze shutting out the sun's rays like a damp blanket. Finally, an immense city, protected from the swamps by dikes, appeared. In its center we made out the rectangular structure of a *prolo* landing way toward which the chief navigator was piloting the ship. Moment by moment the city rose to meet us until at last, eight weeks and five days after arising from Imperium, Zongainia, the keel of the spaceship touched the steel landing cradle at Dunsaan, planet of Alpha Centauri.

As the last propulsion plate was turned off and the full weight of the *prolo* pressed the hydraulic landing rails deep into their concrete beds, the door was opened and the gangway run out. For a moment air rushed into the spacecraft, a peculiar pungent air, its odor reminiscent of cypress swamps, and then a number of men ran up the ramp to the door. One of them, evidently of some authority, demanded to see the commander. She was at once sent for, while the official waited impatiently in the control room. We five "passengers" made ourselves inconspicuous in a corner and watched. In a few moments Ver Vera Nadji, the commander, entered to be at once fairly leaped upon by the waiting man.

"Thanks to all our ancestors that you are here!" he cried in Zongainian. "We thought that your ship had been caught..." He paused. Vera Nadji seemed astounded.

"Caught?" she repeated. "By whom?"

"You don't know? But then you have been out of touch for sixty-one days... We have our latest information from the Ethero beam transmitter at Waiko...two days ago...the message said that 'all unconvoyed *prolos* are to remain in the fortified dockyard'... It's war, Vera Nadji... If El Zoia has not ordered the battle fleet together already, he will within ten days."

VERA NADJI fell back in horror. "I thought they would settle it peacefully... The Interstellar Commerce Commission was in session..."

The man laughed. "The Interstellar Commerce Commission...Bah! Since Vera Miraza was Presonio it has done nothing but aggravate matters."

The commander of the *prolo* shook her head. "It will be terrible. Zongainia will win, of course. But for us it will mean scores of battleships destroyed; thousands killed. For them, a planet ravaged, a whole race wiped out. They are idiots, Ver Muot!"

The official nodded. "Do you suppose they will come here?"

Vera Nadji shrugged. "Perhaps. But you have batteries, Ver Muot. And you also have battle *prolos*. So what if they do?"

Ver Muot shivered, replying, "I am more interested in being commandant of a repair station, than a dead hero on a wrecked *prolo*."

The woman laughed, and then turning suddenly toward us cried: "Ah! yes, Ver Muot—and I have more colonists for your 'Discontented Club' here," she beckoned him after her. "May I present Lord Mitchell Hanavan of England; Prof. Sheridan Milroy of the same country; Dr. G. A. Cummings, America; Prof. Herman Pfeiffler, Deutschland; and David Lawrence, America."

We all bowed and smiled in turn, while the official murmured, "A day," a few times and then added something relative to our immediate removal to the foreigners' enclosure—the "Kont-se-el-Heligz." Vera Nadji deputized our friend Ver Moti to conduct us thither and at once fell into violent discussion with the dockyard commander.

BEYOND PLUTO
BY JOHN SCOTT CAMPBELL

The four made no move—they only watched us with yellow glittering eyes.

Illustrated by
Frank R. Paul

Our attention divided between the strange new world we were entering and the impending war, we descended from the landing way and got our first view of Dunsaan at close quarters. I confess it quite struck all thoughts of war from our minds. The city spread for miles in every direction, a heterogeneous assemblage of flat-topped white adobe buildings, none more than twenty feet high.

The walls were pierced at irregular intervals with round-screened windows and doors, in and out of which went the inhabitants. And such creatures they were! White, about four feet high, two-legged, like men, but there the resemblance ended. The whole upper portion of their bodies was covered with a rubbery white mantle of skin under which a score or more flexible and retractive tentacles undulated. The brain was contained in a limp lobe at the top of the mantle; the mouth, as we later found, lay underneath. The creature's single eye, fastened on the tip of one tentacle, constantly swayed back and forth as it walked. Looking at them one had an unforgettable sensation of flabby bonelessness— of a certain softness such as is associated with polyps. I think Prof. Pfeiffler was the only one not overcome with revulsion.

"Vell," he remarked with gusto as we entered the first street, "Ve got to dissecd von uf doze!" This didn't improve our impressions much. Ver Moti laughed. "They're from Duranko," he explained. "Sister planet of Dunsaan—same system. Intelligence a little below us but rather clever in certain lines…quite deaf and dumb. Your friend Ver Milroy will have a time learning their sign language."

Apparently there were no streetcars in Dunsaan. The entire three miles to the foreign settlement was made on foot. We threaded our course along avenues crowded with the odd white creatures who displayed no curiosity concerning us, until at last another white building under the brow of one of the city's protecting dikes appeared.

"This," said Ver Moti, "is the 'Discontented Club.' You will find a quite nice group in there—they play cards and smoke and drink and have all the other disgusting little habits you like so well. So I imagine it won't be too hard."

He knocked on the front door, which was opened after some time by a huge fat man smoking an immense Dutch pipe. "Vell," said he in English, "vat iss id now?"

Prof. Pfeiffler, his eyes lighting, poured forth a stream of fluent low Dutch to which the other, immensely startled, responded eagerly. Separating the two with difficulty, we entered the building. Ver Moti officiated in making the introductions, and then left us, bag and baggage, and not very much of that, in the main room. Our fellow exiles seemed very kind and friendly, showing us rooms on the upper floor and asking us numberless questions.

The house, a big bare structure, once used as a warehouse by the Zongainians, contained five Englishmen, one Frenchman and seventeen Boers. The Englishmen were of the two ill-fated parties that had preceded us up the Nile; the Frenchman, the sole survivor of a detachment of the Foreign Legion that had penetrated the forbidden land from the west, while the Boers had wandered in by twos and threes in the course of elephant hunts and treks after gold.

We noticed almost immediately a sort of separation between the English and French, and the Dutchmen. They lived in different parts of the building, ate apart and, as we found, did not even converse unless absolutely necessary. Our curiosity as to this state of affairs was soon satisfied, for that evening at the mess table the leader of the Englishmen arose and after introducing himself as 'Arry 'Awkins made a semi-official speech that was very illuminating.

He commenced by stating that at the time the second party entered the wilderness in 1914, the Great War was just beginning and that the Dutchmen, upon hearing the news told in a more or less partisan manner, immediately took the side of their neighbors against England. This feeling was not mitigated by the recent, to them, Boer War, in which several had received wounds. During the years of idleness here in Dunsaan a bitter controversy over the outcome of the war had arisen, and it had become one of the important topics of discussion.

Both sides imagined how its course was running; each favorable to his own faction and each hopelessly convinced of his own correctness. Besides this the natures of the two nationalities tended to drive them apart. The English were forever talking and planning about escape; while the stolid Boers, satisfied with an easy life and naturally disliking the idea of physical danger, preferred to remain where they were. Other things further aggravated matters until the exiles were anything but the happy family they might have been. The Frenchman had fought a duel with a Dutchman and killed him. His companions complained to the commander, Ver Muot, but the latter refused to take any action, asserting that the quicker they killed each other off the happier he would be. At this juncture we had arrived with our store of news and fresh ideas, like a sea breeze on a desert. Oft-times, however, a sea breeze can fan embers to a flame. And, as it turned out, this is what we did.

HAWKINS was impatient for news from the world. Taking turns we stayed up most of the night narrating the wonderful events that had transpired during the last fifteen years. The Boers came in, too, but made little comment. Hawkins nudged me as we ascended to bed and whispered delightedly something about, "Blimey, but our victory doesn't help their digestion."

Next morning at breakfast in the English quarters Hawkins, after suddenly opening every door for listeners and peering from each window, told us all to draw near. Then he began to speak in it low voice, punctuating his discourse with many suggestive gestures and mysterious glances.

"It might look," he commenced, "like we was laid by 'ere for duration—an' maybe it woulda been, if 'Arry 'Awkins 'adn't been along. Has soon has Hi harrived on this blasted planet, Hi thought to myself: "Arry,' Hi thought, 'hit's hup to you to get hout of 'ere. Hit may take a long time but you're a long ways from old Lunnon, so don't get himpatient, 'Arry, me boy.' Well, we 'adn't been 'ere two months when Sir Percy, 'e was as commanded us, gawd bless 'im, discovered one of these 'ere space flyin' boats lyin' in the swamp out 'ere has neat as you please with honly 'er engine gone and most of 'er side bashed in. Sir Percy said she 'ad been in a wreck an' hafter they pulled hout the machinery they left 'er 'ull to rot. Right away Hi saw the way we could pick up and leave these blighters hanny time we choose by just putting in a new hengine an' patching hup 'er 'ull. So we started in swipin' hiron plates and parts of a hengine and Sir Percy got 'old of some plans—and there we was.

"But blimey, hit was slow. There was big iron castings and hall kinds of gadjets that Hi don't understand yet, to sneak in, and hoften we went a fortnight without gettin' has much has a blinkin' bolt. But old Sir Percy 'e was a good un, 'e got everything there and put together right. When we found hout that, we didn't 'ave no instruments to navigate with. So we 'ad to start hall over again. But then hit was five years ago last month Sir Percy died of fever. Hafter 'e was buried our luck left us. Hi was the only one as 'ad the nerve to swipe anythin' but none of us was sure 'ow to put the bloody swag onto the boat. Jenkins 'ere was for startin' hout without the instruments, but Hi says 'We've got plenty of time; don't worry an' maybe 'Arry 'Awkins can think hout a way.' So all we've been doin' for three year, come next September, his to pick up hextra hinstruments and load 'em into the machine."

He paused for a moment in his talk to peer out the window. Evidently finding all satisfactory he hunched a little closer and almost whispered:

"These Dutchies, the blighters, don't know wot we 'as up our sleeves. Hif they did they would tell the Colonel, 'e what calls isself Ver Muot, just out of spite because they are so mad we won the war. They want to stay 'ere, they do, an' they can until they rot, for hall Hi care. Hall we needs is a good mechanic to read the plans and fix the hinstruments and then the Colonel and the Dutchies can go to 'ell. Blast 'em!"

We listened to this picturesque discussion with immense interest and, as may well be imagined, plied Hawkins with questions afterwards. In this manner we learned that the repaired *prolo*, a sixty-foot craft, was partly imbedded in a pre-carboniferous swamp about five English miles from the city and on its opposite side. It was this distance that necessitated a long detour around the outer slope of the dike that made the Englishmen's visits to their ark so rare. The Zongainians, however, did not watch their prisoners very closely as escape seemed highly improbable, and besides for some months they had been taken up entirely with their "bloody war," as Hawkins put it.

This led the conversation to the mysterious talk between Ver Muot and Vera Nadji on the transport. Hawkins knew very little, save that there was some kind of trouble between Zongainia and a place called Kanan, evidently another planet. The impending war seemed so distant from our interests that we five newcomers soon considered it as unimportant as did Hawkins. Its main effect would be to make our jailers forget us, that was as far as our thoughts went.

CHAPTER TEN
War!

AFTER a week or so of settling down to satisfy Hawkins' sense of what would appear proper to the authorities, we made a midnight trip to the hidden *prolo*. Climbing out of a back window facing the dike, the five of us were joined by Hawkins and the Frenchman. Without a word they led us up the embankment over the crest of the dike—some eighty feet high—and part way down its other side. Cautioning us to be careful of our footing, Hawkins proceeded ahead. Heavy dank odors ascended from the morass below and now and then I heard thumps and splashes as though some large amphibians were moving about. The darkness was absolute for Dunsaan was moonless and its thick atmosphere prevented any starlight from filtering through. If it had not been for a dim phosphorescence, which outlined the ground, we could not have gone a step.

After nearly three hours, Hawkins slowed down and began peering close to the ground. Soon he gave an exclamation of pleasure and picked up the end of a light, woven-wire cord. Motioning us toward him he whispered, "Watch where Hi walk and keep 'old of the line, this swamp is bottomless." Then slipping the cable under his arm he clambered down the bank to the flat. Hanavan, Milroy, Cummings, Pfeiffler and I followed, while the Frenchman brought up the rear. At the bottom of the dike Hawkins, with the confidence of one on familiar ground, proceeded out upon a long spit of quaking land, between black pools of water.

Ahead the cord stretched, rising dripping from the slime and soon covering our hands with ill-smelling liquid. No word was spoken. Hawkins skillfully stepped on long scaly logs, jumped across menacing pools and occasionally passed over a more or less solid island of rank grass. On either side I heard the scurry and splash of animals, but evidently the denizens of this Dunsaanian swamp were very timid, for we never saw one.

At the end of another hour of exhausting travel, a dark metallic mass loomed before us, and Hawkins stopped. He fumbled with the door, opened it, and after carefully wiping his feet climbed in. We followed, thanking Heaven for having a floor underfoot again. Hawkins immediately made a light and showed us over the craft with pride. Everywhere the work of a master mechanic was in evidence. Steel ribs had been bent into shape, or replaced; plates had been welded on. The engines, complicated things, as yet confusing to us, were all in place. Oiled, their fuel tanks full, they were ready to hurl the *prolo* into space as soon as the instruments were in place.

While Hawkins was showing us around, the Frenchman brought out the all-important plans. Lord Hanavan and Prof. Milroy, who were the only ones familiar with the Zongainian written language, pored over them saying little. The Frenchman and Cummings, the latter of whom also knew French, struck up a conversation in that tongue. Prof. Pfeiffler, armed with a flashlight and a light crowbar, went to the nearest Island in search of specimens, while Hawkins entertained me with a lengthy history of his early life in the neighborhood of Billingsgate. Time passed quickly and soon the green ray of the first sun struck across the swamp to announce the coming of another day. The seven-hour night was over.

Hawkins was not worried; as much as three days had often been spent at the *prolo* without exciting suspicion. Opening a cupboard he brought out some anti-sleep powders to carry us over until we should return. "These 'ere Zongainians," he remarked, "'ave a blinkin' powder for hevery hoccasion."

The short day was spent in much the same manner as the night. Hanavan and Milroy were evidently "getting" the plans for they took more anti-sleep powders and dissected one of the spare instruments with many knowing nods and Zongainian words. Between the equally lengthy anecdotes of Hawkins and the Frenchman, I fell gradually asleep. The last thing I can remember was the Frenchman saying: "—*et quand Marie m'a vu, elle m'aimait tout de suite, comme toutes les autres...*"

With the setting of Dunsaan's twin suns we prepared to return. Lord Hanavan, though his mechanical experience had been limited to motor boats and radio, had succeeded in installing the telescopic meteor-lookout and the speedometer, and he assured us that the plans were not half as difficult as they appeared.

The green sun vanished, and after a short period of orange twilight the intense night of the planet descended.

The return journey was started uneventfully, hardly a word being said by anyone. Through the dim radiance of the luminous plants we trudged, each occupied with his own thoughts. Near midnight Hawkins turned sharply right and up the embankment. Some paces behind we followed, groping for the grasses of the crest. Looking upward I discerned the cockney's sturdy form silhouetted for an instant against the city's glow; then with a whispered gasp of warning he rolled back upon us.

"A crowd in front of the 'ouse…Zongainians…those Dutchies…"

OUR hearts scarcely beating, we carefully elevated our heads over the parapet. The building was flooded with light, a hundred Zongainians and a good thousand of the weird white people surrounded it. In the middle of the group near the door were the treacherous Boers and the four other Englishmen, facing Ver Muot and his guards. We could not hear what was being said, but it was not difficult to guess. The Boers had found out our plans— perhaps overheard where the *prolo* was…

I felt Hawkins tugging at my sleeve.

"Back to the boat! Hi say—has quick as we can make hit! "

I started to wriggle down the dike when he seized my ankle. "Not that way—we 'aven't time. We'll 'ave to chance hit across the city."

Back we scrambled to the top of the dike where, hidden by the long grass, we crawled a hundred yards beyond the floodlights and then down into a dark street. Led by the wonderful Hawkins we scurried along, ducking into the yard-high doorways when the mantled white people passed. Fortunate it was that they were, deaf, otherwise our loud breathing would surely have betrayed us. For a time we seemed to have eluded any search party, but our hopes were soon shattered.

The Frenchman suddenly shoved Hawkins against the wall, hissing— *"Gare! La prolo…* Eeet ees there!" We crouched for a moment, watching the slender form go silently by, her searchlight flicking from street to street. Running now, we started out afresh. Again the *prolo* passed and again we were fortunate in hiding against the wall.

I thought we were hopelessly lost when between two buildings I saw, massive and grass-covered, the dike! Faint with the reaction, we struggled up its face and slipped down until our feet were in the morass. Hawkins searched frantically a few moments and then holding tight to our lifeline we started out over the swamp. Haste was imperative, for a faint glow indicated that dawn would soon be at hand. For centuries, so it seemed, we floundered through rank grass and blackish water before the steel walls of the *prolo* came into view. Never did I see a more welcome sight! We piled in, this time one may be sure, not stopping to wipe our feet.

"We will 'ave to start hat once!" gasped Hawkins as soon as he had found the knob which turned on the glow light. "They'll scour these swamps till they find us, that's wot they'll do. We got to be gone before daylight."

Hawkins and Hanavan went into the engine room to start the motors, while Milroy and the rest of us screwed down the windows and door. Our terror of capture drove all sane reasoning from our minds; even Lord Hanavan utterly forgot that half the instruments were unmounted and that we were quite without charts of the starry void into which we were going.

Fortunately the *prolo* was well supplied with fuel, food and oxygen. Indeed, the assiduous efforts of Harry Hawkins and his companions had filled every nook and cranny of the cabin to overflowing. We were not, however, in a mood to throw away provisions for comfort.

Thanks to the frantic efforts of Hawkins and Lord Hanavan the motors were started and the ship was ready to rise some time before dawn. We all assembled in the main cabin and after a pause, a sort of mental gathering of courage, Hawkins turned on the propulsion plates. The craft heaved out of its muddy dockyard with a sucking sound and immediately poked its steel prow into a dense thicket of fern trees. Hawkins backed it out, the stern overturning a tree in the process; and then realizing that the swamp was a little dangerous for windows he brought the *prolo* straight up a thousand feet. There we hesitated.

"Our *camarades,*" cried the Frenchman. "Our friends who have worked through all zee long years to make zees escape! Are we to leave zem behind?"

Hawkins, filled with emotion, could not reply. But Lord Hanavan did. "To descend now would mean certain capture," he said slowly, "we can do them a greater service by returning to the world and sending help, than by giving up this ship over which they have labored... Let us go on..."

As the *prolo* ascended beyond the last vestige of Dunsaan's thick atmosphere, the twin suns arose above the horizon. Their light, though weird in its duality of color, had nevertheless a cheering effect upon us. Below lay the dark bulk of Dunsaan, with its fetid swamps and its weird inhabitants. Above, the starry universe glowed incredibly distant. And we seven voyagers from the world hung between the zenith and the nadir, like Mohammed's coffin, in a steel space-flying machine, about whose operation we knew next to nothing.

Now that we had left the closeness and excitement of the swamp, we realized with awful clarity the position we were in. Hawkins knew the general direction of the sun, but since everything ahead would vanish as soon as we went faster, visual navigation would never do.

"Hif Sir Percy was only 'ere," wailed Hawkins, "'e knew hall about 'ow to do it."

But Sir Percy was, perhaps fortunately for him, beyond care of escape.

OUR hopes had reached their lowest ebb when Prof. Milroy, who had been looking at Dunsaan through the glasses, suddenly seized my arm and cried, "One of their *prolos*...a big one...it's coming toward us!"

Hawkins looked—then I. Milroy was right. Already the strange craft was near enough to see without binoculars, a tiny metal spindle gleaming in the sunlight. For an instant we were seized with a terror that we had been sighted, but reason soon told us that our smallness would prevent our being visible at this distance. Steadily the *prolo* arose; it was heading toward the part of the sky where the sun lay. Almost simultaneously the idea flashed upon us—the way to get back to the earth. Follow that ship!

Immediate action was necessary. It was already past us. Leaping to the control chair, Hanavan turned on the power. We were fairly thrown to the floor. For an instant the universe reeled around us; then Hanavan had the car straightened out. With ever-increasing velocity we tore after the fleeing *prolo*, pressed flat by the violence of acceleration. After a few ticklish moments we commenced to gain on the bigger craft. Lowering the acceleration rate to conform to that of the *prolo* ahead, we had a short conference. Watches were appointed and upon Cummings' suggestion a special couch was laid beside the controls for the navigator to rest upon when the acceleration became too great.

The hours slipped by and the twin suns of Dunsaan reddened into oblivion. The weird color changes of our speed became apparent all around us; only the *prolo* showing dimly ahead retained its true hue.

At the end of four hours Hawkins was relieved by Milroy. Hanavan and the rest of us took sleeping potions.

When I awoke ten hours later the sky was a dead black. Dr. Cummings at the controls was lying flat on his back, staring upward through the glass roof at the other *prolo*. Looking around I discovered everyone else to be asleep. The ship was perfectly quiet, and—save for the lights on the instruments—quite dark. For a long time I lay still, my eyes upon the dim form of our guide. I noted that we were considerably closer, evidently because of the difficulty of seeing. The lights in her control room glowed like a big star, hovering motionless in a velvety immensity.

Somehow I felt an interest in the occupants of the other ship. I wondered who they were and what they were doing. It reminded me of watching boats pass one at night on the ocean; only here the ocean extended to infinity and that friendly light ahead was our only link with life. My mind filled with thoughts like these, I had begun to drowse off again when a violent lurch of our *prolo* half threw me from the bunk. Hastily regaining my feet I saw that Dr. Cummings was sitting up, gripping the control levers tensely, and staring upwards. I followed his glance to see the ship ahead moving swiftly sidewise.

"Changed its course," hissed Cummings. "Wake the others…"

I started to do this when Cummings countermanded his order.

"All right now. They're going straight."

I relapsed into a dozing state again.

I do not remember how long we followed the *prolo* across space. It may have been a couple of weeks, but I am not sure. After eight or nine days the other craft began to decelerate. Almost crashing into her, we did likewise. Lord Hanavan was greatly disturbed.

"It took four weeks acceleration before we were halfway to Dunsaan," he explained. "If we start to decelerate after only a week or so it means *that we are not going to the Earth!*"

Beyond any hope now we followed our guiding star that was so false, through all of its many maneuvers for over a week, steadily slowing down all the time. Stars began to reappear; they passed through the colors of the spectrum and became fixed. It was apparent that we were either moving extremely slowly, or were stationary. But nowhere was there a sign of a sun or a planet. The *prolo* before us hung motionless in the sky, as if waiting for something.

Waiting. But for what? Time only could tell. We put in the hours as best we could, installing more instruments and a little rapid-fire gun that Sir Percy had acquired. It was mounted in an airtight chamber, built in the control-room floor, with its muzzle, when ready for action, projecting into the vacuum of space. Hawkins entertained us with stories of escapades in London during his youth… One always watched the big *prolo*. We hardly noticed that our weight had dropped to nearly zero.

Three days passed in this fashion and then, while we were listening to one of the Frenchman's stories, Hawkins on watch called out.

"Ahoy there! There's hanother blinkin' *prolo* 'ard haport, an' hup a few points."

The Frenchman's story was suddenly interrupted. Looking in the direction indicated I made out the fish-like form of another spaceship slowly approaching our guide. The latter made no movement. For some moments we watched this meeting and then

Milroy, with his glasses, made out two more *prolos* dropping slowly downward from above and behind us. Soon these were visible to the naked eye, and more had materialized out of the void. All assembled with the first ship in long lines. It suggested battleships arranging themselves in a convoy. At once we thought of that overheard conversation back on Dunsaan. The war…

CHAPTER ELEVEN
On Kanan

IN scores now the *prolos* silently appeared and fell into place. Huge craft—one had a feeling that they were not passenger or freight ships—and droves of smaller ones, some no larger than ours. It was like a review or a parade. Engrossed, I watched the lines form and then start slowly away. Now upon each ship there appeared a blaze of light, a signal of some kind. I became conscious that Milroy was speaking.

"I say, if we can get in with those fellows, they'll think we are in their party. Let's go over to that group of small ones above and get into line."

It was a good suggestion. While Hanavan, who was the best navigator, operated the controls, the rest of us cleared the boxes of food and fuel from the control room to make it look shipshape in case anyone should look into our glass roof.

The ten miles or so to the swarm of small *prolos* was soon covered; Hanavan deftly maneuvered our craft into line and then, following the blazing light of a leader, we picked up speed. Weight returned with acceleration and within three hours Doppler's effect had extinguished every star. But now, before and behind for thousands of miles, we could see a miniature Milky Way, the pilot lights of the fleet. It is a wonder to me now that we were not discovered at once in our deception. Our ship had no signal lights, nor neon-tube number outside and for all we knew might have been crowded into another craft's place. But whether by accident or carelessness, we were not apprehended. The immense fleet numbering many thousands, swung majestically across the sky, our little fugitive *prolo* a part of it.

For six days we accelerated; then reversed and commenced to slow down. Another six days and we would come to a stop. Then—

Five passed. The stars reappeared magically and, evidently to prevent confusion, the artificial stars of the fleet commenced to blink.

Ahead of us a misty glow like a dim nebula came into being. The line of lights pointed in its direction. We felt a certain tenseness—something seemed about to happen.

Something did. In empty space about fifteen miles ahead there was a terrific explosion. A gigantic sheet of greenish flame spread soundlessly, enveloping a dozen *prolos* in its folds. For half a minute it lay across the sky and then faded away, leaving the battleships twisted, redly glowing wrecks. Instantly along the line little pinpoints of blue fire began to appear. For five minutes this continued, then ceased. A pause...then far, far to one side the sky was lit with tiny green flashes of flame that grew and faded. We waited, amazed. Then, without warning, another sunburst of fire leaped up, closer this time, for I distinctly saw a sixty-foot craft like ours crumple and grow red hot a mile away. Now the little blue sparks began to fly in earnest. Every battleship fairly glowed with them. In the distance came the answering flame bursts. Suddenly we realized what we were witnessing. Our fleet was in battle with the enemy. Men were being killed by the thousands around us, and at any moment we might be engulfed by one of those gigantic shells.

Then I noticed that our fleet had divided itself into two lines; one was turning toward the invisible enemy while the other, in which we were, continued in the direction of the round nebulous patch.

Not disappointed at leaving these rather dangerous pyrotechnics behind, we increased speed again. Lord Hanavan filled the little gun's chamber with air and, after going over directions again, loaded it. It could fire two thousand shots before reloading was necessary.

Two hours passed. The battle had vanished long ago. Our half of the fleet, barely moving, neared the destination. Its luminous corona now filled half the sky, while in the center we could discern a ball about the size of a full moon. Dr. Pfeiffler suggested that it might be the planet Kanan.

Now there was a change in the fleet's formation. The line turned, presenting its length to the planet and forming a wide crescent, then advanced. Thirty minutes passed. Slower and yet slower went the armada, as though its commanders were suspicious. Without warning every light vanished. We turned out our cabin lamps, depending upon the dim glow from outside. And then in front of the crescent, the sky became a green inferno. By the hundreds; by the thousands, the enemy shells burst. Some *prolos* more advanced than others were destroyed, while right and left the ships glowed again, this time with the fleet's answering fire.

The planet's atmosphere became speckled with green. Then the crescent hurled itself forward. Flinging himself upon the controls, Hanavan urged our little craft on too, while he shouted to Hawkins to be ready at the gun.

"We're in it now!" he cried. "It's fight or die!"

There was no time for thought or reflection. Though all was silent save our own excited voices, I could imagine the deafening roar that would sound if there was air in the void around us. On we rushed, sometimes surrounded and once actually touched by a green flame. Ships on either side went down—but still the thousands of the Zongainian fleet poured in. The planet grew and grew until it filled half the sky. A faintly audible whistling from the outer skin of our ship betrayed our entry into its outer atmosphere. As we descended the air grew luminous…I caught glimpses of streaks of lightning, but whether these were a natural phenomena or part of the battle, I cannot say.

Near our little *prolo* we saw another battleship, huge, shadowy, slipping ghostlike through cloudbanks. Through the windows came the first thunderous echoes of the battle, now louder as the air grew denser. Suddenly we saw other space flyers below, like a shoal of whales. They sprang into life the instant we sighted them. Spurts of green flame came spitefully from their sides and shells with heavy concussions, bursting about the Zongainian battleship. The shockwaves threw our little craft about like a leaf in the wind. The Zongainian battleship, still dropping, returned the fire. I had the satisfaction of seeing one of the enemy turned end upward and drop. A faint crash, arising from the depths, told of its end.

FOR five minutes the air was filled with bursting shells. The larger Zongainian *prolo* now had a gaping hole torn in her side and her drop was becoming more pronounced. Lord Hanavan directed the nose of our tiny ship toward an enemy battleship below and I pushed the firing button. The opposing craft was immediately surrounded by a ring of fire and backed away, evidently disabled. But now the ground appeared. Clouds of smoke obscured the view, so we had only an occasional glimpse of Titanic buildings, grotesque twisted masses of wreckage…shattered battleships…

The Zongainian battleship, her stern dropping lower and lower, struck against a tower. With a roar the mass of masonry fell, and then the giant *prolo*, giving a last burst of fire, fell heavily into the city, leaving a dozen buildings in ruin in her wake. At the same instant there was a blinding flash of light, an ear-splitting concussion, and amid a shower of broken glass and hot metal our little craft fell into the chaos below. With this all consciousness ceased for me.

My return to the land of the living was preceded by a tortuous succession of nightmares, in which I was pursued across a limitless blue void by a pack of steel monsters with gaping jaws. Flames darted from their mouths and bolts of lightning, like pointing fingers, indicated me to my relentless enemies. After an eternity of mad chase across space, I began to hear a faint pounding, a metallic ringing like a blacksmith's anvil, interposed with heavy dull thumps. Strange odors were wafted to my nostrils and, as if at a great distance, I heard the confused voices of many people. Gradually I became conscious that I was lying on my back on some kind of a couch, and that my limbs and head were curiously numb and heavy feeling. For some time I lay still, not opening my eyes, and trying to remember what had happened last.

The vague meanderings of my mind were suddenly interrupted by footsteps, and a voice near at hand. It spoke in Zongainian.

"Well, how has time treated our six runaways? Have any more died?"

I could not quite catch the answer, but a sudden gripping feeling passed over me. Who had died? Making a desperate effort I opened my eyes, and then commenced to blink them in amazement. For an instant I thought that I was the one who had passed on and that I was already in some trans-stellar inferno. I was lying on a narrow cot along with a hundred or more similar beds upon a steel shelf much like the gallery of a theater. Fifty feet overhead a twisted metal roof curved, ending abruptly in a long jagged tear. Out in front of our shelf was an area of crumpled spaceship's and shattered buildings heaped in an incredible confusion and, as I discovered by hard peering, covered with hundreds of tiny men who were clambering about hauling on ropes, pounding and hammering and operating machines.

Now and then the light of some welding apparatus would glow like a firefly, sharply silhouetting its operator in the gray gloom. This amphitheater was bounded by a serrated scarp of immense buildings—all battered and seemingly ready to fall at the least shock. After staring at this chaotic spectacle for some minutes I turned my head, observing that it was covered with a rubbery bandage, and looked at the speaker who had awakened me.

He was a tall Zongainian dressed in a sepia cape and wearing a turban-like headdress. Seeing me move he came over to the cot where I recognized him to be our officer friend on the outward trip, Ver Vlygar Moti.

"A day," said he, using the universal Zongainian greeting, "or rather a night, for these Kanan days are hardly bright enough for such a term. Well, you seem to be on the way to recovery. We thought you were gone when we hauled you out of your *prolo*. How did you ever get here? We leave you safe in Dunsaan for life and in the next fifty days you come shooting right into the midst of the biggest war in ten centuries, and alive too…"

"What happened?" I asked. "Where is the fleet and where are we?"

"In Kanan," replied Ver Moti. "As far as we know the Zongainians have won, but our battle *prolo* was disabled at the same time yours was. It fell into the city of Kanan. Our ethero communication apparatus was hopelessly smashed so we cannot call for aid. The crew—about five hundred who are alive, not counting the hundred and twenty wounded—are trying to dig out a small cruiser and repair it. But have patience, your wounds will be healed within ten days…and in the meantime you need rest. If you persist in asking questions we will have to give you sleeping potions, like we did to your friend Ver Hanavan."

WITH a few more words delivered in a similar tone, Ver Moti left me with my thoughts and the contemplation of the scene before me. I wondered how serious the plight of the stranded Zongainians was. Their battleship, which lay diagonally across two buildings in the background, was wrecked beyond repair, and in the twisted chaos of the amphitheater, I could find no ray of hope. At any moment a Kananese *prolo* might fly overhead and have the Zongainians at its mercy.

For an hour or so I watched the scene and then after drinking some warm milk-like fluid I fell into a sound sleep.

And so a week passed over Kanan with its eternal misty twilight and we lost souls in the hands of fate. D'Arcy, the Frenchman, had been instantly killed when the *prolo* struck; the rest of us, protected in a measure by the steel roof, were only cut up generally by glass and torn metal. Injuries, which without earthly medical science might have proved fatal, or resulted in lifelong mutilations, were conquered by the wonderful surgery of Zongainia. And Ver Moti assured us that we would not bear a single scar as a memento of the mishap.

Each day more of our rubbery wrappings were dissolved off, until at the end of eight days everyone except Hawkins could leave his bed.

In response to our earnest wishes to help, Ver Moti finally conducted us to the headquarters of Vera Nadji, one-time commander of the battleship. Her rooms were located, as were the quarters of the crew, in one of the least damaged buildings facing the square.

Vera Nadji received us warmly, wanting to hear about our escape and considering it to be a joke on Commandant Muot.

Then becoming serious she told us more of the situation. The city of Kanan, capital of the planet of the same name, had been completely evacuated some time before the battle. Just where these people were (the city, she said, housed more than seven hundred million) no one knew. The Kananese land army was somewhere about, but exactly where was a matter of conjecture. The *prolo* fleets of the two combatants, after the first engagement above the city, had vanished into space and as far as we knew could still be locked in combat.

The last word Vera Nadji had received was that the Zongainian First Fleet had the enemy on the run. Since that time, eight days ago, she had heard nothing. The cloudy sky remained empty; the immense city deserted.

The only hope of the crew lay in a damaged hundred-and-fifty-foot cruiser, which was half buried in wreckage across the square. Here the technicians and mechanics from the Zongainian battleship worked continuously. Chemical blowtorches made the steel and concrete debris flow like water, while the engineers patched and replaced the machinery inside.

As soon as we were recovered, we all went to work shoveling concrete to make a landing place. We worked almost frantically, watching the foggy sky with one eye, and by a sort of mass suggestion praying patriotically for Zongainia's success. We were so much like ants struggling there in that Titanic city. Its thousand-mile streets impressed me, at least, much more than the millions of light years of the universe.

There is no night in Kanan's eternal half-light and so I cannot tell in days how long we were there. It seems as though it might have been years. But Lord Hanavan who alone kept his watch going, is sure that this lull, if such activity might be so termed, did not last over three weeks.

At that time the small *prolo* had been disinterred and placed ready for operations upon the crude landing way. Fuel and other supplies were being rushed in by the crew and Vera Nadji—along with her communications experts—was busy tinkering with the ethero receiving set, the remains of which had been recently installed on board. We escaped prisoners, who in the general democracy caused by the disaster were somewhat privileged characters, were in the lower storeroom, forward of the generators and coils, packing food crates on top of the condensers.

Overhead sounded a steady tramping as the crew crossed the control room with their loads. The air in the little windowless chamber was stuffy, and so after half completing our task, we sat down to rest. Hawkins said he wanted a drink and went outside to get it. The rest of us sat for about five minutes talking intermittently about something or other—probably our fate when Vera Nadji's crew rejoined the First Fleet.

I can remember that Prof. Milroy was making some remark about inscriptions he had found in a half-wrecked building, when utterly without warning, there came a deafening roar and a concussion that hurled us and our crates together upon the floor. The *prolo* seemed to almost stand on end for an instant and then fell back on its bed. For a moment there was utter silence and then a bedlam of cries and shrieks broke forth. We heard footsteps running back and forth above and some one shouting that Vera Nadji was wounded. Then all else was blotted out by another blast at a greater distance. It was followed by the slip and thud of falling masonry and a long-drawn tinkling as of glass. We lay for a few seconds, partly stunned by the first explosion, and then Lord Hanavan shoved a box to one side and scrambled to his feet.

"Another battleship..." he started to explain, when a lurch of our craft made self-preservation of prime importance. This time, however, the *prolo* moved by herself; a hum from the motor-room told that we were rising.

CHAPTER TWELVE
A City of Terrors

PICKING ourselves up as quickly as our bruises would permit we hastened to the ladder leading to the control room. Above was a scene of indescribable wreckage. All of the "non-breakable" glass from the front windows was lying in tattered shreds on the floor. The instrument panel was buckled against the partition, while the wind whistled through hundreds of rents in the steel sheeting. About a dozen people were in the room, some of them with blood streaming from open cuts; one was in the navigating seat, while others were at work upon some kind of a gun.

A mile below were the towering buildings of the city and almost directly underneath hovered a thousand-foot *prolo*. As soon as we appeared, Ver Moti—his face bloody from a cut—leaped toward us and shouted to bring up a power cable. He made a vague gesture toward the gun and then below. "Kananese..." he added hastily. "Surprised us. They are bombing the camp...haven't discovered that we are gone yet..."

At that instant another figure appeared, one arm held limply against her body. It was Vera Nadji.

"Use bombs," she snapped at Ver Moti. "The auxiliary coil is out. Can't spare power for the gun. Drop a *kanfrene* on them..."

Ver Moti fell back a pace, his face whitened. "But," he stammered, "our comrades..."

"They will have to take the chance if they are alive yet," answered the commander. "Let the Kananese know we are here. We can lead them away from the square..."

Ver Moti left on the run, without another word. Cowering back into the passageway we watched the proceedings.

Ver Moti, leaning out under the broken window, pointed a small gun down and fired several times. Sticking my head from a porthole I saw tiny green flashes on the back of the battleship. Immediately our craft wheeled and rose sharply, while the enemy commenced to ascend. In response to the navigator we swung sideways to take advantage of the floor propulsion plates, and then shot off at an angle. A second after we had started, the air behind turned a brilliant green with bursting projectiles.

Now the chase began in earnest. The battle *prolo*, moving ponderously, filled the air about us with shells, while it arose from the Zongainian encampment. The crew of our smaller *prolo* lined up at the windows and returned the fire with their handguns, but apparently without effect. While this was going on I noticed Ver Moti coming up from the storeroom with a small metal case. With remarkable care he laid it upon the floor and took from it a small black bottle.

Drawing Vera Nadji back he handed it to her saying, "Better do it soon. They may get us at any moment."

She said something we couldn't quite catch, and then began to issue commands. The *prolo* turned sharply about and started back, ascending above the larger ship. With a feeling of horrified anticipation I kept my eyes glued upon the tiny oval phial in Vera Nadji's hand. Now I saw that Ver Moti had taken several more from the box and was passing them out to the crew. One by one he gave each man a bottle and then he came over to us.

"Here," he said, a *kanfrene* bomb. If everyone else misses, throw it. Wait until the last…"

At that instant the ship commenced to climb again and Vera Nadji shouted, "Now!" From the front window I saw her arm flash out, hurling the little bottle outward and downward. Breathlessly we waited as seconds followed seconds. Then on the roof of a building just below the enemy craft a volcano seemed to erupt. An immense sheet of flame leaped up, completely enfolding the battleship. I glimpsed skyscrapers going heavenward *en masse* and then the sound wave hit us.

Just what happened to the Kananese battleship I don't pretend to know. We five earthlings who possessed no sea legs at all landed on the floor *en masse* too, and while we were picking ourselves up, the *prolo* left the vicinity of the explosion at a velocity of three thousand miles per hour. Later Ver Moti told us that the enemy craft was probably melted by the heat. *Kanfrene*, he said, was a Zongainian word meaning "bad atom," and its explosive violence was due to the release of atomic energy.

After the destruction of the Kananese battleship Vera Nadji did not linger in that part of Kanan. Other *prolos* were sure to come and then all would not be "restful to the nerves" as Ver Moti put it.

After an hour or so of traveling above the city, our commander ordered a descent made upon a gigantic and partly wrecked landing stage. Surrounded by thousand-foot beacon towers it lay—a plateau of metal and concrete a dozen miles long—lying diagonally across the roofs of a hundred buildings. Seen from above we could make out that one end had sagged downward, possibly from the collapse of some structure below. Here and there amid the twisted girders and crushed masonry lay a glittering pond of mercury, spilled from the shock-absorption cylinders.

Under the guidance of Vera Nadji herself we dropped vertically past the towers, and finally more than two hundred feet below the stage floor we settled to rest in one of the larger mercury lakes. It was the ideal retreat for the repair work we had to do. The thick-walled buildings with their round windows arose on three sides, while on the fourth we were sheltered by the overhanging platform above. Almost as soon as the motors were stopped we all set to work on the little *prolo*.

A foraging crew was sent out to cut sheets of flexible glass for the torn windows, while a marvelous electric welder did wonders patching up the crumpled side of the roof. No less efficient was the bandaging applied to the cut and bruised crew; the blood was washed off, the wounds expertly closed by the ship's surgeon and a syrupy liquid, which immediately congealed to a flexible transparent solid, was poured on.

EVERYONE turned—even we outsiders—to finding jobs. Lord Hanavan was soon an expert glass fitter, while Prof. Pfeiffler and I found work feeding flux into the hopper of the welder.

The scene is one that will remain long in my memory. The towering steel columns of the landing stage, the black immensity of the abysmal streets; and reflected brilliantly in its bath of mercury—that wonderful machine which had brought us hither—the *prolo*. Over the whole scene flickered the green lights from the welding machine, while the toiling Zongainians cast hundred-foot shadows on the building walls. Their low voices and the occasional clang of metal on metal were the only sounds in all the city. All else was gray, silent, forbidding.

After seven hours of work, Vera Nadji at the welding machine gave the command to rest. Tired and hungry, we crowded into the control-room where food was served. Here the first mention of the future was made. Our commander, finishing her gelatine hurriedly, stood upon the navigating chair and spoke. Her words were calm, confident of success.

"Within a day and a half," she said, "we can return to the pit. We will take on all of our comrades who still live and then seek the fleet. Let us hope that Zongainia has given these Kananese a demonstration that they will not forget."

Later, while most of the crew slept, our old friend Ver Moti explained in a low voice the cause of the trouble between Zongainia and Kanan.

I cannot remember all the complicated reasons he gave, but the basic cause seemed to be trade rivalry. Property of the Zongainian "Interstellar Transport Association" had been confiscated by the Kanan government under pressure of the Kanan Transport Company, and demands for reparations met with diplomatic insults. The trouble was evidently of long standing. There had been friction between Kanan and Zongainia since the first Zongainian spaceships had landed there.

"That," said Ver Moti between yawns, "was around the year 1350 according to the Christian calendar." Ver Moti fell asleep in the midst of a discourse on price wars between planets, but it did not bother us in the least because we were already far away from interstellar battles, dreaming of a snug little planet that lay in sunny ignorance of the giant universe that lived and fought around it.

"Morning" brought fresh labors for all. While repairing the auxiliary induction coils it was discovered that the supply of wire was exhausted. This seemed a rather insurmountable difficulty, especially as we had no wiredrawing machine. But the resourceful Vera Nadji had the solution. In the buildings around and below us, she said, was enough wire for a million *prolos*. After some discussion it was decided to send Lord Hanavan, Prof. Milroy, and myself to retrieve it, as we were about the least useful members of the crew.

Preparations for our departure were simple. We were given wire cutters, electric light and some concentrated food for lunch. Ver Moti stopped work long enough to tell us where to look for wires, and then after solemnly shaking hands with Cummings, Pfeiffler and Hawkins, we took our departure.

Prof. Milroy was delighted with the opportunity to be alone. "Finally!" he cried, rubbing his hands together, "I can study those inscriptions and the buildings. What we might find inside them… What contributions to anthropology… Oh, we shall have a day!"

After which he almost fell into the pond of mercury and so became silent for a time.

Scrambling over the heaps of debris, we soon entered the nearest building. Lights on, we walked in a line down a vast echoing corridor, which extended seemingly forever before us into the darkness. Now and then shadowy halls led off to one side into unknown regions, but a fear of losing our way kept us to the main passage.

The instant the *prolo* was out of sight and sound, a cloak of gloom seemed to settle upon all. Not a ray of light penetrated the enormous structure and only the echo of our own hushed voices disturbed the silence. Everywhere the passageways extended like the vaults of a crypt, decorated here and there with garish murals of goblins, or whatever deities the Kananese had. Ahead our shadows marched; while behind the darkness crept in stealth upon our heels.

At first Prof. Milroy's scientific ardor made him oblivious to all except the decorations and inscriptions on either side. But bit-by-bit his voice became hushed until he only whispered an occasional monosyllable to one of us.

I tried to imagine the city when it was full of people, but somehow it was impossible. The concave floor suggested a sewer inhabited by rats only; while the hideous figures painted on the walls hinted of inhuman horrors around the corner. We tried to concentrate on the search for wire, but the eye continually wandered ahead where the shadows fled before our lights, or behind where they came after us. To one who has not been in the buildings of the deserted city of Kanan, it is impossible to describe the formless terrors that grew upon us.

It was not a fear of death or of the supernatural. Indeed, had a live ghost appeared we would have welcomed him as a brother in this far planet. It was an unimaginable thing, a sort of sinister essence waiting…waiting for us to descend beyond all reach of the Zongainians, when it would…

MY reverie was broken by the voice of Hanavan in the lead. "A light ahead. I think we have passed through the building, as Ver Moti said."

We hastened on and shortly were standing on a sort of balcony overlooking the street. Three hundred feet below it lay two wide stone avenues with a canal in the center. Overhead the buildings soared perhaps a thousand feet. They were massive things with enormously thick concrete and stone walls, but somehow the entire scene lacked the mechanized, the civilized appearance of Zongainia's streets. Blocks of stone and a canal in the middle. No sign of machines or tracks or any of the appliances of science that marked the difference between a modern street and one of Rome or Babylon. One felt that it was primitive and incredibly old.

After spending some time on the balcony, Prof. Milroy found a passage running parallel to the street and separated from it by a wall pierced at intervals with windows. Down this we walked, the beam of Hanavan's light following the upper molding. We had not gone fifty feet when out of a side hall there came a thin ribbon of

BEYOND PLUTO

BY JOHN SCOTT CAMPBELL

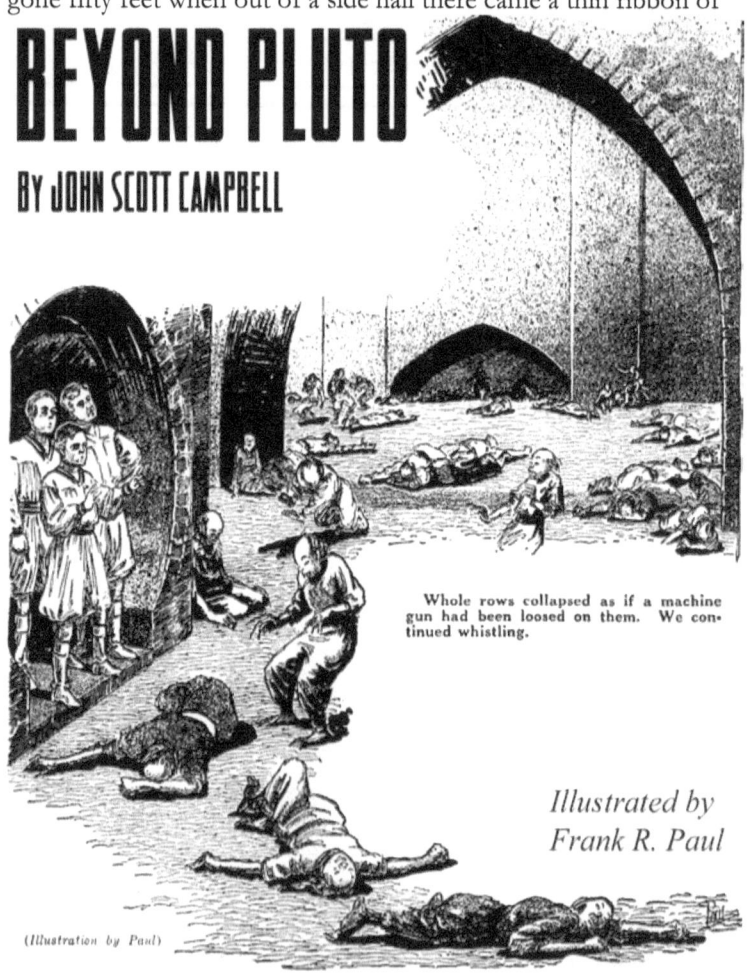

Whole rows collapsed as if a machine gun had been loosed on them. We continued whistling.

Illustrated by
Frank R. Paul

(Illustration by Paul)

metal covered with transparent insulation and fastened to the wall with some kind of glue. This we ripped down, cut and placed in a coil where it could be found on the way back. Then on again.

The hall descended gradually until after we had progressed a half-mile, there appeared a large ornamental door leading directly onto the stone paving. With a sigh of relief we hurried into the open, away from the gloomy passage. At the edge of the canal were a number of flat slabs of stone and here we stopped to eat. According to Hanavan's watch we had been gone three-and-a-half hours.

Lunch of Zongainian concentrated food does not take long and so, after doubtfully considering the canal water, we started out with our thirst unslaked. About a mile down the great street there was an intersection where we could make out a heap of wreckage and a mass of twisted wire. Toward this goal we turned our steps, following the canal. Once Milroy saw a large yellow eel-like thing in the water, but our lack of fishing lines or hooks saved it. And once we were all startled by a raucous squawking from the upper floors of a building. We never saw what kind of a creature it came from.

The distance to the pile of wreckage was much greater than we had estimated, for after an hour's steady tramping it was still quite a distance away. Prof. Milroy grew tired and suggested that we try inside the building again. Accordingly we entered the nearest door where almost at our feet we found a big roll of fine wire, the ideal thing for the damaged induction coil. After a short rest it was decided to go straight through the building instead of retracing our steps the length of the street.

To a sane person this may sound foolish, but our nervousness had made us anything but sane. Our first relief at getting into the open was now replaced by a fear of being seen by someone or something hidden in an upper window—by some queer twist of reasoning we thought that by keeping to the darkest halls we might sneak through without being found out. Whatever it was, I felt reasonably certain we could hide from it. During all the time we had been in the city we had found nothing alive.

However, we entered the structure and—choosing a ramp leading in the general direction of the spaceship—started up. We marched on for four solid hours thereafter without catching the slightest glimpse of light. The hall, now wide, now narrow, wandered on in a course gradually more tortuous. In the walls were innumerable round locked doors. Hanavan said they must be the entrances to apartments. Fatigue and a growing horror of our condition quenched any curiosity.

Near the beginning of the fifth hour after leaving the street we discarded the bundle of wire. Bitterly we cursed it and the day we set out on this mad adventure. A little later we came to a halt.

Physical exhaustion prevented further walking—no matter where we were. After discussing the question of sleeping in the open hall we proceeded to batter down one of the doors in an endeavor to find a reasonable amount of shelter. The door soon gave, but when we entered the chamber we received a terrible mental shock. Standing in a group in the center of a round chamber were four people; weakened, hideously yellow and all pointing or making some kind of gesture at us. We sprang back and Lord Hanavan raised the wire cutter—our only weapon.

The four made no move—they only watched us with glittering yellow eyes. For ten seconds we stood in the doorway as motionless as those before us, and then Hanavan slowly lowered his weapon. We peered closer and then Milroy managed to gasp out, "They're dead! Embalmed! Stuffed!" The next instant we fairly tore out of the room and in spite of our exhaustion ran far up the corridor before pausing. Avoiding the now sinister round doors we finally huddled together in a remote corner of the passage. After extinguishing all lights, we lapsed into a fitful slumber broken by nightmares of pursuing fiends from dusty burial chambers.

CHAPTER THIRTEEN
In the Enemy's Camp

I WAS aroused some seven hours later by Prof. Milroy, who clapped his hand over my mouth and hissed, "Not a sound…something's coming…" I sat up hastily to discover by sense of touch Lord Hanavan on hands and knees, listening. For many minutes we waited, hearing nothing. Milroy insisted, in whispers, that he had heard footsteps and a dragging sound, and Hanavan once silenced us to listen long for the repetition of distant laughter. It never came. Perhaps it was the creature, which had called in the street.

In any case it was apparent that unless we could soon escape from these endless passages we would go insane. At first we feared to put on our lights, but once it was done we felt better. The hall was empty as far as the beams would reach.

Before resuming the trek we had a short conference. Lord Hanavan wished to return to the street the way we had come, but Milroy and I opposed him. There were too many side tunnels, too many forks. And besides, the thought of passing that open door and the grisly statues inside would have deterred us.

It was finally decided that the best course was to ascend to the city roof where we could go in a straight line and find the wrecked landing stage more easily. But how to get there was the question. We commenced marching as we talked, keeping to those passages which had some upward slope. An hour or more passed this way when around a corner appeared a light. Hurrying to it, we found ourselves looking out of a window far above another street. Below lay the same wide, double-stone avenue with the sluggish canal in the middle. But the encouraging thing was the sight of a broad, flat roof, which was less than fifty feet overhead.

Prof. Milroy essayed a weak cheer, and we started again. Less than a hundred feet brought us to the bottom of a ramp, at whose other end I could discern the gray sky. We fairly ran up that last passage. Abreast, Hanavan and I smashed the door open and sprang out onto the roof.

For some moments we cavorted in celebration, so great was our joy at escaping, and then we commenced to observe our surroundings.

The ramp terminated upon a platform upon which we stood. On three sides it sloped gently down to a flat gravelly plateau, extending a hundred yards to the nearest street. Across that another building roof—at about the same level—continued. Mile after mile the roofs extended, a vast plain crossed with chasm-like streets and dotted at intervals with skeleton-frame towers. Far away we could dimly make out through the mist a mass of immense buildings. Hanavan pointed to these and said, "That's evidently the 'down town' section. We are only in the suburbs."

Now that we were comparatively free, the next job was to find the *prolo*. This would have been simple except for the fact that we had not the slightest idea which way to go, and that the landing stage was nowhere to be seen. Hope ran high, however, so choosing at random we started along a street toward the nearest steel tower.

Hanavan's idea was to climb it, but after less than half a mile we found the route blocked by a cross street. Somewhat discouraged we sat down on the parapet and ate a little more of the concentrated food. It occurred to us that it might be a good idea to be sparing with our rations. Some ten minutes passed, when Prof. Milroy leaped to his feet with a whoop of joy and, pointing skyward, commenced a wild dance. Following his arm, Hanavan and I looked up past a steel tower into the haze, and there cruising slowly in our direction was the *prolo*. Crying something about the visibility of a moving object, Hanavan started running toward it in an erratic course. I followed, first spitting out in great relief the unpalatable Zongainian food tablet.

The *prolo* evidently sighted us immediately, for it accelerated and dropped lower. As it neared us I saw a door open on one side and several heads appeared. Suddenly I collided violently with Lord Hanavan. He was standing still, wildly beckoning to Milroy, a hundred feet ahead. Out of breath, he turned to me. "That's— that's not the same *prolo*...it's larger..." Not comprehending his words, I looked more closely at the now near craft. It was larger and of a different design. The next instant it was hovering thirty feet above us and I could see the faces peering down. They were angular...yellow...foreign looking.

Swiftly the ship descended until its landing rail grated on the roof. Immediately a dozen men sprang out, all armed with the tiny Zongainian small gun. In Zongainian they cried, "Who are you? From what *prolo* do you come?" Struck by a sudden fear we could not answer at first. The leader of the party appeared to become angry, and then he commenced to laugh. The others joined him, giving vent to a high-pitched cackle.

"Oh," he chuckled, "you are surprised to find a Kananese cruiser above Kanan? You thought they were all wrecked or captured by your invulnerable First Fleet? Ha, but you have much to learn! The First Fleet, the mighty First Fleet won't be boasted of much longer..." And with that he burst out laughing anew until he fairly wept.

Now indeed, we knew the fullness of our misfortunes. No sooner had we found our way from the city than we walked like very babes into the enemy's arms.

WHILE the Kananese were still indulging in their hilarious glee, Lord Hanavan addressed Milroy and me in a low voice in English. "Don't mention Vera Nadji and the ship or they'll get them all. Say that we were marooned by a Zongainian battleship. Make them think we're friendly..."

The commander, attired in a long yellow robe, approached us.

Come, my friends from Zongainia," said he, "you must not keep a cruiser of the Imperial Kanan Fiong waiting. You are going to have a rare honor; that of witnessing the end of your countrymen. You shall see the flagship *El Zongainian* itself crumpled to molten wreckage. Oh, it will not be long. Come!"

The crew closed in about us and knowing that resistance was useless we followed.

The *prolo* immediately arose vertically to a height of many miles, affording a wide view of the city, and then proceeded in a horizontal direction. He, of the yellow robe, approached.

Bowing to us he spoke, suavely.

"May I introduce myself. I am Ver Unkar, 19th Imman in the Navy of Lao Refi, Imperator of Kanan, Owner of All Souls, Arbiter of Life and Death, and Future Emperor of Zongainia. Have you names, Zongainians?"

Lord Hanavan, as spokesman, drew himself up and replied: "You are mistaken. We are not Zongainians; but unfortunate explorers from another part of their planet, who were dragged into this conflict against our will. We make no cause with them, and desire only to return."

The Commander, Ver Unkar, commenced to laugh again, and then stopped. "I would not believe you but for your complexion and accent, but you may be right. We shall see when we arrive at our citadel. Now to the point. We find you wandering, like lost *shivars* on the roofs. You could not have flown there, therefore, the Zongainians must have left you. I judge you don't like your abductors any too well. So tell us all about it, and Kanan may return you to your world when its fleets sweep the universe of Zongainian scum. What have they done to you?"

I had known Lord Hanavan for an archaeologist and explorer, but I confess that during the next half-hour he impressed me as being a first-rate actor. He described our adventures minutely and alluded to El Zoia, Ver Moti, and the others in terms that would hardly be complimentary to them. He ended by describing how we had been ruthlessly cast away to die in order to make more room on the *prolo*. Ver Unkar listened sympathetically, his yellow countenance expressing a variety of emotions, from anger to fierce joy, as we thoroughly described the bombing of the Zongainian encampment.

When Hanavan was through, he asked us many questions bearing upon the size and strength of the First Fleet; its system of cruising and of attack, and other points, all of which Hanavan answered in the fashion designed to give about all the information on what the Zongainians did *not* do.

After the interview we were fed, a meal more earthly than we had tasted for many days. Then we were securely locked in a tiny windowless chamber by Ver Unkar.

As soon as our captor's retreating footsteps had died out, Prof. Milroy spoke:

"Now we are in for it. Everything we do gets us further from any chance of returning to Earth."

"Somehow," answered Hanavan musingly, "the soft words of these Kananese are more foreboding than the open threats of Zongainia."

Prof. Milroy made an effort to cheer up.

"At least we will have an excellent opportunity to study a most interesting species at close range. And then, too, we shall eat— which is something. You know," he continued, warming to the discussion, "these people impressed me as being Mongolian— yellow skin, angular features... I would like to study one's skull...

And did you hear them talking among themselves? Their language—it was quite unlike anything I have heard—like the chirping of birds. They seemed to talk on a regular musical scale. If we could only get a recording... My! Perhaps it will all turn out well after all."

"They seemed," said Hanavan, "to have some plan up their sleeves to finish the Zongainian fleet. There is no reason to favor Zongainia, but I have a feeling that it won't improve our chances to have these Kananese win. I wonder what they are going to do?"

He looked at Professor Milroy as though expecting an answer, but that great savant was busy with a pencil, writing musical staves on the wall and singing scales softly to himself. Hanavan then ceased his discussing and we proceeded to take an inventory of the room.

After the passage of nearly two hours there was a change in the motion of the Kananese cruiser; it ceased its forward movement and dropped rapidly for a time. Then it decelerated; started again, moved horizontally, until finally a sharp jolt told us that it had landed. Outside our door were footsteps and voices, sounding like soft flutes running up and down *arpeggios*. We waited as patiently as possible until finally a hum sounded, the bolt was magnetically withdrawn and Ver Unkar entered. He was very businesslike and seemed worried.

"You will be conducted to the Intelligence Bureau—they will have complete charge from now on." He peered into the room suddenly at Milroy's musical notation, his eyes opening wide in surprise. "You speak Kananese?" he demanded, suspiciously.

"No." Milroy discovered that he did not know the Zongainian word for music, so he mumbled, "mathematical game," and hurried to our escort in the hall.

AS we were marched into the control room of the ship, Lord Hanavan, attempting to take a cheerful attitude, commenced to whistle Tipperary, when Prof. Milroy seized him by the arm. "Don't do that!" he hissed.

"Why?"

"Don't ask me," responded the other in the same low tone, "but don't sing or whistle. Our lives may depend upon it!"

Led by four tall blue-robed Kananese sailors and followed by a similar number, we descended from the *prolo* to the secret citadel of the city. The craft lay with many others on the floor of an immense room, through whose roof we had evidently come. This chamber, which must have been fully two miles square and eight hundred feet in height, was filled with toiling Kananese. Here and there weird machines shot sparks into the air. But save for the voices, there was none of the noise usually associated with a repair place. But the voices! They were indescribable. It was like the tuning of a vast reed orchestra, or the sound of wind in the pine forest. Nearby groups of workers could be distinctly heard "tooting" softly up and down the scale to each other. But the more distant voices merged together into a soft rhythmless music, rising and falling in cadences like the echoes heard in a seashell.

For several moments we three hesitated spellbound at the gangway, taking in the sight and sound until our guard, puzzled as to the wait, indicated by gestures for us to move on.

My recollections of the Kananese citadel are exceedingly vague. I remember that it impressed me as being huge, barbaric, and very old. The rooms were built of stone instead of composition material; while the more modern electric wires were glued along the molding, as though placed much later.

The passages through which we were conducted to the Intelligence Bureau were filled with busy men and women. Everywhere the place buzzed with industry; each turn unfolded wider vistas of machine shops, forges and laboratories. The ancient halls fairly echoed with the piping of the laborers.

We did not have to wonder to what end all this activity was directed. Ver Unkar's words stood always before us, "the First Fleet…won't be boasted of much longer."

After a quarter-hour's walk our escort halted before an imposing black stone doorway. On each side stood guards, with whom the blue-robed ones parleyed. After a pause the door swung open and we were admitted. Within was a sort of anteroom whose sole occupant was a short, stocky man in a brilliant red cape. As we entered he swung about and scrutinized us closely. He seemed to start the least bit as his eyes rested upon us, and then he spoke to the leader of the guards in Kananese.

Another wait. The man in the red robe strode impatiently up and down, paying utterly no attention to us. The eight guards leaned against the walls and chirped quietly among themselves. Finally, a small door at the other end of the room opened and the yellow face of a Kananese protruded. Immediately "Red Robe" entered and the door closed.

Hanavan and I sat down on a black stone bench, while Prof. Milroy edged nearer the guard, with his ears cocked. Twenty minutes passed, when the door opened again to let the man in the red robe out. Keeping his back to the door, he walked straight toward us. As he neared the bench he held out one hand in which I saw a folded piece of paper. Then he spoke in Zongainian:

"The examiner will see you at once, Zongainian dogs. See that you pay him respect…" After which he swept out the door without another glance. But upon the polished floor at our feet lay a tightly folded bit of paper. Looking sideways at the guards, I stood in front of Hanavan—hiding him for an instant—and then we all entered the door at the far end of the room.

The interview with the examiner was short and almost identical. Lord Hanavan did all the talking and managed it, quite adroitly, but for some reason or other the examiner did not take kindly to us. Dressed in a bizarre uniform and headdress he scowled more and more darkly, and finally cut Hanavan off short.

"Don't go any further," he said, "you are probably lying anyway. So you want to be sent back to Zongainia to tell where our stronghold is? You will consider yourselves fortunate to live—if you do. I'll take no chances on spies here."

He laid his fingers upon a little key, whereupon the door opened and we marched back into the arms of the guards.

Ten minutes later we were listening to their fading footsteps through the iron doors of a small, vaulted stone chamber.

CHAPTER FOURTEEN
The Mysterious Message

THE instant they were gone Lord Hanavan dug in his pocket for the piece of paper the man of the red robe had dropped. On it was inscribed in angular Zongainian characters:

"Keep courage. Work is done here for Zongainia. Watch and listen."

We re-read it several times and then Milroy commenced humming in a wandering, tuneless way, while his brow wrinkled with thought. Lord Hanavan carefully destroyed the note, making some remark about an uncomfortable place. I contented myself with examining the chamber minutely.

The room was constructed of square blocks of grayish stone, and from the worn appearance of the floor, had been in use many years. From the vaulted ceiling hung a single glow lamp whose wire entered by the ventilator. Dragging one of the benches under this I poked my arm into it as far as I could reach, but encountered only the stone sides of a rectangular tunnel. A gentle draft of warmish air came steadily in.

After a bit we talked together of Kanan, of the Zongainian fleet and of the mysterious man and his note. Lord Hanavan became reminiscent and described his house in London, his club, an elephant hunt in Burma, the unwrapping of a Pharaoh's mummy.

Prof. Milroy wound up his watch.

We wondered what Dr. Cummings, Pfeiffler and the little Englishman were doing. And we wondered who was going to win the war.

An hour or more passed; Lord Hanavan was yawningly suggesting that we get in some sleep, when there sounded a gentle scratching at the door. We rose to our feet. By its very slowness the sound suggested stealth. We moved so as to be behind the door when it opened. For twenty seconds the intermittent scraping continued, and then the door soundlessly swung in. A head appeared; glanced at us and then as quietly the door was closed. In the center of the room, finger on lips, stood the man in the red robe.

We waited, saying nothing. The other appeared to be listening, and then breaking into a smile he spoke:

"It was rather risky to come here so soon. But they are suspicious; they might move you any time before I could see you. It is necessary for you to know what to do."

Hanavan started to speak but the other cut him off.

"I know what you want to say. I understand your curiosity—but time presses. You can tell about yourselves later. You are Zongainians; that is enough for me. Listen carefully."

He paused, stepped swiftly to the door, and then returned to us.

"The Kananese scientists have discovered a magnetic beam that has the effect of crystallizing any steel coming within its field. It can turn the most highly tempered steel into a mass of brittle crystals in a second. Unknown to Zongainia, the Dictator, Lao Refi, has had built a gigantic magnet projector. It is their plan as soon as everything is ready to send a part of their fleet to attack the First Fleet out in space; to retreat to the citadel and drop to shelter behind a magnetic screen. Then the great beam will be turned on our ships, changing their girders and steel plates to crystals. The *prolos* will simply collapse.

"The mightiest guns, the thickest armor, will not save them from destruction. Not only will the entire First Fleet be lost, but El Zoia, who has come on board the flagship *Zongainia*, will be killed. The projector is above the repair shop—it is…"

He stopped suddenly and then opened the door a crack. He turned to the room for an instant, whispering:

"Guards coming. The fleet must be warned. If I am captured…" he broke off and darted into the hall. With a soft click the metal door closed.

We had no time to cogitate upon this rather surprising interview, for within less than thirty seconds five Kananese soldiers and an official-looking person with a black, kimono-like costume entered.

"I have been sent by the examiner," said he sitting down upon the bench. "When our great Emperor, Lao Refi, crushes Zongainia, he will open to your world the boon of Kananese civilization. No longer will your countries remain in the ignorance Zongainia has cast upon you. Your warring nations will be united under a Kanan government; we will manage all. Now the mighty Lao Refi does not wish to act without due consideration of his subjects, so I have come to learn of the customs of this little planet that our Governor may know whither he goes."

After this rather elegant, but suspicious introduction, he of the black robe rubbed his fingers together, glanced at the five guards lined before the door, and then commenced:

"You, Ver Hanavan, are from the Empire of England?"

"I am from England."

"It is the mightiest nation of Voya, is it not?"

"One of the mightiest."

"And you, I understand, are among its greatest?"

"No. My title is hereditary."

The other paused, regarding the ceiling. Then...

"I would be interested in securing a cross section of life in England, for statistical purposes. May I ask, what is your average day?"

Lord Hanavan looked annoyed.

"I don't understand you," he replied.

"What do you do when you awaken?"

"I arise." The other glanced sharply at him.

"Don't be facetious. You dress, and then order your palanquin—"

THE word had to be defined. Hanavan explained carefully that palanquins were not used in England.

"I beg your pardon. What does one use in England?"

Hanavan paused a moment, seeking a translation, and then replied with the name of the small Zongainian land vehicle—the *lokeg*. The man in the black robe raised his eyebrows as though noting something, and then visibly masking his thoughts he proceeded.

"Possibly before you order your *lokeg* you send messages across the city by runners to friends or business associates?"

This time our friend knew the word. "No, I would use a telephone."

Again the Kananese raised his eyebrows. His voice became softer and he leaned forward as he asked the next question.

"And if perchance the day is foggy, your servants light candles—"

"No. They would turn on the electric lights. May I ask to what purpose is this interview?"

"Its purpose," murmured the other, "is almost fulfilled. "One more question." He smiled at us in an oily way, as though pleased with himself. "Should you wish to hurry across the waters to France, you would bargain with some worthy fisherman for your passage—"

"Your question is senseless..." started Hanavan, and then at another steely glance from our inquisitor, he shrugged his shoulders. "I would buy a ticket on a...a motor glider."

At this hastily compounded Zongainian phrase, the Kananese abruptly stood up.

"That is all," he snapped, "come with me."

Vaguely alarmed over this odd visit we followed the guards down the great hall.

It was soon apparent where we were going, for less than ten minutes later we found ourselves face to face with the now glowering examiner. A few words were exchanged in Kananese between the black robe and the examiner, and then the latter turned upon us.

"Spies! Liars! Zongainian snakes!" he spat out, "You hope to fool us? Ver Iod was too clever for you. He has been to Voya, to England, only forty years ago. He questions you and suggests things that were done there two hundred of your years before, but you, who think you are wary, reply with tales of what may not be in England for another hundred years. Know, careless fabricators, that there are no *lokegs*, nor motor gliders outside of Zongainia.

"Know you that the brave Iod saw naught but wagons pulled by animals, in England? Know you that the Voyians use mineral oil for lights and not electricity? If you are the best spies El Zoia can send, then Zongainia is verily a nation of imbeciles!"

We listened, dumfounded, to this tirade. It was soon clear what mistake had been made. The Kananese had endeavored to trap Hanavan into an ignorance of his supposed native land, but because we were forty years ahead of the England Ver Iod knew, we were suspected of lying! It was no use denying, for the examiner's crowing might easily be turned into wrath, and in the present circumstances that was not to be desired. Lord Hanavan shrugged his shoulders and replied that he depended upon the righteousness of our cause and the examiner's justice.

That person was somewhat mollified by this and informed us that the justice of the noble Lao Refi and his administrators was infallible.

No more questions were asked and no information as to our disposal was volunteered. Our curiosity did not cover that topic to the extent of asking possibly provoking questions, so the three of us were marched out of the office without further ado.

We met the escort in the antechamber; they formed before and behind, and out the door we went. In the hall the front half of the escort paused, their backs toward us, while the rear section was getting out of the door. At this instant I felt someone bump against me and a hard cold object was forced into my hand. Startled, I turned in time to see a man attired in a dull gray cape, vanish into a nearby doorway. Without looking at the strange package I jammed it into my tunic and came into step.

We were taken this time in a different direction, and to judge from the steady climb, somewhere near the roofs. Finally we entered a corridor above, which sounded the subdued hum of some sort of electrical machinery. Oddly one of the guards offered information. "Transformers for welding machines," he said. I did not believe him.

The march soon ended in a tiny metal-walled room with a thick iron door. The solid thud of its closing carried away any hope of escape. We were here for keeps.

BY this time we had become so used to mysterious happenings, or rather our senses so blunted, that I showed Hanavan and Milroy my package with little excitement. It consisted of a curious-looking revolver-like instrument and the usual roll of paper. But this time the message was of interest.

"Zongainians: Whether you ore El Zoia's agents or not, I do not know, but in your hands now rests our victory or ruin. You are in the strongest prison room in all Kanan. The walls and door are of tempered steel. Guards will come with food within one dek. Then is your chance. Make your way to the projector as I direct. This weapon, if you know not its operation, will throw projectiles twenty to the second, when the thumb button is pressed. I can do no

more. My capture will occur within a quarter-day at the most. I give you my equipment and the blessings of Meta."

There followed some directions for finding the magnetic beam apparatus and a roughly drawn diagram. That was all. Hanavan examined the weapon for several minutes and then placed it on the bench.

"It's worth the attempt," he remarked. "At least it will end up doing something."

At this, Prof. Milroy, who had been paying little attention during the last few minutes, came to life.

"I don't think we will die," said he. "Keep that thing concealed when the guards come… I do believe philology will have a practical use after all."

Our attempts to get some explanation were met with an assured, if somewhat cryptic shake of the head. Finally, we sat side by side on the bench, while our colleague drew staves upon the wall and whistled and hummed intermittently.

For two hours we experienced one of those maddening waits that seem always to occur just before action. Milroy's whistling degenerated to the repetition of an unmelodious succession of notes, while his face bore an ever-widening smile. Finally he spoke:

"Well, gentlemen, I have it. When our friends enter, if you will allow me to…"

There sounded a sharp click. We faced the door, watching. A pause and it swung open.

Two Kananese entered while three others, armed, waited outside. Evidently the examiner was taking no chances. Those who had come bore several covered jars, which they proceeded to deposit on the table, without comment. This done, both turned toward the door, when Prof. Milroy walked slowly toward them and commenced to whistle that inane melody. Instantly the two stopped and wheeled about. Milroy continued to the end and, after a pause, repeated it with a variation. The effect upon the Kananese was amazing. Their repulsive features bearing what was very evidently the strongest of emotions, all five crowded into our cell and surrounded Milroy. He, not in the least embarrassed, continued to whistle speaking to us between breaths, in English.

"Out the door...while they are under the effects...slam it...when I come..."

Realization of what was happening began to come as we followed his directions. The guards stood in a half-circle about him, staring with glassy eyes.

"Mesmerized," murmured Hanavan, "by those tones."

There was little time for reflection, however, for hardly were we out of the room when Milroy joined us. He stopped his solo in mid-note and seized the door. "Quick, before they recover..."

The massive panel was closed, while from within came the click of some hidden locking device. We were free...in the citadel of Kanan.

As we hastened down the hall I confess I was more interested in the way in which our friend had hypnotized the soldiers than in our predicament. Hanavan shared my curiosity, though he glimpsed more of the truth than I, but Prof. Milroy gave but the briefest of explanations. Between hurried steps he told us,

"Musical scales and progressions seemed to be the basis of their language, and from the fact that a solitary person would make these sounds I inferred that their entire temperament was based upon tonal sensations. In a word, that their thoughts were made up of sound, instead of the pictures that cross our minds. And that emotions are to them simply tonal progressions...did you notice how the examiner chirruped when he was angry.

"So I concluded that any desired emotional state could be induced merely by the right tune, as it were. The problem became one of determining that tune. Fortunately, I have had plenty of time to listen and observe; the rest was only a matter of working out their psychological scale. The progression I used upon those guards consisted in alternate dominant sevenths and parallel minors, and induced the condition of surprised immobility, a state very convenient to us."

"That's your masterpiece, Sheridan," exclaimed Hanavan; "the last word in interpreting foreign languages. It's too bad the Royal Society cannot hear about it."

Suddenly Prof. Milroy in the fore, halted, finger on lips. We were at the end of the straight corridor. Ahead it turned sharply to the right and ended within fifty feet, in a tall metal door.

Listening, a confused patter of feet and a distant piping of voices was heard. Evidently beyond the panel lay one of the busy "streets" of the citadel. After vainly trying to locate a keyhole through which to peep, we held a council of war.

CHAPTER FIFTEEN
Milroy's Music

ACCORDING to the chart, which we now studied closely for the first time, it was necessary to traverse that passage for nearly five hundred feet. Our course marked by a red line now branched left, through a series of chambers each marked with a small red triangle surrounded by three dots...the Zongainian symbol for danger. At the end of the third chamber was the representation of a spiral staircase and the word *Unalt*—up. Here was another of those little triangles—what they meant we could not guess, but that caution was intended we felt no doubt. Beyond the stair was a short passage marked "pass; contact 7-29, 14-12, 2-18," and above that a circle with the word "magnet."

"The directions seem complete enough," I ventured, "but how did he expect us to pass this hall?"

"Shoot our way through," replied Hanavan. "Or perhaps overpower and change clothes with three Kananese. Excepting that it is rather doubtful if fate will present us with three alone... Too bad we locked those guards in."

Suddenly Milroy sprang up.

"I have it!" he cried delightedly. "Why use force when there is an easier way? Don't forget their 'Achilles' heel.' All that is necessary is to induce a state of catalepsy and Kanan is ours!"

"By Jove! Mass hypnotism..."

"Exactly! I have been thinking...the effect of a single note might be much increased if we could contrive to sound a chord..."

An hour and a half later, after about the oddest preparation for a battle that I can think of, we opened the metal door to the hall. For an hour Prof. Milroy had covered the walls with musical notations, and had whistled and hummed and perspired. Finally he wrote on three staves an eight-measure harmonization and we, like a "barber-shop trio," put our heads together and whistled, until each part was memorized.

"We've got them now," chuckled Milroy in triumph, as the door opened.

However Hanavan kept the gun ready.

The view that met our eyes as we stepped out was a familiar one. The passage, some eighty feet wide and half as high, was crowded with hurrying Kananese. Their ceaseless piping ran like the gurgling of a brook. At first we stood unnoticed on the threshold of the corridor, and then a man stopped, peered at us intently and began to back away, his voice raised in a quavering siren-like call. Instantly all other sounds stopped. The rolling current of humanity abruptly halted, and a thousand faces were turned upon the cause of the disturbance.

There was a moment of utter silence while their eyes sought us out. Now was the chance! Like the leader of a church choir Milroy waved his hand—one, two, and, we began. During the first measure there was no response, and an odd tingling sensation went wandering down my vertebrae. Forming my lips with difficulty I continued. Another measure passed; I saw that the expression of those nearest the door had changed. Their eyes seemed glazed. One rocked slightly. On we went into the first variation, then results. Someone in the front row sagged, limped to the floor. Another raised hands to face, staggered back a yard, and toppled. At once they began to fall everywhere. Whole rows collapsed, as if a machine gun had been loosed upon them. Before we had half finished our piece the entire audience was unconscious. With a sign, Prof. Milroy ceased.

"Old sayings illustrated," he remarked, stepping carefully over the recumbent bodies, "behold the audience after the musicale."

As may be imagined, it did not take us long to cover the distance to the side turn. Around the next bend could be heard a mounting volume of reedy voices raised in excitement, as the ceaseless traffic came upon the vanguard of the unconscious. With a fearful backward glance we hastened into the first of the small chambers marked with the danger sign.

Hanavan ahead, pushed open the narrow door and stopped. He whistled in surprise and entered. "My word! Just look at this…"

We crowded after him and then halted too. Before us was what was evidently a guardroom for there were stacks of weapons against the wall, but the guards lay, every one of them, in sweet slumber upon the floor!

Prof. Milroy was gleeful. "Danger number one disposed of, eh? If we only had a public address system, the war would be won!"

Stopping only to pick up an assortment of small weapons, we hastened on toward the second room from which we could already hear a powerful hum. It was separated from the first by a similar door, but the instant we opened it we realized that trouble was at hand.

Pausing together at the entrance we peered into a long chamber filled from end to end with electrical apparatus. Glittering coils of a greenish metal, great cubes of crystal and sheet silver, and a maze of switches, electrodes and circuit breakers turned the place to a veritable Steinmetz nightmare. From the farther end came the flickering blue glow of a mercury-vapor rectifier, while seated beside it was an elderly-appearing Kananese. The hum of the transformers had evidently drowned out our psychological trio, for the instant we stepped into the room the old man was on his feet, and reaching up to a switch.

"Ready?" queried Milroy. He raised one hand to start the music when the Kananese acted.

Down came the big switch and at the same instant, with a crackling roar, a curtain of flaming electricity descended before us. Shrinking back against the wall we soon found the origin of this display. Along floor and ceiling were rows of ball electrodes from, which leaped hundreds of arcs, interlacing, joining and breaking until they formed a lacy sheet of electricity completely across the room. To even approach it meant sure death, while as we suddenly realized, the continual roar prevented the thin sound of our whistle from being audible to the little man beyond.

For a moment we seemed defeated. We could not use the gun, for even if the guardian were killed his fiery curtain would remain.

RETIRING to the far end of the room we waited for the Kananese to make the next move. If we had expected him to call for help we were mistaken for, after making some adjustments upon the switchboard, he strolled in a leisurely manner up to the crackling wall between us. Here he made a long and careful inspection, seemed to nod his head, and returned to his seat by the transformers. He touched the lever, when from behind us sounded

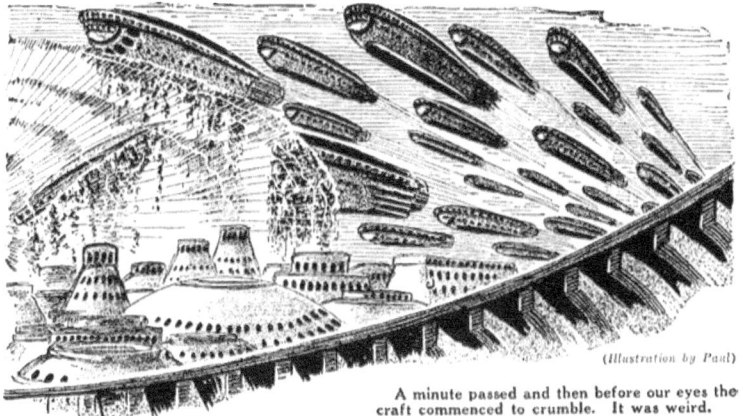

(Illustration by Paul)

A minute passed and then before our eyes the craft commenced to crumble. It was weird.

a gentle thump; the entrance door had dropped into place. It was not necessary to try it to know that we were locked in.

Hanavan prowled about the end of the room for a moment, poking at dials and levers, in the hope of finding a duplicate of the switch for the arc. No luck.

"It looks like the game is finished this time. We can't get our voices through—even with an amplifier. The crowd will be at our backs within a few minutes, and in a half hour the First Fleet will be in the range of the projectors."

"We might try to sing very loudly," suggested Milroy, "one can hear the whine of the transformers plainly through the screen."

Hanavan shook his head. "No," he said, "they are much louder..." Absently he twirled a dial. Immediately the tone of the transformer changed pitch, rising to a high whistle like a siren. Startled, he spun the little wheel in another direction, and was rewarded by a prolonged howl from the apparatus across the room.

"Frequency control," he muttered and was about to leave it when Prof. Milroy sprang forward.

"Frequency control to them, but our salvation!"

"What? What do you mean?"

"Controlled pitch! Play our notes on the transformer! As effective as whistling! Give me five minutes and this barrier will be gone!"

It was considerably less than five minutes when Prof. Milroy was ready. Paying no attention to the clamor of voices from the guardroom behind us, he seized the dial and after a few preliminary howls from the coil, he commenced to broadcast.

The little old man at once began to take interest. I watched—my heart in my mouth—waiting for him to collapse. But he did no such thing. Instead, he stared at us for a moment, nodded his head with vigor, and reaching up shoved the big switch back into place. Instantly the electric wall vanished; our path was clear to the end of the room. Making sure that his hand was far enough from the switch, Hanavan and I hastened across the chamber where the Kananese was smiling at us in the friendliest manner.

"Grab him," commanded Milroy. We did so, encountering no resistance. Milroy at once left his dial and hastened across the danger line. He had hardly reached us when the whole demeanor of the Kananese changed. The smile on his yellow face turned to a snarl and he commenced to struggle.

Our colleague regarded him a second, then pursing his lips he whistled softly. The prisoner relaxed, gave a soft squeak and tumbled from our grasp onto the floor.

"Come," reminded Milroy, "time presses."

At the farther wall of the instrument room was a narrow portal, beyond which lay the spiral staircase. Leaving the unconscious guardian heaped in his chair, we began to climb and Milroy explained:

"It would have been of no use to hypnotize him, so I tried another 'tune.' It merely caused the feeling of extreme affection for the universe in general and us in particular. A sort of love song, as it were. Of course, the effect ceased with the music, hence the lullaby."

From above came a vibrant hum, its intensity increasing with each turn of the spiral. It suddenly occurred to me that the sound came from the magnet projector; that that machine was already in operation against the fleet. We increased our pace.

We had ascended some five hundred steps when the top appeared. It consisted of a small chamber, less than six feet in diameter, roofed over with a spherical dome. On one side was a two-foot panel of blue stone, in which were imbedded a hundred or more copper disks; otherwise, the walls were of seamless metal. We stood for a moment staring blankly, when Hanavan, the sheet of paper in his hand, peered more closely at the metal buttons.

"There is a character cut on each one," he cried. He looked at the paper speaking his thoughts aloud. "Pass: contact: 7-29: 14-12: 2-18..."

Now I noticed fastened to the wall above the plate, two metal spikes connected by three feet of shining copper cable. For some reason, in this emergency our minds worked more rapidly. Hanavan seized the pins and cable while Prof. Milroy, pencil in hand, studied the panel. In a moment he checked two of the disks. After a pause he found another pair and marked them, and almost immediately located the last two numbers given in our directions. Hanavan, following them up, pressed his two spikes firmly against the contacts. There was a snap of sparks, while overhead I heard a click. Next, he connected the second pair of disks with the same result. Now the last two. The steel points were jammed into the copper. We waited a second, when silently half of the circular wall commenced to rise. Through the opening crack beneath came a flood of bluish light, while the hum of electric machinery became overpowering. Moment by moment I caught a widening glimpse of glittering steel, of dials and switches, of coils and insulators.

NOW the door was fully open. Gripping the little Zongainian gun, Lord Hanavan led the way into the chamber beyond.

We entered a room more than two hundred feet square. Its walls were composed of vertical columns and plates, while a hundred feet overhead was a cylindrical roof resting on wheels. We gave but the briefest of glances to the room, for our attention was immediately focused upon the towering mechanism that occupied its center. That we were looking upon the great magnetic projector itself, there was no doubt. Mounted upon a massive crystalline stand it resembled nothing more than a huge earthly telescope, save that the core was built of thousands of laminated iron plates and coils of wire.

Standing before the switchboard at the base of the instrument were a dozen men, with their backs to us. Even as we looked one of them pulled out a switch. A hollow rumble sounded above. We glanced up to see the whole ceiling sliding sideways. Beyond was revealed the dull, gray sky of Kanan, but in it were *prolos*—hundreds of them—dropping slowly past us. Far above, its remote crescents passing out of our field of view, was a gigantic armada of spaceships, thousands upon thousands…sweeping magnificently down upon the last stronghold of Kanan.

Involuntarily we thrilled at the sight, and then our attention was attracted to the group at the switchboard. One was talking in Zongainian.

"Will they not be surprised…what's left of them." He laughed. "And their fool spies! I would love them to be standing here now so they could see what happens to those who oppose…" The Kananese man had turned around and now he was facing us, his eyes wide in amazement and fright, his yellow face slowly whitening.

The others swung about at his silence. Instantly one made a motion with his hands. There was a sharp crack and a dim vision of a bluish spark. Lord Hanavan, in the lead, gave a sharp cry and staggered back raising his gun at the same time. Again the Kananese fired, and then Hanavan found the trigger button. There was a crackling rattle and the group of Kananese seemed to literally explode before him. In a cloud of smoke and flying bits of metal they ran a few steps, only to fall in that merciless hail. Explosive bullets—the Zongainian gun fired explosive bullets! Suddenly the barrage stopped. Hanavan was leaning against the nearer wall, his face white and drawn. He held out the gun. "Take it… Make them…turn magnet…upon Kananese." He closed his eyes as I took the weapon.

But now our attention was focused upon two who had escaped the general slaughter. These poor cowering wretches were on their hands and knees wailing what were evidently pleas for mercy, in their own tongue. Prof. Milroy, without pausing, whistled a few notes and pointed through the roof to the Kananese battle *prolos* now directly overhead. I backed him up with a suggestive shake of the gun.

I do not know which was the more potent, but under the combined influence of the gun and Milroy's hypnotism, the Kananese returned to the control and focused their dreadful telescope until it was bearing squarely on the center of the nearer fleet. Milroy, inflexible, gave the command. The power was turned on. A score of huge tubes flickered with a blue radiance, white six-foot coils on the magnet glowed red. A strange thrill passed across my body…the magnetism, or was it but a nervous state?

Tensely we waited, eyes glued upon the gray fish shapes above. A minute passed and then before our eyes the enemy crafts commenced to crumble. It was utterly weird, the slowness with which those giant living monsters turned to shapeless clouds of wreckage. One by one they changed, lost form and merged into one mighty rain. Girders, armor plates, guns, and tiny specks that might have been men, fluttered endlessly down, down to the roofs. Minute followed long minute until we discovered that the sky was empty again save for the distant crescent of the Zongainians. We blinked, unable to realize that the Kananese Imperial Fleet was gone…wiped out in a dozen minutes by their own weapon.

For hours it seemed I remained staring through the roof at the empty gray sky and the swarm of the First Fleet, moving infinitely, slowly toward the citadel. I do not know how long I would have remained thus had not I caught the image of a shadow moving swiftly in front of a dully-radiating coil. The next instant I looked down and my eye met that of one of the Kananese who was glaring with a deadly malevolence at me and slowly raising a slender metal rod.

Milroy must have seen him at the same instant for he gave a sharp cry of warning. Automatically my thumb found the button of the barrel of the gun. The Kananese threw himself forward and up and vanished into a haze of smoke. Now I saw the other man running, crouched low, toward the instrument panel. I started to shift my aim, when with a last great leap he reached his objective. The next second a glare like a lightning bolt flashed out. Instantaneously I saw the Kananese silhouetted against the coils, one hand grasping a shattered tube, his body completely encased in a gauze of sparks. Then darkness, punctured by leaping blue flames…a crashing roar of loosed fury…a dim vision of arcs playing up and down the length of the magnet. And then with a splintering sound it toppled, ponderously, majestically.

Shattering girders and lesser pieces of apparatus it fell, crushing into ruin half the chamber and bringing down with it the hopes of Imperial Kanan.

CHAPTER SIXTEEN
A Close Victory!

FOR a moment we stood motionless in semi-darkness, and then, without a sound, Lord Hanavan collapsed to the floor. We ran to his side, when from the still open doors came voices, running footsteps. The stairway! We had forgotten the stairway!

Prof. Milroy, with rare presence of mind, seized the gun and ran to the door. After hauling Hanavan out of the zone of fire, I returned to his side. As I arrived the voices rose to a sharp crescendo. Flinging the door wide Prof. Milroy turned his weapon downward. From below there sounded a sharp, strangled cry, followed by a prolonged and horrible screaming. His face ashen and his body rigid, Milroy held the weapon until the metal steps collapsed for thirty feet. Then he snapped it off and closed the door.

He gestured toward Hanavan.

"Dead?"

Without waiting for an answer he listened for a heart beat. He arose in relief. "Still going...no sign of a wound..." He shook his head, as though trying to clear his mind, and then walked unsteadily to a metal bench, where he slumped down.

For several seconds I remained standing at Hanavan's side, attempting to collect myself, before I remembered the fleet.

Half-fearing to find it gone, I looked up through the open roof. It was still there. So near that only its center could be seen, it drove downward, silently, ominously. Rank after rank of thousand-foot battle *prolos*; endless columns of smaller cruisers; a myriad of gnat-size bomb droppers, all drawing together upon the exposed entrance to the Kananese workshops and citadel.

Even now the magnetic ray should have been at work destroying the armor and steel beams of those ships. Somewhere the Kananese commanders, the examiner and the Emperor, were waiting and wondering at the silence, perhaps not knowing yet what had happened.

Suddenly I realized what it meant. Zongainia would he victorious...we would be rescued...we could return...

All thoughts were stopped at that instant, for with a blaze of colored lighting and a shattering blast of thunder, the first rank of the attackers opened fire.

Prof. Milroy leaped up at the sound. Without withdrawing my gaze from the roof I noted a light blinking rapidly upon a side switchboard. That was the Kanan military staff calling for help.

Now the very floor was shaking with the impact of shells and bombs. The Zongainian fleet had changed directions. It seemed to me to be circling and dropping gradually lower. Green bursts of flame in the sky showed that Kanan could still retaliate. But as the minutes passed these became rarer and rarer.

Ship after ship passed over. Now they were scarcely a mile away. A bursting shell threw a shower of cement and glass through the roof. As we scurried for the alcove where Hanavan lay, Milroy shouted in my ear, "One of those is coming here any minute. If we don't leave soon..."

I gestured toward the unconscious archeologist, but Milroy was busy across the room with a little oval door. He shouted something over his shoulder, inaudible in the din, and the door opened, revealing a tiny round chamber. Returning to me he cried, "Elevator...to the roof..." At my look of dismay, he returned, "Stairs gone. Must signal...only way... Help me with Hanavan..."

Another avalanche of debris forced us to make a quick decision. Half carrying, half dragging our friend over the crumpled remains of the projector, we managed to enter the elevator where Milroy, by some marvelous intuition, pressed the correct starting button. The door clicked shut, bringing the thunder of the battle to an abrupt stop, and the car rose swiftly; Milroy sat heavily on the floor and held his head in his hands. His whole body, physically exhausted, was giving way in spite of his heroic will.

"We have only a slim chance that they will see or recognize a signal," he murmured, "but we..." With a jolt the elevator halted, another door opened, and the tumult of the attack drowned further human words.

We were on the roof and in the shadow of one of the steel towers, overlooking the entrance to the Kananese stronghold. But what a change had taken place! The entire roof had fallen in. The camouflage was off, while half dozen Kananese *prolos*, cornered in their own pit, were fighting their last battle.

The First Fleet had gathered in a circle about the place, where it hovered motionless. From each *prolo* there poured a veritable stream of projectiles, under whose relentless impact the structures of the city crumbled like eggshells. Flames licked the skyline amid billowing masses of smoke, while countless buildings quivered and exploded from external and even internal blasts.

The workshop floor where we had landed was buried many feet deep by the wrecked roof and the riddled hulks of *prolos*. There seemed to be hardly a dozen Kananese ships left in sight, and some of these even lay disabled on the surface, still firing. Tighter yet grew the ring of the First Fleet. That the end was near was apparent.

I became aware that Milroy was shouting inaudibly at me. I took a step back when, without warning, the roar ceased.

A crowd of echoes was heard for a few moments, and then silence descended—utter and deafening by its very intensity. A line of red flames flickered quietly across the pit; some masonry fell with a light clatter. I looked at Milroy. "What is it...?" He did not reply. Again I turned my eyes upon the pit.

THE Kananese *prolos* were rising silently, each toward a Zongainian craft. Dimly I made out lines of minute things that were men filing out of the buildings into the open. For a moment smoke blotted out the scene. Milroy's voice, small and distant and bell-like, broke the stillness.

"They are surrendering...giving up...it is all done!" Abruptly he sat down, tried to speak, and then crumpled in a heap on the steps.

Suddenly I realized that we were invisible here and that we must signal. I shouted and waved my arms; then, seeing the futility of such signs, seized the gun and turned it upon the pit. Again and again it crackled, until I saw a *prolo* turn toward us. In a moment it was overhead. Faces looked out, not the sickly yellow masks of the Kananese, but the round tanned features of Zongainians. I attempted to shout, to point, but the effort was too much. The universe leaped in circles about me, and then blackened. I felt myself falling, arms about me...voices...movement...darkness.

"Meta ela Meta! In this word there is no defeat! *Meta ela Meta!"* These words uttered in Zongainian by a resonant bass voice heralded my return to the land of the living. To my opened eyes there was disclosed a low steel room, its floor covered with pneumatic beds and prone men. A faint hum came from somewhere…engines! I raised my head to look for the speaker, when the voice came again…from a small black box at one end of the room.

"Word has just been received from the flag ship that Lao Refi, Emperor of all Kanan, has surrendered personally, and is now aboard the *Zongainian*…"

At this there arose a babble of conversation from the other occupants of the room. Now I noticed that all wore the molded bandages here and there on arms and legs. Another glance about the room convinced me. The steel walls and floor, the faint vibration of electrical machinery, all pointed to one conclusion. We were in the hospital room of a Zongainian battleship.

The patient on my left turned on his side and said to me: *"He* thought he was going to retire on a pension after making a mess of the job of Emperor, but El Zoia had him by the neck. When the people and the army found they had to choose between losing an emperor or having the city bombed, they rendered him up in a hurry. Ha! But this is *the day* for El Zoia."

Seizing upon the first thing that came into my mind, I asked, "What *prolo* is this?"

"Brought in unconscious? This is the *Zongainian.*"

"Where are we?"

"I can't tell within a half light year, but we are somewhere on the route to Zongainia."

My heart gave a sudden leap. Zongainia! The Earth! We were going back!

I lay back on the pneumatic bed and listened to the voice from the loud speaker. It evidently came from Zongainia, broadcasted across the Universe, by a ray a thousand times faster than light. As I listened a sense of unutterable repose and comfort came over me. The voice continued.

"…The country is waiting only for the coming of the flagship *Zongainian* and the fleet to celebrate the victory. The people are already swarming about the government Ethero station for a first television glimpse of their beloved El Zoia. Ver Menisto has crowned his career as statesman and scientist by a military achievement of the highest order."

"Is he on the ship?" I asked. "El Zoia, I mean."

"Yes."

I lay back again. I wondered why no one approached my bed; why this wounded soldier spoke as though I were but a comrade; why we had not been sent to the Commander—and then suddenly the truth dawned upon me. Picked up in the turmoil after the fight dressed in Zongainian garb, tanned by the sun of Egypt to a betel brown, we had been placed unrecognized among the thousands of wounded to be returned home. My breath came faster as new hope grew within me. Glancing about I soon made out the forms of Prof. Milroy and Lord Hanavan. Turning again to the man beside me I attempted to make conversation.

"Which *prolo* were you on," I asked.

"The *Voya V*," he replied. "I was carrying ammunition when we got it...tore the whole side out of the old *Voya*. I thought we were all through but the city roof broke our fall. I was conscious all the time. One of the first landing parties from the *Ahtz*, I believe, picked us up."

He scratched his bandage and then looked at his wounds through its transparency.

"Those landing expeditions were all failures," he remarked. "Before we went down, I saw the *Muniun-116* drop three thousand in a street. I don't believe half of them ever returned."

He regarded the ceiling meditatively, but at that instant a number of men and women, evidently doctors, entered. I lay back on my couch again, wondering if I would be recognized. Shortly after, I fell asleep.

More than a week, by earth's time, passed before Hanavan, Milroy and I could be called well. Our illness was nervous rather than physical, and such I gathered could not be treated so speedily. However, we were given every comfort, so recuperation came rapidly. Toward the end of the week the ward was almost empty of patients, and we had all the privacy we could desire for planning.

BOTH Lord Hanavan and Milroy had had the same idea as I. If we could mix with the 80,000 odd members of the crew there was a possibility—the barest possibility—that we might make our way north, out of the country to the Sobat. Thence on a raft to civilization. If Cummings and Pfeiffler and the Englishman were prisoners on board, we might contrive to free them, too. Otherwise, all we could do would be to bring back a rescue party from England. An army division, if necessary, and force the Zongainian dictator to give them up. Oddly, we still thought of Zongainia as a beautiful but half-barbaric country. Even after what we had seen of its strength. Lord Hanavan, who had once been a Colonel in India, never thought of the military strength of Zongainia in terms of a *prolo* fleet over London!

After the passage of a week, more or less, we were pronounced "ready for duty." Rehearsed beforehand, we duly reported that we were members of the landing party from the *Muniun-116,* lost on the roofs. After being registered under names made up beforehand, we were assigned places as "inductor-men," in the engine room, and as far as the Zongainian staff was concerned, we were cared for.

Owing to our position in the center of the *prolo,* we did not for a long time comprehend just how huge the *Zongainian* was. Naturally we avoided asking suspicious questions, but while off duty Prof. Milroy, rummaging in the engineer's office, found some rather astounding data. The *Zongainian* had a beam of eight hundred feet, a length of 5170 feet, and weighed on earth, some seven million five hundred thousand tons. Its normal crew was 78,000, it had 800 30-inch rapid-fire guns, and 4000 five-inch guns. Its armor plating was four feet thick, and its engines developed a horsepower of three hundred million!

Our job during the fifteen or more weeks of the return voyage was that of caring for two of the immense induction coils that supplied high-tension current to some motor. The coils were more than thirty feet in length and by their proximity to our sleeping quarters kept us continually charged with electricity. Within the first five minutes, Hanavan's watch became magnetized and stopped. Milroy's long, fine hair stood out like an aura about him, making a really excellent electroscope.

Our quarters consisted of three trough-like berths, one above the other, in what might be termed the starboard dormitory. Five thousand men slept there, occupying the berths in rotation; and it was necessary to be out immediately, after the first gong sounded, to make room for another person finishing his six-hour shift. Food was rationed out at the beginning of each shift, and we ate on duty whenever we were hungry, consuming both the gelatine and the package in which it was issued.

Upon several occasions we caught glimpses into the main power room of the craft, but a limited scientific knowledge prevented any comprehension. The place was vast; hundreds of feet square and high, and filled with Titanic electrical apparatus—coils—condensers—fifty-foot vacuum tubes, whose glow cast weird reflections on the ceiling.

As nearly as we could understand, the purpose of all this apparatus was to generate electric current of a certain frequency and waveform that, when sent through ranks of mineral crystals, caused electromagnetic impulses creating a sort of interference phenomenon with gravity.

We ate and slept within a five hundred-foot area and not once during the whole trip did we catch a glimpse outside.

All things must end, however—even this interminable voyage. Day by day the bulletin board in our sleeping room announced a smaller velocity, and a shorter distance to cover before we should reach the Earth. Our fellow-workers talked now of the coming landing, of friends, parents, wives or husbands, of homes. We three, in our turn, became animated by a great excitement, which leaped higher as the news came that we were inside Neptune's orbit—A. N. 8 it was termed on the bulletin board, after the sun's astronomical name Alf Nueri.

Uranus' and Saturn's paths were crossed during the next day without sighting them. Jupiter's orbit was passed at a distance of two hundred million miles from the planet. Then we decelerated five days among the asteroids. At Mars, fifty million miles from the earth, an escort of some thousands of *prolos*, the "Asteroid patrol," met the First Fleet. In common with a number of the other engineers we went to the windows for our first view of the sun.

It was very disappointing. The Sun, dull in comparison to the other giants of the Universe, glowed beneath. Over to one side a tiny, ruddy, heavenly body gleamed—Mars. And far below, a silvery blue star of intense brilliancy attended by a dimmer companion, lay the Earth. We looked at it—too filled with emotion to speak. About us the crew, shouting to each other, danced and laughed with joy.

After we had returned to the sleeping room, Lord Hanavan drew Milroy and myself toward him.

"Landing in Zongainia," he said, in a low voice, "won't automatically mean walking up the steps of the Royal Society. Once we leave the ship we will be on our own in a city and country almost as unknown as Kanan. One slip may mean capture. That everyone will be rejoicing will aid us somewhat, but we must be careful. Our immediate course can be decided by *where* we land. If it is in the city of Imperium it will be very difficult. If we descend in the northern city—Andorks—we will have only a short distance to travel to the valley...the basalt cliffs...the Nile..."

Others of the crew entered the room at this instant and all conversation ceased.

It was now only a matter of hours until we should land. Weight increased abruptly as deceleration was raised. Up the great hallway toward the control sounded voices...running steps. Orders to stand by our coils and switchboards came from above. Vague shiftings and movements betrayed the maneuvering of the *prolo* as it approached its landing place. We waited...

Then deceleration increased once more. A faint whistling echoed from outside. The atmosphere! Then our motion seemed to slacken; we moved forward, stopped again. A long pause ensued and then a sharp tremor, a metallic thump. Orders appeared on the ground-glass signal screen: "Shut down power."

The hum of the generators slowed. Like the descending whine of a score of sirens, the massive motors were turned off. Voices sound up the hall; the sharp hiss of air and a breath faint, but unmistakable, came down to the engine room. We sniffed long and then laughed idiotically at each other. It was the fresh tangy breeze from the lake! We had landed; the voyage was over.

CHAPTER SEVENTEEN
The Mysterious Stranger

AND now I come to what is one of the strangest parts of our whole adventure. A half-hour after the *Zongainian* had docked, with about four thousand more refugees from other ships, we were disembarked and told to report to the Prolo Shops at Andorks the next day. We marched down an enclosed gangway and onto a balcony. We paused for a moment, confused, and then remembrance flashed upon us. We were overlooking the Imperium landing way from the very walk where a half-year before we had been led to our prison ship, but what a difference there was now.

At that time we had been helpless prisoners, confused, comprehending nothing of the language; not knowing whether we would see another dawn. Now we stood attired in the uniform of the Zongainian Navy, masters of the tongue and, as it turned out, heroes in the eyes of everyone. With a crowd of some two hundred others, we marched down the hall and into the main lobby of the great interstellar depot. In this immense room, which measured more than seven hundred feet square, milled a vast crowd of people, colorful in their light costumes; cheering wildly and throwing Zongainian confetti in the form of iridescent bubbles of some sort, upon the column of returning soldiers.

Through a lane in the crowd we went, and so out upon the street.

Here also were uncounted thousands of people, extending between the towering buildings as far as the eye could reach. Dazzling beams of colored lights flickered back and forth from spotlights on the balconies. Music—strange, throbbingly triumphant, and beautiful—floated down from nowhere. From the steps of the depot we caught a momentary view of the whole spectacle, and then still with the main body of soldiers we descended and were swallowed up in the mob. It was not difficult to make our way down the street, for unlike European crowds, the Zongainians were courteous in their excitement.

One by one our comrades dropped off, going to their respective homes before reporting to Andorks, until finally we three found ourselves, late in the evening, on the outskirts of the zone of celebration. About us the buildings were lower, while the glass ceiling had ended some blocks back. Overhead it was cloudy; the colored lights of the city were reflected back like an aurora. Once we caught a glimpse down a long avenue of the White Tower, arising an incredible distance and bathed in rainbow hues. And once in the midst of a turmoil of music from a square we were startled by a familiar piece of earthly music—Liszt's Second Hungarian Rhapsody.

There were fewer people here and they seemed intent upon getting to the central area as soon as possible. Stepping into the arcade of a building, we took a moment to discuss further movements. Now that we were actually back, all our former assurance departed. The city of Imperium, which had seemed so unimportant when the Universe lay between us and the world, now assumed vast proportions. We suddenly realized that we had a hundred-mile hike ahead of us before we could even leave the in-habited area of the country, and then without sufficient clothing or shoes, and with only the little Zongainian rapid-fire gun, which was hardly suitable for game. We would then have to make a long return journey down the Nile.

"We might go on to Andorks with the rest," suggested Prof. Milroy, "and have a seventy-mile start."

Unfortunately we had no idea as to the point of embarkation; indeed, I doubt if we could have found our way back to the landing way. We dared not ask questions and feared that an attempt to walk the streets all night might result in arrest; or whatever was done to vagrants in Zongainia.

Rapidly now courage oozed out. We were as lost in Imperium as a Hottentot would be, alone in New York City.

As conversation lagged, I noticed a man standing at the sidewalk railing that overlooked the street proper and who was regarding us steadily. I nudged Hanavan and indicated the watcher. For a moment we looked in silence, and then Hanavan murmured, "We must not let him know we see him. We may be suspected...we may be breaking some law..." he stopped abruptly, and I turned about. The man had left the railing and was walking toward us in a leisurely manner. We crouched back into the doorway, horrified. My heart leaped; I looked up and down the street, but escape was impossible. The other doubtless had weapons...

Hanavan whispered, "Bluff it out. We have a chance yet." I essayed to brace myself up, with sorry results. Luckily the shadows hid our faces.

In a moment the strange Zongainian was at our side.

"From the fleet?" he asked, pleasantly.

Hanavan nodded adding, "The *Zongainian.*"

The other was agreeably surprised.

"Has anyone invited you for the evening?" he inquired next.

Hanavan paused, uncertain as to the answer. Finally he said, "No."

"Well, that will be fine," replied the other, apparently well pleased. "With twenty million families looking for one of you returning heroes as a guest at the celebration, you are rather at a premium." He paused. "I have apartments in the Sixteen Meriot Building. My private car is on the street below. If you will..."

We would. I was cold and damp with perspiration from the reaction as we descended to the street and climbed into the orange-colored vehicle.

Without a sound, the stranger started his machine and we were soon moving at a rapid pace toward the White Zongainian Tower.

As soon as we were under way the driver turned to us. "My name is Ver Anul..."

WE hastened to introduce ourselves by the names given on board the *Zongainian.*

Ver Anul then proceeded to ask many questions about the war, about the siege of Kanan, and the ease with which it had fallen.

"It is a matter of much wonder to the government, I hear, that the Emperor allowed—literally invited—the First Fleet to defeat him. And there have been reports that some strange accident overtook the greater part of their fleet. However, a commission has been appointed to investigate the matter. Their findings may be announced tonight."

A pause followed and then Hanavan very carefully began asking about the celebration. Ver Anul, however, did not appear surprised, and talked all the rest of the way. We gathered that there would be a ceremony in the largest auditorium in the city, which, broadcasted through telephone wires, would reach everyone in the country as well as the three hundred thousand in the hall. Ship commanders and soldiers were to receive decorations, the terms of the treaty were to be read and Ver Menisto, the all-conquering El Zoia, was to make a speech. Before the ceremony we were to have lunch in Ver Anul's apartment. Further explanations were cut off by the arrival at the apartment building.

Ver Anul shared his suite with another man and three women, all unattached business people who lived together like a happy family sharing parlor, bedroom and bath. Each had a soldier guest for the evening who kept us in the background by their conversation about the war. Dinner, the usual jellies and thin wafers and sour liquid, was soon over. Ver Anul, with profuse politeness, escorted us to a chute and handed us the little metal guides. It was no time to back out, so with averted faces we dropped off one by one. The chute ended in a sort of station where one could enter the cars of the pneumatic subway. Our host indicated a car and entered after us. Twenty or more people were already there, reclining on tiers of bunks that made the place suggestive of an American Pullman car.

We were in the car scarcely five minutes when it halted and everybody hastened out. We found ourselves in a vast square under the open sky and facing the facade of a great building. Glowing windows three hundred feet high stretched for two miles on either side, while a glimpse of moonlit water beyond showed that we were near the lake. The square was covered by an immense crowd which must have numbered hundreds of thousands, but Ver Anul knew his way for he pushed through to a small door near the main entrance. Showing a round ticket of some kind to the doorman, he pushed in.

"Reserved," he explained. "In the first row of seats."

"He must be important," whispered Prof. Milroy in English. "I wonder why he picked us up?" Hanavan shrugged.

The next second we passed through a short corridor into the auditorium. I was prepared for something huge, but the size of this room was overwhelming. Its ceiling, hung with heavy curtains, was more than six hundred feet overhead, while the floor extended over two miles back. Seated upon the floor and the mile-wide philology balcony was the audience—three hundred thousand people.

At the nearer end of the hall was a large platform occupied by a number of seats and by a device we surmised to be amplifying apparatus for the speakers. Directly behind this hung a white screen almost four hundred feet square whose purpose we could not guess.

Ver Anul went at once to a vacant bench where we all sat. He spoke to a number of other men and women nearby and they, I noticed, glanced at us with interest.

The first few rows of seats in front were separated from the rest by a light fence. In this space gathered a thousand or more people, all evidently officials of the government, or officers of the fleet. Several hundred other soldiers in their tunic-uniforms and light capes took seats across the room.

After a short wait all the lights dimmed and went out, save those on the platform. A spotlight from the microphone stand illuminated the speaker's seat. A few moments passed during which the vast assemblage became quiet and then a figure, which I immediately recognized as El Zoia, ascended to the platform. As he stepped before the microphones, a brilliant light was projected on the mammoth screen and, standing more than three hundred feet high, a clear colored picture of him appeared.

Every movement, every feature must have been visible from the farthest end of the hall. A murmur arising from the audience died down. The tiny figure on the platform inclined his head, followed exactly by the image above; and then his voice, amplified a million-fold, sounded from behind the screen.

His talk was short and concerned itself with anecdotes and descriptions of the campaign. In spite of our limited knowledge of the Zongainian literary tongue we could see that he was a born narrator. Within five minutes we had completely forgotten our situation, and were entirely engrossed in his charming tales.

After an hour of this, he introduced a short bearded man, the first such we had seen in Zongainia, who was the commander of the First Fleet. This man, whose name I believe was Ver Loxus Throm, complimented the officers and personnel of the fleet and introduced another—National Secretary is the nearest English translation of his title—who discussed the economic results of the war. Then the Dictator took the platform and called up a dozen or more *prolo* commanders to be decorated with a silvery cloth headdress, not unlike those worn by modern Arabs. Murmurs of approval from the audience greeted each decoration. Next some fifty officers were awarded scarlet hoods for exceptional bravery, and one spoke into the microphone and televisor. Ver Anul leaned over and whispered in my ear:

"The big event of the evening has not come yet. It will be a...surprise."

I made little of that remark and, attributing it to my ignorance, continued to watch the proceedings. For perhaps an hour these decorations were given out, and then El Zoia took the stand.

"We now come to the presentation of the hood of Ela Meta, the highest honor possible to a Zongainian soldier, which tonight will be given to three of the crew of the *Alf-Nueri*, for bravery in the face of danger, unvarying tenacity of purpose and devotion to their country. Their names will be engraved for all time in the memory of Zongainia for having saved her fleet from destruction. Their names are: Lord Mitchell Hanavan, of England; Prof. Sheridan Milroy, England; David Lawrence, United States."

The murmurs of the audience broke into a roar of applause, which drowned out even the loudspeakers. We lay back upon the bench, amazed, stunned. Ver Anul seized Milroy and me by the arms and cried:

"Up, up! Go up to the platform! He's waiting..."

We staggered forward, unable to think, and blinked into the lenses of the televisor. I became conscious that El Zoia was speaking to us; of gigantic figures upon the screen that were our own; of a continual thunder of voices from the hall; and of a gold-colored hood being placed over my head; and then, our minds reeling, we were literally carried off the platform and out of the side entrance, while three hundred thousand people yelled madly for three escaped prisoners who had just been recaptured.

CHAPTER EIGHTEEN
Homeward Bound

THE mental reaction from the events of the past few hours kept us in bed until noon of the next day. I doubt if we could have slept at all save for the gaseous sleeping potion blown in through the ventilator. As it was, however, we got a good dose of slumber—the best thing possible after what we had passed through.

I awoke first, quite without memory of what had happened. I was lying under a glass panel frame like a counter in an American store. This enclosed bed, for such it was, was one of six in a big square room, flooded with sunshine from windows and a skylight.

Outside lay a wide formal garden, a small lake, and beyond, a mounting range of forest-covered hills. My mind still groping, I sat up and nearly cracked my skull on the ceiling of the sleeping compartment. At this, jolt recollection came in a flood. The landing at Imperium...the strange man who had picked us up in the street...the auditorium... I held my head between my hands for a moment. Suddenly my attention was attracted by a muffled shouting and thumping. Startled, I looked into the next bed in which Prof. Milroy lay, tangled in the cape he still wore, shoving and pushing at his enclosure.

Seeing that I was awake, he made motions indicative of escape and gestured toward the other bed-cases. I now observed that each contained a slumbering figure; whoever they were they had not awakened. At this moment Prof. Milroy found the mechanism opening his bed and the top rose like a jackknife bridge allowing my comrade to roll out onto the floor. His first act was to direct me by many gestures and shouted phrases, to pull down a lever inside, causing the glass case to open. The next instant I stood beside him.

His first words were an exact echo of my own thoughts. "In Heavens' name, what has happened? Where are we?"

I shook my head. "On Earth, that's sure. In Zongainia awaiting deportation, probably."

Milroy walked to the window. "At least," he murmured, "we can get another glimpse of the old world. Look, a butterfly."

I ran to his side to see. A wave of feeling swept over me as I looked out. Trees, grass, clouds, birds and insects, the golden light of our own sun. For minutes we stood silently at the window, absorbing through every pore the warm sunlight, and the familiar earthly beauty of the scene.

Finally, Milroy, turning away with an effort, pointed to the other beds.

"Who are they?" he asked of the empty air. Hanavan..."

We hurried to the nearest. Inside was a short, stout figure, lying on his back and giving vent to snores audible even through the soundproof case—Prof. Pfeiffler! I rushed to the next case—yes, there lay Cummings, sleeping quietly, his face somewhat tired-looking. Milroy, ahead of me, cried out that he had found the little cockney, Hawkins. And in the farther bed, Lord Hanavan was just in the act of awakening. It can be well imagined with what impatience we three waited the awakening of the rest of our companions.

What had happened to them after we had left the disabled *prolo* on our ill-fated search for wire? Had they been transported here on board the *Zongainian?* Did they know how we had been tricked into coming to the celebration? That the mysterious Ver Anul was an agent of El Zoia, we had no doubt now. How long we had been watched could not be guessed. Hanavan tried to open Dr. Cummings' bed, but could find no fastening outside. We had to wait.

Lord Hanavan went to the window where he remained for several minutes before turning to us.

"No escape there," he mused. "They're watching, we can be sure of that. Our fate, I guess, is in the lap of the gods."

"El Zoia, you mean," muttered Milroy, "the gods haven't a chance here."

"Well, in any case, we are going to see Dunsaan again, or a more distant place." He paused to watch a humming bird outside. "You know, I cannot understand yet his reason for last night—El Zoia's, I mean. His action seemed contradictory to his nature. He may have a love of the dramatic; a sort of grand gesture before the execution to impress his subjects."

From behind there sounded heavy footsteps. A voice, deeply melodious and never-to-be-forgotten, rang out—in English:

"I may have to deport you yet, gentlemen, you seem to know too much about me."

We spun around. In front of the now opened door he stood, attired in a white tunic and cape, hands on hips and beaming on us as if immensely pleased. We remained silent.

"In your land," he continued, "stories usually end happily. I trust this one has."

Hanavan found his voice. "It has ended?"

"First installment," replied Ver Menisto. "To be continued."

Prof. Milroy now spoke. "You seem to know about the magnet projector in Kanan…"

"Nothing mysterious there, Prof. Milroy. My agent, whom you saw, told all about it."

"So you allowed us to work our way back on the *Zongainia* thinking we were unknown…?"

"Precisely." He pointed to one of the beds. "I believe our learned Deutscher has awakened…Prof. Pfeiffler. We spent many a delightful hour on the return trip. His Zongainian is…well…he speaks with such an odd accent. But I learned a great deal of zoology."

PFEIFFLER sat up, blinking, and then raised the glass case.

"Guten tag, mein Herr Menisto. Vell, und here iss all der rest uf der oxbedition." He stood up, stretching. "Dot vass a vine bardy ve had last nighd. Vasn't id?"

Now Cummings was awake. He climbed out, said good morning to El Zoia, and laughed at our stupefaction.

"Your friends," explained El Zoia, "shared my suite on the *Zongainian.* We became quite well acquainted."

For some twenty minutes we talked thus, telling experiences, describing impressions, for all the world as though in Hanavan's London drawing room. We were completely carried away by El Zoia's informal manner.

We walked out upon a white stone porch overlooking the garden, the wide valley and in the remote distance the city of Imperium, which lay far below and to the south. About us lay a magnificent villa—palace rather—of white stone-like material, six floors high and covering acres.

"This," explained Ver Menisto, "is my regular home—when I *am* at home. We are in the province of Palata—recognize the Latin in Palata and Imperium, Milroy? And those mountains mark the northern border of the country."

He paused. Hanavan filled the breach. "We have been wondering for some time as to the—the disposal which will be made of us. We..."

"Of course," he replied, "and I have my mind quite made up on the subject. Your greatest desire is, I imagine, to return to your world?"

We did not answer. Hanavan stood at the railing, looking at the slender spire of the white tower in the distance. Some small birds of an iridescent green fluttered on the balcony.

"I have been studying you carefully," continued El Zoia, "You are scientists, semi-civilized, men of honor. I understand your thoughts and fears of returning to Dunsaan, or even of remaining under compulsion here. And so, perhaps because I am not utterly unemotional, or because you might escape anyway, I am going to send you back—send you back home. Your pledge of silence will be enough. You have worked well for Zongainia, and as courageous soldiers of Zongainia, you are thus rewarded."

He stopped. For a long moment we all remained in silence, then Lord Hanavan spoke:

"We give our word." That was all.

Ver Menisto hesitated for an instant. Then his entire manner changing he cried cheerfully:

"Well, now that that matter is settled, we might spend the rest of the day seeing a little more of Zongainia. I have a small *prolo* here and we ought to cover most of the country before sunset."

I can remember little of the afternoon. We soared for hours in the tiny open flyer, sometimes high, sometimes skimming the surface of the lake. Now that our minds were no longer occupied with worry, the beauties of the country were more apparent. A wide basin, containing the capital and the lake, and flanked by three rich valleys constituted, with the magnificent mountain mass, the main topographic features of the region.

Here and there the plain was colored by cities, while silvery roads ran in geometric lines. In the extreme clarity of the air on the plateau every detail could be made out, buildings, streets, the odd streamline ground vehicles, and the monorail trains, like the one we had first seen on that day so long ago. El Zoia navigated the machine himself, pointed out cities and rivers like a veteran tourist guide.

Finally, late in the afternoon, we descended to the roof of the tower… The same landing crew helped us out, and in the office below the same secretary bowed and ushered us in.

Ver Menisto now telephoned, using instruments quite out of sight, and made arrangements for a ship to carry us away.

"No use to send you on a long trip on foot," he explained. "We can land you in London in an hour."

As sunset approached we supped in the office—a delicately flavored gelatine and the bitter drink. For some reason the food seemed better than before, possibly because it was the last meal we would eat of it. There was little conversation. El Zoia, in a corner confined himself to brief answers to questions. The rest of us, overlooking the lake and the mountain watched the sunset—so like that on the eve of our coming.

Finally, the meal was through. In response to some orders given without our knowledge, an attendant entered bearing six complete suits of clothes secured I cannot imagine where. It is difficult to describe the effect these heavy, dark things had on us. I had a disagreeable sensation of putting on a straitjacket as I struggled with the shirt and collar. After twenty minutes to effect this change, a voice on the telephone announced that the *prolo* was waiting. Ver Menisto ascended with us to the roof.

"I believe I will go with you," he remarked. "If it is foggy at London we can drop you at Hyde Park."

We climbed aboard, the engines hummed a higher note, and the *prolo* arose effortlessly from the roof. The last gleam of light had vanished from the mountain and the yellow afterglow of the sun was fading over the western hills. Overhead the sky glowed a deep blue, while in its depth an occasional star shone steadily. El Zoia saw us watching and pointed.

"A. N. 2...Venus. You would be interested...a unique world..."

As the velocity increased, the city slid ever more swiftly beneath us. Its luminous streets gathered together until they took on the semblance of a giant spider web. The mountain, a dull white now, fell away on the right. Ahead a somber dark plain extended north. The jungle, the desert, Egypt...England...

Somehow as the lights of Zongainia vanished one by one I felt a regret, a vague wish to stay longer, to see more of this land. In the darkness of the cabin, visions of the world, the old familiar world of houses and streetcars and noise, and rush, became clearer. I began to reconstruct mentally the broken thread of my existence, cut so suddenly...was it only six months ago? Cummings and I would go back to New York and write up our paper on metaphoric rock deposits of North Africa. There would be questions to evade, curious acquaintances to avoid, inconsistencies to cover up about those six months.

It was now completely dark, only the thin wail of the upper atmosphere told that we were traveling more than eight thousand miles per hour. Above, glittering in a velvety black sky, lay the Universe. Were these stars real? Yes, they were real enough, for beneath our feet the steel floor of the *prolo* vibrated with the powerful motors. Real now, but I felt that they would soon vanish into nothingness with the *prolo*, after we had landed.

The hour passed quickly. A reflected gleam from the crescent moon told of the Mediterranean, miles below. And then the *prolo* dove downward into the thicker air; the whistle of the wind increased and gradually a dim orange glow appeared in the mists ahead.

"That's old London all right," said Milroy, in a shaky attempt at humor, "look at the fog!"

Suddenly we decelerated. Out of the vapors came the outlines of buildings, towers and a vague confusion of traffic arose. The spectral shape of the Parliament building passed close—dull and squatty beside the white Zongainian Tower—and then branches scraped against our runners, leaves whipped past the window, and we had landed. Someone opened the door and extended the ladder gangway.

"Hurry, don't want to be caught by a bobby," whispered El Zoia.

We descended to the damp grass. A gentle rain was falling. We waited. In the doorway above, El Zoia stood—his white garment shining in the glow from a distant streetlight.

"Remember," he cried softly, "when you want to come back, Zongainia will welcome you…"

The *prolo* swiftly arose. "And…goodbye." He raised his arm to wave and then the trees blotted him out. A slight breeze rustled the foliage and the mist wet our stiffly pressed suits. For many minutes we stood as men in a trance, and then Pfeiffler said:

"Leds…leds get in before ve get all vet."

THE END

LIFE-GIVING ENERGY FROM A WORLD OF COLD DEATH!

It was, quite simply, the most phenomenal engineering feat ever accomplished in the history of mankind. Its actual scientific name was a long one, much too long, so it was simply called the "Artery." The Artery piped raw power from the distant planet of Pluto, all the way to an impoverished Earth, and the success of the Artery project was, in a real sense, life itself to its creator, Norman Bayerd.

However, now the same politicians and scientists who had steadfastly opposed Norman Bayerd all along were there to bedevil him yet again. But even worse than their meddling was the actual sabotage that threw off the Artery's beam and threatened mankind itself…

CAST OF CHARACTERS

BAYERD

He was the brains behind the Artery, the most powerful energy producing device ever created—and it became his obsession.

PATEL

He believed in seeking energy with new methods outside of the Artery.   Bayerd believed he was out to destroy his life.

ELLIOT

He was Bayerd's close ally and a true believer in the entire Artery project—but could he be trusted?

MENDOZA

This savvy Councilman was Bayerd's closest political friend, sent from Earth to oversee the Artery process.

GILCHRIST

Another powerful Councilman from Earth, only his mission was to try and discredit the entire Artery project.

ARTERY OF
FIRE

By
THOMAS N. SCORTIA

ARMCHAIR FICTION
PO Box 4369, Medford, Oregon 97504

*For more information about Armchair Books and products, visit our
website at…*

www.armchairfiction.com

Or email us at…

armchairfiction@yahoo.com

CHAPTER ONE

"YOU'RE a liar!" The pent violence of the voice hissed in Norman Bayerd's ears, jarring him from his reverie. He stood on the edge of the precipice, feeling a sudden vertigo, a sense of disorientation, so that the star-flecked sky of Pluto into which he had been staring seemed to writhe and pulse like the black surface of something alive.

Then he was over it and filled with a quick anger. Just for an instant he had felt somehow divorced from the reality that stretched out before him. You could lose yourself in the blackness of that sky, he told himself.

Standing on the very brink of creation... Looking out through the infinite distances and knowing that there was nothing between you and the nearest point of light but endless emptiness. Nothing, not even the tiniest speck of rock—nothing but the sheer impassable loneliness of interstellar space.

"I'll break your swinish head," a second voice said.

Bayerd moved to the edge of the precipice, his heavy forelegs raising puffs of volcanic dust, which arced in low parabolic sheets back to the corduroyed rock, rock that still showed the flow patterns of ancient lava. He looked out over the vast polar tableland that stretched from this one prominence to the horizon, searching for the two figures near the southern tip of the great smelters. He adjusted his vision to infrared to take advantage of the heat radiating from the smelters and the ionization chambers and stepped up the magnification. The two men were near the far end of one of the massive conveyor belts that brought the pulverized uranium hydride from the great beds to the south. The image of four-legged massive bodies danced before his eyes, wavering in the schlieren distortion of hot hydrogen spewing from the decomposing ore in the smelters.

"NO BOCHE speaks to me so," the first voice. One of them raised a mallet-like fist.

Bayerd remembered the frantic search for uranium on the planets...

"Amazonian grave robber!" the second voice sneered, and both figures moved in for contact.

"Stop it," Bayerd yelled. For an instant both figures froze motionless amid the glowing towers and throbbing chambers of the plain.

"Trubner...Sanchez..." Bayerd demanded, "what's got into you two?"

"This smelling pig has a tongue that wags at both ends," Trubner said.

"Cut it out," Bayerd replied quickly. "Another crack like that and I'll put you on report."

"Whose tongue wags too much now?"

"You too, Sanchez. We're cutting our deadline too close without any private wars."

144

"Sanchez is to blame," Trubner said thickly. "He and his lies about the Liechtenstein robbery, and…"

"You heathen Germans would steal food from your mother's grave," Sanchez cut in hotly.

"I said that's enough," Bayerd snapped. "We've no time to fight amongst ourselves. Every minute the Artery is out of action means the power shortage Earthside becomes more critical. The Liechtenstein census trouble is just a taste of what's to come."

HE PAUSED for a moment, thinking of home and the darkened cities and the building tension. It was only a matter of time until the situation blew up in their faces, unless…

He cut to the command net and said, "All right, can all of you hear me? Check in." Trubner and Sanchez acknowledged immediately with Chang, Girard and Muletti coming in seconds later.

"Gentlemen," Bayerd said, "we're two thirds through our count-off. That gives us barely four hours until beam time. The power shortage back home is now a 'class A emergency'. That means power rationing to private homes and to all but critical functions. We've run into delays here that we didn't anticipate."

He paused, listening to the murmur of agreement.

"We can't afford the luxury of quarreling amongst ourselves," Bayerd said. "Chang, you're senior here. I want a report on the next man who shoots off his mouth. You're all under military jurisdiction here, and I'll use every bit of that authority—up to and including court martial proceedings—if there's any more of this bickering that we've had over the past couple of days. That's a promise, and I'll make it stick."

HE CUT from the circuit and snorted in disgust.

Complete gibbering idiots, he thought. He switched to the 'A' net and said, "Elliott, did you get all of that?"

"They're all pretty jumpy with the power shortage and the political situation Earthside," Elliott said quietly. He sighed and for a moment Norman Bayerd had the odd illusion that the man was standing beside him, rather than being nearly three and a half billion miles away in the Black Field Station orbiting nearly a million kilometers from Terra. But, Bayerd thought wryly, even that wasn't true. Actually Elliott was perhaps fifty feet away if he were on the station's metering bridge, less if he were in the Commo room. The paradox made for some confusion in thinking, unless...

"I've got some news that should take your mind off your troubles," Elliott said dryly.

"That sounds ominous." Bayerd adjusted his sight to watch Girard and Muletti far inside the accelerator area as they stripped a foot-thick shield from one of the towering resonators of the accelerator. The chambers of the accelerator itself stretched far beyond his vision like a fantastic metal Midgard serpent encircling Pluto's arctic circle.

"Our guests are coming a day early," Elliott said.

"Mendoza and Gilchrist? Mendoza promised me he'd keep that rabble-rouser out of our hair until after beam time."

"Apparently the good Councilman from Greenland has found some new ammunition. He's bringing a friend of yours."

"Who?"

"Patel," Elliott said.

FOR A SILENT moment, Bayerd considered the implications of the statement.

Patel!

He'd rather have ten Gilchrists on hand rather than one Patel. He'd counted on Mendoza's presence to act as a counterbalance to Gilchrist, but Patel's presence more than tipped the balance. The political atmosphere could get tense.

"How long have I got?"

"Barely an hour."

"What are they trying to do?" he demanded angrily. "Catch us with our house dirty?"

"Looks like it. We wouldn't have even this much warning if Mendoza's secretary hadn't radioed us from the Antilles Shuttle Field just after they took off."

"After fifteen years, that little bastard comes back to haunt me."

"Patel? You think this is a personal attack brewing?"

"What else—?" Bayerd asked. "He's been after me ever since the Fissionable Resources Committee hearings fifteen years ago. Don't worry, though. I clipped his wings once and I can do it again."

BAYERD thought for a moment and then he said, "I want a news blackout on what's happening Earthside until I tell you otherwise. We can't have any more trouble with the crew." *As if that would solve the major problem,* Bayerd thought. After five years of jockeying for a bigger slice of the very finite power pie, national tempers at home were at the breaking point. The problem among the engineering crew was only a pallid reflection—like the accusations last week that the census reports of the Liechtenstein district had been falsified. If only they could have delayed the Artery changeover a year... No, the situation would only have worsened with the delay.

"Look," he told Elliott, "I've got another hour's work just checking the calibration on the remote metering circuits. Can you keep the firemen amused until I get back?"

"There's the planetarium."

"Good. Take care of it, will you?" Bayerd said and cut from the circuit.

For seconds he stood, feeling the tensions of his body.

Patel...

This was the end. As if there wasn't enough pressure on him. It would be so good, he thought, just to lie down and rest; he should never have allowed them to talk him into coming back on duty to handle the changeover.

But he realized that he would have insisted, had they not made the offer. That some other hand should touch this creation of his was unthinkable. Norman Bayerd had worked and fought for the Artery until it was the very core of his life.

HE LOOKED back over the plateau on which he stood.

The control station, built on the truncated top of the "Needle," a massive volcanic splinter thrust up from the polar plain, was an organized confusion of cables buried in fused rock, complex instrument banks and control consoles. Actually, once countdown had started, the station functioned strictly as a monitor. Automatic units in a control capsule buried in a pit on the plain initiated the transmission. This directed the stream of plasmoids that was the Artery upward at the proper angle; it controlled the density and orientation of the magnetic lens generated by the orbiting lens stations two and a half million miles sunward in Pluto's warped orbital plane.

He turned his eyes downward, scanning the polar plain from the base of the jagged stone tower of the control station outward, pausing on the bottomless crevice that ringed the stone outcropping like a ragged moat, moving outward through the jet shadows that striped the irregular plain toward the sprawling units of the Artery. His gaze took in the vast curve of the accelerator it-self; the glowing stokers, storage towers for their product; the great ionization towers—all the vitals of the Artery that rose like a vast creature from the dead rock. It stretched its octopoidal arms over the polar region and far south via the great conveyors to suck the very substance of the planet out of the continental beds of uranium hydride and turn it into the pulsing blue beam that would hurl sunward in a few short hours.

THE WHOLE panorama with its eerie half-lights and strange brilliances was like something compounded of the fire and brimstone of the Christian hell of his childhood. Pluto, with its endless stretches of centuries-old snow and blackness that filled the vacuum plains and airless mountains like some yeasty dough in colorless ferment when they first came—had changed from a Norse hell to a Christian hell. It was a place of energies where a creature of flesh and blood could not survive an instant, where the very space was laced with surging magnetic fields that would magnetolyze a man's body fluids to their component gases in seconds. Where the alpha and beta particles from the power pile—accelerated to near light speeds where their vectors coincided with the accelerator fields—would blast a fatal path of ionization through animal tissue regardless of the shielding.

Yes, he thought, they had indeed turned it into a Christian hell, a thing built on the pattern of warped images from some medieval heretic, shivering in anticipation of fire and brimstone. Not that it made too much difference, he thought. No man could live an instant here. Were there any part of him that owned the weakness of flesh and blood, or carried a deadly dependence on protein and body fluid, he would cease to exist in an instant.

Metal, he thought, looking down at his thick metal torso and seeing the radiation from the generator making power in his vitals, *to live in hell you have to be a man of steel.*

For a moment he looked up into the black sky. Seeing the stars, he wondered how much further one must go to be there.

CHAPTER TWO

BAYERD completed the final check on the monitoring board for the orbital lens stations. He checked to see that the tape, which recorded each reading and adjustment against a time scale on its edge, was threaded and properly positioned. Then he closed the base of the console, got to his feet, and paused for a moment to rest. He was *tired*—so fatigued that he had trouble keeping his attention on his work.

Just a few more hours, he thought. He felt a warm hand on his shoulder then and in an instant his whole orientation changed. He was a flesh and blood man, enclosed intimately in the pantographic harness of a Schrenk transmitter, again existing in a small cubicle on the "S" level of the Black Field Station, millions of miles sunward from Pluto.

The transition had been near instantaneous with the speed of a c-cube radio impulse. He drew his face from the vision mask, cut the power that left his puppet body cold and lifeless atop the Needle, halted the recording tape within the unit, and started to remove his arms from the sleeves that enclosed them.

"Everything check out?" Elliott asked as Bayerd stepped from the seat of the unit.

"Everything so far," he said, rubbing his hand across his forehead. "Why aren't you with our guests?"

"They're below at station center. I wanted to catch you before we started the circus." He handed Bayerd a message flimsy.

"What's this?"

"I CHECKED Commo just before our guests arrived. You know, the usual routine of checking the log against the morning transmissions. This one wasn't entered."

"Looks like a communication code," Bayerd said, scanning the sheet.

"It's not one of our routine codes. Can't make it out. If I hadn't been running a spot check, it would probably have been erased from the tape automatically at the watch change."

"I don't like this coming on the heels of Patel and Gilchrist's arrival," Bayerd said slowly.

"Do you think Gilchrist might have an agent planted in the station personnel?"

"You know these men better than I do. What's your idea?"

"Doc Beckworth, Chang, Girard, Muletti, Trubner, Sanchez," Elliott said, checking them off slowly. "No—I can't see any of them working for Gilchrist. Maybe one of the group we had here during the major operation, but they've all gone back."

"Whoever sent this message," Bayerd said tiredly, "probably knows there are only the eight of us left on the station. That's fairly common knowledge. If there's a plant, he's still here. Otherwise the message wouldn't have been sent."

He folded the message and placed it in the pocket of his tunic. "You get back to our visiting firemen," he told Elliott. "I have a few things to do before I join you."

"Right," Elliott said and left.

AS SOON as the door closed, Bayerd found a seat on the low case of the Schrenk unit's oscillator and sat breathing heavily. Thank heavens, he thought, Elliott had left when he did. He felt the throbbing in his temples and the pain at the base of his skull from the old injury. He found the vial of capsules the doctor back home had given him and took one. Without water, the capsule made a hard lump in his throat; he sat for several minutes after the lump had faded, waiting for the lax calm to steal over him, waiting for strength to ooze back into his tired muscles. Finally he left the cubicle, walked down the long corridor line with Schrenk unit cubicles—most of them now unused—and found a tube, leading downward toward the center of the station.

The center of the Black Field Station was a hollow sphere, nearly five hundred meters in diameter, laced with silver cables like the traceries of a careless monster spider. It was cut by fragile catwalks, thrown up with no apparent regard for "up" until one realized that "up" was away from the center of the hollow sphere. Quite apart from the hollow interior's function as an auxiliary station in the Black Field, it served a somewhat more frivolous purpose needing darkness.

BAYERD pushed from the personnel tube and made his way over one of the catwalks in the darkness. He was still feeling faintly nauseated and he anchored himself to one of the cables in the darkness without a sound. He could hear a murmur of voices and saw vague, man-size blobs of darkness floating near the center of the sphere, their forms outlined by the light from the projection on the walls that enclosed them.

For a moment he felt a secret thrill at the vast panorama spread across the darkness. Not even death, he thought, could be frightening with such a thing to leave behind him. For the first time in the last hour he felt better, more secure. To hell with the Patels and the Gilchrists, he thought. A hundred years from now, when the Artery still blazed across Earth's night sky, who would remember *them?*

Even after years of familiarity, the illusion was breathtaking. It was as if he were floating in space with a blazing wealth of stars surrounding him. Then the sense of disproportion grew as he saw that he was viewing the solar system out of scale from a vantagepoint above the plane of the ecliptic. The sun was unnaturally small; far out, he could see the exaggerated point of light that was Pluto.

From Pluto's displacement in relation to the ecliptic, Bayerd decided that the time was just past perihelion but before Pluto had crossed Neptune's orbit. That marked the time as just before the turn of the millennium. He could understand Elliott's reasons for picking this period rather than one more recent.

HE WATCHED as Pluto enlarged for the instant that Artery transmission began. A brilliant ribbon of blue, swirling with sub-tones of pulsing green, darted from the point of light upward at an angle and then bent sharply to parallel the ecliptic as it touched the field of the Alpha Orbital Lens inside Pluto's eccentric orbit. The lens was microscopic on this scale, but the image enlarged for an instant to show the five lens stations revolving around a common center, while the incredibly dense magnetic field that they generated within their mutual circle warped the beaded beam of the Artery from its original path.

The ribbon of cobalt light traced its path slowly toward the sun, curving in opposition to the planetary motions of Pluto and the Earth, its velocity a pedestrian quarter the speed of light. The increasing radiation-pressure of the sun was making itself felt as the beam passed the orbits of Jupiter and Mars, introducing a new distorting influence upon the beam.

The tiny image of the Earth-Moon system enlarged now; the Moon trailed by the tiny nodal plane lens station in its metastable orbit. The beam, almost at Earth's orbit but well displaced above the ecliptic, touched something in its path and disappeared. Whatever the interfering object was, it did not scatter the beam; but the blue streamer emerged from the area at a snail's crawl, as though in some fashion it had shed most of its quarter light velocity.

"AT THIS point," Elliott's voice cut the darkness, "the major portion of the beam's kinetic energy has been absorbed by the Black Field. It then passes through the Earth-Orbital Lens, and is deflected downward through the Nodal Plane Lens that trails Luna to the plating surfaces on the Moon."

"Humph," a harsh voice rumbled, "why get rid of all that energy? Needless waste."

"If we didn't, Councilman, we'd probably melt down a good hunk of the moon during the course of operations, not to mention losing most of the transmitted metal by reflection."

The glowing beam, scarcely moving, intersected the Earth Orbital Lens and turned sharply down toward the ecliptic. It was showing a tendency to spread now as it slowly approached and touched the Nodal Plane Lens. There was a moment of suspense as the lens redirected the beam perpendicularly to Luna's surface and it crept slowly toward contact. The blue radiance touched the surface of the Moon; it flared faintly, and contact was made. The two worlds, Pluto and Luna, were joined in a thin band of glowing U-235 plasmoids, a pulsing umbilical cord of ions.

"Marvelous," Councilman Mendoza's voice said from the darkness. "Like Archimedes and his lever."

"Marvelous?" the harsh voice grated. "So was the dinosaur."

"Lights," Elliott said and the interior of the station was suddenly flooded with brilliance.

BAYERD freed his line and pulled himself across the intervening distance to the five men who were floating in random orientations in the center of the station. Beckworth, the station's M. D., was holding the small control box from whose side a thin cable snaked up to the projector positioned on one of the catwalks.

"The dinosaur was a necessary evolutionary step, Mr. Gilchrist," Bayerd said.

"You know Commander Norman Bayerd?" Mendoza asked, his nervous white smile punctuating his dark skin.

"We've met," Gilchrist replied in a rumbling voice. He was short and beefy with a ragged fringe of yellow-gray hair circling his otherwise bald scalp. "At the committee hearings fifteen years ago," he added. "Patel, come here and say 'Hello' nicely to the man." He turned and beckoned at the small, olive-skinned man who had stayed somewhat apart during the exchange.

"Hello, Norman," Patel said, his large liquid eyes glistening. "It's good to see you again."

Bayerd nodded without speaking, feeling the quick warmth on his face.

Bayerd checked his watch and said, "We have ninety minutes to beam time. Elliott will assign you Schrenk units and you can observe our final checkout. There'll be alternate robots for each of you on the Needle and below on the plain."

"Good," Gilchrist said. "I want a good look at this dinosaur of yours."

ELLIOTT turned and led the way for one of the personnel tubes. Bayerd remained in the same position as the group moved out. As soon as they were out of earshot, Patel, who had remained to the last, said, "It is *good* to see you again, Norm."

"No doubt," Bayerd replied.

"I had hoped we might talk."

"I have nothing to talk about."

"After this was over, Diane thought you might like to spend a week or so with us and the children."

"Do you think you can change all that with a few pretty words?" Bayerd demanded.

"It's not right," Patel said, "for a daughter and…"

"I thought it was quite clear," Bayerd said, moving away, "I have no daughter."

Mendoza was waiting for him at the entrance of the personnel tube. As soon as Patel had pushed silently past them, Mendoza said, "Norm, watch your step, will you. Those two are up to something."

"When did Patel climb on Gilchrist's bandwagon?"

"HE'S BEEN around Council Hill for the last year or so. Some private committee. He and Gilchrist got together when the power crisis started giving the Council headaches."

"That political hack," Bayerd said softly.

"No—he's bull-headed and about as single-minded as they come, but give the devil his due. He wants a way out as badly as we do and he can be dangerous if he's crossed."

"What's keeping you two," Gilchrist yelled from the tube at that moment.

"Right with you," Mendoza called.

"Before you go," Bayerd said, "I want to know something. Do you have anyone spotted on my crew?"

"What do you mean?"

Bayerd told him about the message in the unauthorized code.

"I don't know," Mendoza said. "It might be an agent planted by either Gilchrist or one of the individual countries involved in the Liechtenstein affair. Trying to dig up something to embarrass the administration."

"Whatever the explanation," Bayerd said, "I don't like it one damned bit."

CHAPTER THREE

IN THE last half-hour before countdown, Norman Bayerd ignored the visiting party. He could not, however, completely dismiss them from his mind. Their presence was an ill-perceived mass, hanging over his head. He wished again that they might have delayed the changeover another year, but he knew that he was only running away from the problem to be solved.

Anyway, there was another factor. Sixty wasn't so old, he thought; but every time he returned from this strong metal self to the flesh and blood shell in the station, he felt as if he had crossed from the "living" to the "other-than-living." This vicarious existence was something that breathed new life into him, knowing that the world on far Pluto was a world he'd built—complete, an intimate part of his life. A part that would collapse into the rubble of history and be forgotten if Patel and Gilchrist prevailed.

Ever since Pluto had passed out of Neptune's orbit, after perigee in 1989, it had moved in a path more and more displaced below the ecliptic. The eccentricity and inclination of the orbit had changed Pluto's orientation to the ecliptic all the while its distance from the Earth had increased. The problem of control had grown greater and greater as the beam, originally parallel to and displaced above the ecliptic, now cut through the plane of the ecliptic for its contact with the Black Field and Earth Orbital Lens.

THE changeover had become imperative after the turn of the millennium. It had taken the engineering team six months to change the positions of the two lenses and the Black Field, jockeying the fragile stations in a broad path perpendicular to the ecliptic while still maintaining their proper motions. During the period, of course, the Artery could not transmit; the Earth's fissionable reserves had steadily dwindled, forcing an even tighter rationing than that, which prevailed when the beam was in operation.

Fortunately, the rationing system was already well established. Terrestrial power demands had caught up with the new supply of fissionables from the Artery scarcely five years after the beam was in operation. Rationing on a complicated formula, weighing both population and industrial development had been the only answer. The political situation had been tense before the changeover. Now tempers had flared again and again in the World Council, and threatened to explode in open violence over the week-old scandal following the discovery of the attempt to falsify the count in the Liechtenstein district during the current census.

IN THE LAST minutes before final checkout, Bayerd remained on the plain, away from the group on the control point. After he had checked the vapor tower of the main smelter, and the grid temperatures of the first bank of ionization chambers, he moved across the plane and out of the accelerator to the control capsule. The ceramic shield that covered the electric winch that would lower the capsule into its hundred-foot pit in the rock, had been stripped half away. The faceplate and remote visual pick-up that scanned the capsule instruments had been moved back on their gimbals to facilitate the final adjustment of the capsule mechanism. Once the controls had been set and locked on the capsule, it controlled the wide-spread functioning of the units within the accelerator circle by a dozen coaxial cables buried deep in the rock, as well as the orientation and density of the Plutonian lens.

A signal from the Needle could override the capsule and cut the beam; but the capsule and the massive computers buried beneath the plain handled the actual transmission at speeds impossible to an organic nervous system. Once the Artery was in operation, only the capsule site was accessible. The raging magnetic fields near the accelerator would completely destroy control of a Schrenk robot. The capsule would transmit an initial calibrating segment of the beam. Then, twenty hours later, it would make any necessary adjustments from data fed back to it by the Earth Orbital Lens Stations, and begin continuous transmission.

HE PAUSED by the capsule and looked out over the plain, feeling his inner self fill with pride. What a magnificent concept. Without the Artery they would still be chasing the pot of gold at the end of the rainbow as Patel had wanted. Patel and his single-minded search for a new power source! You couldn't harness the hydrogen reaction—that had been proven—and what else was there but the old standbys, uranium and plutonium fission? With the twenty percent conversion you got with the Black Field, that meant a lot.

When the vast beds of U-235 rich ore had been found on Pluto, the power famine on Earth had been critical. It was commercially impractical to bring the metal back by ship. The drain on world resources of merely building the ships would have been fantastic. The Artery had been a heaven-sent solution to the dilemma.

Who cared how much energy you burned at the source? So…so smelt the ore on Pluto; vaporize it, raise the vapor to an ionizing temperature and squirt out the cloud of ions and electrons. You shape them with electromagnetic pulses; bite them into small chunks of plasma with internal particles rotating fast enough to organize it into those almost-living cohesive clouds of particles called plasmoids; accelerate them endlessly in a giant accelerator until they reach nearly a quarter the speed of light and hurl them sunward. Twenty hours later, you plate out precious metal on the Lunar plains.

THAT WAS the concept, ready made, a mere matter of engineering—complex engineering to be sure, but the technology already existed. No striking into *terra incognita*. They couldn't wait for the vain hopes of a new power source; nor was there enough to back that expensive phase of research and still build the Artery. A choice had to be made. They built the Artery.

If there had been any sense at home, Bayerd thought, the power would have been enough for centuries. It wasn't his fault that industry and power usage had expanded so rapidly to meet the new supply. The point was he'd given them what they wanted, and in the process built the best structure man had ever conceived.

He checked the time quickly and called, "Check in!"

"Trubner. Ionization chamber full potential."

"Girard, how about smelters?" Bayerd asked.

"Intake full idle. Reservoirs at ninety percent."

"Field stability?"

"Sanchez here.   Accelerator field oh point oh-oh-five variation at reserve."

Quickly he took the reports from Muletti at the far side of the accelerator below the horizon, and Chang, who was running a final remote check on the computers far below. He checked the settings on the capsule once more, made sure the screws were tight on the verniers and said, "Trubner, grab Girard and get the capsule sealed and seated... Gentlemen, ten minutes to count-down."

HE watched two figures detach themselves from the shadows about the blue-hazed ionization chambers and move toward him. For an instant the scene was unreal, as though he was displaced miles from the site. He shook away the sensation, stepped back a pace and deactivated the robot. A brief adjustment, and he was in the alternate robot atop the Needle, feeling somehow vaguely depressed after the surging emotions of the plain.

There were three active robot bodies and, when he switched to the normally unused 'B' net, he heard Elliott explaining the functioning of the metering stations, while Mendoza and Gilchrist occasionally made comment. He started to break in on the conversation when one of the three inactive bodies standing on the far edge of the area straightened and moved toward him.

Bayerd turned to look out over the tableland below, trying to ignore the robot that he knew must be Patel. He switched to the 'A' net to rid himself of the three-way conversation between Elliott and the Councilmen. Below him the whole plain was aglow with energy except for the deep fossa ringing the base of the needle as a moat rings a castle, cutting it from menace.

"It *is* magnificent," Patel said quietly.

"The culmination of every engineering technique since the pyramids," Bayerd said.

"With something of the attributes of them," Patel said.

When Bayerd did not answer, Patel asked at last, "Have you ever read Shelley's *Ozymandias?*"

FOR SECONDS, Norman Bayerd struggled with the anger surging within him.

Elliott's voice cut into his thoughts, "Norm! Three minutes."

He switched to the command net and moved quickly to his station at the accelerator monitor, where flickering meters told of the varying potentials below and the prognosticated azimuth of the beam on transmission. Elliott took his position at the console that monitored feedback information from the Plutonian Lens as the others withdrew and waited silently. Elliott keyed the warning signal, waited thirty seconds, and then checked to see that the team below had withdrawn.

"Thirty seconds," Bayerd announced as the timing light on his board glowed. "We are now on automatic."

The twenty-second light glowed on Bayerd's board as Elliott took up the count down. Impatiently Bayerd lowered the volume and thought. *A minute from now and it's ended. Only Patel and Gilchrist left and their fangs are pulled.*

Like mice nibbling at the feet of a steel colossus.

"Fifteen seconds," Elliott announced tensely.

"Lens check-out."

"Computer reading forty-five two three two."

"Orbital lens?"

"One thirty four...thirty six...fifty eight."

"Check." Bayerd released the override switch. The count-down began as a taped voice said, "Ten, nine, eight..."

HE checked his own readings again. Right on the nose. The beam would strike the lens at just the right angle, and arrow its way sunward. The Artery would be whole again in just twenty hours.

"Three...two...one...zero!"

"Look, look!" There was a quick intake of breath from someone on the net as the three visitors peered upward at the band of pale blue springing from below the horizon and piercing the sky. Bayerd switched to ultra-violet vision and the beam blazed as though a giant brush, dipped in liquid fire, had been raked across the sky. Below it, the space above the smelters was a riot of swirling color like a phosphorescent oil slick on black water as secondary radiation excited the escaping hydrogen and painted the sky with Geissler colors.

The group was lost in the sudden wonder of it and he could only stand and drink in the beauty spread across the sky. Only in the last instant did he hear Elliot shout, "My God, cut it!"

AUTOMATICALLY, his hand lashed out for the override switch. Something arched within the console and sudden brilliance bloomed on the plain below. An invisible sponge wiped the colors from the sky.

"Something happened," Elliott said. "The angle was wrong at the lens."

"Did you stop it?" Bayerd demanded.

"I managed to reorient the lens before the board went dead."

"Did you stop the whole transmission?" Bayerd demanded.

"Almost all," Elliott said. "All but about a thousand-meter segment."

"Will somebody explain what happened," Gilchrist demanded.

"The transmission was wild," Bayerd said. "There's a thousand meter segment of the beam heading sunward."

"Heading for where? The lens…dead space…what?"

"Councilman," Bayerd said, feeling a constriction in his throat, "I wish I knew."

CHAPTER FOUR

HOW COULD it happen?" Elliott asked quietly. "What could have gone wrong?"

Bayerd looked out over the deserted metering bridge of the Black Field Station and shook his head. "I don't know. The monitoring board was calibrated just the hour before.

Something went wrong badly enough to cause arcing and fusion of the cable to the capsule."

"Any word from the crew yet?"

"No," Bayerd said. "The shield was damaged. They have to cut through it before they can raise the capsule. What I'm interested in now are the results from the Earthside computers."

"They've had the data for two hours now," Elliott said.

"I know it," Bayerd snapped. "And we can't do a damned thing until we know. Chances are the beam will cut through the system and head into interstellar space, but..." He moved along the bridge to one of the monitoring screens. Idly he taped a combination on the console and the screen flickered and came alive. The view was from one of the lens stations. Against the blackness of space the points of light that were the other five lens stations were a new constellation moving slowly in concert as they revolved around a common center.

TO the pickup, the stations were perfectly stationary. It was the star-flecked backdrop of space that seemed to revolve counterclockwise about the fixed constellations. Separated somewhat and at a greater distance, Norman Bayerd could see the five subsidiary stations that generated the Black Field forming a second circle of points. The slightly brighter, sixth point of light was the Black Field Control Station from which the field was propagated. It gave him an odd sensation, watching the point of light that was his present position, rather like the old illusion of the picture of a man looking at a picture and so on, down into the infinitely small.

"You know," Bayerd said, "this seems pretty coincidental, the arrival of Gilchrist and Patel, the beam failure, and that coded message."

"Take it easy," Elliott said. "Don't start chasing shadows."

"I guess you're right, Bayerd replied with a faint shrug.

BAYERD watched Elliott as he mounted a light ladder and disappeared through a ceiling port. He debated going below himself for a nap. Then he smiled to himself at the use of the word "below" in his thinking. "Below" to a planet dweller meant toward the center of gravity. Automatically you began to think of "below" in a station as toward the center of the station, forgetting that the "gravity" you worked under in a station was actually centrifugal force from the spin of the station—and that as you traveled toward the center of the spherical station, the force of this pseudo-gravity dropped until at the exact center of rotation, you were completely weightless.

But you didn't revise your thinking on such basic terms. You still held to the old patterns of thought, mostly because it was easier, because you didn't want to stop each time you used a direction oriented to a gravity field and decide the correct term. "Below" and "down" were always toward the center of the station but in exactly the opposite direction, toward the outer shell when you were talking in terms other than that of movement between levels. It did make, he thought, for some odd contradictions.

HE DIDN'T hear Patel until he stepped from the ladder to the deck. The small scuffing sound of a foot on metal broke him from his reverie and he turned as the Indian placed his other foot on the deck.

"What do you want?" he demanded.

"Have you got the beam path yet?"

"No," Bayerd said. "We transmitted the data Earthside. Our analogue machines can't handle such a wide variation."

"Too bad," Patel said. "As time goes on, they'll have to."

"I was never very good at innuendo," Bayerd snapped, "so cut it out. You're not playing to an audience now."

Patel sighed. "Do you have to interpret everything I say in terms of innuendo?"

"I've got good reason, I think."

"Look," Patel said, "the last thing in the world I want to do is hurt you. I'd give my right arm to be able to stand on your side of the fence, but I think you're wrong—terribly wrong."

"As has been demonstrated."

"Yes," Patel said, "as has been demonstrated."

"Without the Artery," Bayerd said, turning back to the metering board, "there'll be no fissionables today. You know what that means. We'd have slipped back to a level of technology that could never have supported space travel or the world's population."

"Perhaps," Patel said, "but you haven't done the world any favor. I remember when we first met and you had stars in your eyes when you talked about an interstellar drive. Well, you've shoved the human race into a straightjacket now, restricted him to this one second-rate sun simply because further growth is limited by the present supply of fissionables. We're spending a major portion of the world budget for operating the Artery in just maintaining the status quo. What happens if the Artery can't supply us with even the present fissionables? What happens if we have to fall back on some other resource?"

"Don't try to pretend that this accident threatens the existence of the Artery in any way," Bayerd snapped, turning to face the man. "You'd like to believe that with this little malfunction, the Artery is through."

"If you believe that..."

"What *I* believe is not Important," Norman Bayerd said. "The Artery is my justification."

"And your monument."

"And my monument."

"To endure through the years," Patel said. "Only it won't endure through the years. The existence of the Artery is already practically at an end. Today is just a symptom of troubles to come."

"Today's accident was just that, an accident. Our control of the beam is normally damned good."

"Yes, your control is good—but will it always be?"

"What do you mean by that?"

"Just think about this for a moment," Patel said. "Pluto is outside Neptune's orbit now and moving away from perigee. With an eccentricity of point two-six, that means that its distance from Earth will increase radically over the next few decades. By the time it reaches apogee, it will be well over one and a half times as far from its conjunction with Earth as at perigee in 1989."

"Do you think you're telling me something I don't know?"

"Perhaps you just haven't been willing to consider the implications. What's your feedback oscillation in initial transmission?"

"Less than one ten-thousandth of a second."

"What happens when the target subtends an angle less than that?"

"An undamped oscillation, but..."

"Go on," Patel challenged. "Calculate the probabilities. How many situations like today are going to arise in the next two decades? How long can you continue to operate under those conditions?"

"You can't convince anybody of that."

"Can't I? I can convince you if you'll think about it."

"Anything to destroy the Artery. It's a personal crusade with you. I wouldn't trust any calculations of yours to navigate across a deserted street."

"Because you distrust *me?* Or because you can't face the destruction of this massive symbol of ego."

"Even if there were an element of truth in this, we're constantly improving our equipment," Bayerd said.

Patel shook his head.

"No, Norm, it won't work. You've put all of our eggs in this one basket. Our growth is geared to and limited by the fissionables from the Artery. In forty years, you'll have reached the point where you can't deliver. Even if you refine your equipment, there's a limit—and after that you can't hope to meet the control problem."

The intercom on the duty officer's desk chimed; Bayerd turned on his heel and walked to the instrument. The screen mirrored Elliott's worried face. Bayerd could see he was calling from Commo.

"Norm," Elliott said, "are you alone?"

"Patel's here."

"We've got the results from Earthside."

"Bring them to the bridge, will you?"

ELLIOTT nodded as his image faded from the screen. Bayerd waited silently, avoiding Patel's eyes. He rose and walked to the hatch when he heard Elliott ascending.

"Here," Elliott said, breathing heavily. He handed Bayerd the flimsy pages with their dark brown markings.

"Never mind," Bayerd said. "What's the verdict?"

Elliott pointed silently at the last page.

"Are they sure?" Bayerd asked after a moment.

"I checked with Kepling, the mathematician who ran the problem on the Pelembang Computer. He's sure."

"A one-in-a-million chance," Bayerd said, slapping the papers against his thigh.

"It could be a lot worse."

"Or a lot better."

"What's the answer?" Patel asked.

Bayerd walked over and handed him the sheets. Elliott motioned to him and walked back to the hatch. "Trubner's just reported on the capsule. They've got the shielding off. The cable suspending the capsule was severed by the arc. The capsule's still at the bottom of the well, with a hundred pounds of melted metal debris from the short circuit on top. It may take two days to cut down to it."

"My God," Bayerd said, "and that thing is set to start transmitting the continuous beam twenty hours after the calibration pulse."

"Unless it's overridden."

"But the control circuits from the lookout are gone."

"But not the metering circuits."

"What good do they do?" Bayerd asked disgustedly.

"NONE...BUT they gave us a picture of the capsule settings. The angular settings were way off. The set screws that lock the verniers were all loose."

"Norm," Patel asked behind them, "are they sure of these figures?" He pointed to the flimsies in his hand.

"They're sure," Bayerd said.

"Then the beam will tangent the Earth's upper atmosphere?"

Bayerd nodded silently. He turned to Elliott and said, "Get down to Commo and contact Lunar relay. Get data on every ship in space along the beam path. Also any available magnetic field generators that we might get ship borne within the next fifteen hours. Anything else that you can think of? We've got seventeen hours to either intercept or deflect that beam."

"What about the Pluto installation?" Patel asked.

"Get on it," Bayerd said and Elliott headed for the hatch. Then he whirled on Patel. "Don't worry. We'll get to the capsule before too late."

"If you don't, what then?"

"Perhaps you'd like to blow up the accelerator?"

"You may have to."

"You'd like that, wouldn't you?"

"No," Patel said. "I would not like that. We're too dependent upon the Artery...all of us."

"I'm surprised to hear you admit it."

"Why? It's obvious...but you know what happens when you cut an artery?"

"Huh?"

"When you cut an artery, Norman," Patel said with a worried frown, "you bleed to death."

CHAPTER FIVE

"I'VE RADIOED Earth for complete information on all ships in space within the beam area or about to take off into the area," Bayerd said, scanning the faces of the men on the bridge. Only Chang's face was emotionless. His black eyes were lidded in thought, his face completely composed. The other men Elliott, Patel, Beckworth, the two councilmen—showed varied expressions of worry and anger.

"Damn it," Gilchrist said, "we can't be worrying about ships in its path. We've got to divert that beam."

"Councilman," Bayerd snapped, "that's exactly what we're trying to do. But you need ships to move any equipment into the beam's path."

"What about the Black Field?" Gilchrist demanded. "Can you move the generating stations into its path?"

"Impossible," Chang said slowly. "It would take months."

"The drive units are still orbiting around Terra," Mendoza said. "Can we interpose one of the stations?"

"As a last resort...perhaps. But that knocks the Artery out of business for a year."

"We can't have that," Mendoza said. "We can't survive even six more months without the Artery's fissionables."

"What if we don't stop the beam?" Beckworth asked.

"IF JUST the fringes of the atmosphere are involved," Bayerd said, "the beam will lose only a fraction of its kinetic energy. There'll be heat generated, but not so much that it won't be dissipated without danger."

"And if it penetrates more deeply?" Gilchrist asked.

"A great deal more heat, secondary radiation from the high speed of the beam; ionization; shock waves from the localized heating."

"And what does that mean in terms of damage?" Gilchrist demanded.

"I'm afraid," Patel said slowly, "that it might mean a great deal. The radiation can probably be discounted. Mostly short half-lives. The shock wave could be disastrous. The effect of so much heat generated in the path of the beam would be equivalent to a giant meteor penetrating the atmosphere."

"Chang," Bayerd said, "what's the situation at the capsule?"

"This is not easy," Chang said slowly. "We have lowered four robot units to the bottom of the shaft and are sending down cutting tools."

"Any chance of blasting?"

"Through the metal? I don't think it's advisable."

"Give me an estimate of how quickly you can get to the capsule."

"That I will have in another hour."

"My God," Bayerd said, "an hour? We've got only sixteen before that damned thing is keyed to start spraying plasma all over the system."

"THIS HAD to happen," Gilchrist said. "You can't stake the whole future of a world on a gamble like this."

"Councilman," Norman Bayerd said, "Terra won't have a future if you don't stop pushing the panic button."

"You forget yourself," Gilchrist said, jumping to his feet. Mendoza half-rose, trying to restrain him.

Gilchrist seemed to swell for an instant in his fury. Then he turned without speaking and stalked from the room. Mendoza said, "Damn it, Norm, watch your temper. You can do both of us a lot of harm," and followed Gilchrist from the room.

"You know how most of the commercial space drives operate?" Bayerd asked Patel.

"A combination chemical plasma system?"

"That's right. They throw colloidal aluminum into an arc chamber to increase the arc temperature by a magneto-constriction effect, accelerate the metal vapor jet to supersonic by an eddy-current funnel and then get the last bit of juice out of the fuel by injecting water to oxidize the aluminum. The point is they throw out a wake of colloidal aluminum oxide, and each particle is charged. What would happen if the beam penetrated a large enough cross section of that stuff?"

"Something as tenuous as that?" Patel asked. "It can't possibly stop the beam."

"NOT STOP," Bayerd said. "Just deflect. Each one of those colloidal particles of aluminum oxide is charged. How large a cross section do we need to deflect each individual plasmoid of the beam just the bit necessary to make sure it misses Terra?"

"I can run it on the Station computer," Patel said, moving toward the hatch. "It might work."

"That leaves me pretty much dead weight," Beckworth said when only he, Elliott and Bayerd were left on the bridge.

"How's your supply of pep pills?"

"Stimulants? Well I've a fair supply of PALA—para-amino-lacto-amphetamine—but I don't like to use the stuff except in an emergency."

"This is an emergency in spades," Bayerd said. "Look, we're going to have to keep driving these men for the next sixteen hours at least, probably longer. They'll be dead for sleep and we need everyone. At top alertness, top efficiency."

"All right," Beckworth said, "but you'd better radio for replacements. I want those men off their feet and in bed for at least forty-eight hours afterwards."

He paused, looked expectantly at Bayerd, then said, "And I won't go over a hundred fifty milligrams on any man, regardless of what you say."

BAYERD turned to Elliott. "Give them the situation down below. I want a complete new crew up here in twenty-four hours with another standing by Earthside. And goose them on that ship data. I want cargoes as well."

"Cargoes?" Elliott asked.

Bayerd passed his hand over his head and sighed tiredly. "Playing to a blind hand. Still, you never know what one might be carrying that would prove useful."

"Right," Elliott said and started for the hatch.

As soon as Elliott was out of earshot, Beckworth said, "All right, Norm, sit down a minute."

"Haven't got time."

"You'll take time. I want to take a look at you."

"There's nothing wrong with me," Bayerd said.

"That's for me to say," Beckworth said, pushing him into a chair. He felt for Bayerd's pulse, paused as he checked the count, and then produced a small pencil light from his pocket. After a moment, looking at each eye and pursing his lips, he said, "What are you taking?"

"Nothing."

"Don't give me that."

BAYERD shifted uncomfortably in his seat, and said nothing.

"Tranquilizer?" Beckworth asked.

Bayerd started, then tried to speak. Finally he nodded.

"What for?" Beckworth demanded.

"I've been a little jumpy lately," Bayerd said. "Nothing serious. Got these from my doctor Earthside." He patted the vial of capsules in his breast pocket.

"I think you should be in bed," Beckworth said. "You look like a man who's gone through a concrete mixer."

"Don't talk to me about resting at a time like this," Bayerd snapped, getting to his feet impatiently. "I can't even think in those terms for the next twenty-four hours."

"All right, all right," Beckworth said. "Kill yourself. That's your privilege, but watch your step each minute. Those things, coupled with fatigue, can affect your judgment and your reaction time. And I want a detailed physical on you as soon as this mess is cleared up."

Bayerd shifted his weight uncomfortably, feeling like a small boy who has been caught stealing cookies. "I'll have it done Earthside."

"Huh uh," Beckworth objected. "That's my department. I want an official record on anyone connected with the project. I haven't received one for you from below, and I want to run a few tests."

"Don't be so damned persistent," Bayerd said tiredly.

"That's what I get paid for."

MENDOZA, who had apparently followed Bayerd after he left the bridge, stopped him on "S" deck as he was about to enter the Schrenk Cubicle assigned to him.

"Look," Mendoza said, "give it to me straight. What are the chances of stopping the beam?"

"I don't know. I told you everything I knew at the briefing."

"You don't understand. I've got to know. Things are pretty touchy down below. You don't have the complete picture of the political situation. This could give the Eastern Power Combine a lever in its bid for a bigger ration slice. Up to now, the ration has been on the basis of pre-Artery power usage—modified by population growth. Europe and Asia have always had high birth rates. We've had to do some juggling."

Bayerd rubbed his chin wearily. "I don't see how this ties in with the present situation."

"Well..." Mendoza paused for a second, then seemed to come to a decision, "...you may as well know. All hell will break loose at the next session. We forced this Liechtenstein scandal, accused them of falsifying the census records to up their power allotment. It was easy to do. Small district and not too many people to get to. The idea was to throw doubt on the larger census areas."

"No wonder they blew a valve," Bayerd said. "I wish you hadn't told me that."

"POLITICS is a dirty business when national survival is at stake," Mendoza said. "Don't you see, the West...Amazonia, the American States...are the best hope of pulling us out of this mess. We're the technological leaders, the countries needing the most power..."

"I'm sorry," Bayerd said, shaking his head. "I appreciate all you've done for the project—but I don't want to be a party to anything like this, regardless of what you want from me."

"Damn it, Norm, I'm not asking you to be a party to anything. I'm trying to be honest with you so you'll understand why you can't allow Gilchrist to involve you in any personal issues. Shifting attention from an issue to a personality conflict is the oldest trick in the book. Don't give him the chance."

Bayerd thought for a moment and then eyed the councilman. Mendoza's olive face was shining with perspiration, and his black eyes dropped to the floor when Bayerd looked at him.

"Oh, I know, damn it," Mendoza said. "I get a little sick of the mess myself sometimes. I fight for what I believe in, Norm, just as you do. And dirty if I have to. We're alike in that respect."

BAYERD ignored the thrust and said, "Look, just how dirty will their side fight?"

"Hard to say, what's on your mind?"

Bayerd told him about the changed settings on the capsule.

"My good Lord," Mendoza said. "Whoever would do such a thing? He must be insane."

"Not necessarily. He could have intended the beam to go out into space. The chances were all in favor of that."

"But the capsule…"

"Someone wants the beam shut down for a time. What he didn't anticipate was that the mechanisms in the capsule would continue to transmit the beam, and that we would not be able to get to the capsule in time."

"What are our chances there?"

"That's what I'm trying to find out," Bayerd said, gesturing toward the Schrenk cubicles. "I want to check on the spot and see how Chang's crew is coming."

"Is it possible at all to get to the accelerator?"

"The magnetic fields would disrupt robot control."

"Can't you just cut off the ore supply to the smelters?"

"We've done that," Bayerd said, "but there's about a ten-minute reserve within the accelerator area."

MENDOZA sighed. "Then if you haven't cut down to the capsule in the next fifteen hours, you must stop transmission some other way."

"No one's touching that installation," Bayerd said angrily.

"What do you want? Do you want your equipment intact and that uncontrolled beam running through the system? You said there's enough reserve metal within the system for four days of transmission and what may not happen in that time?"

"You can't touch the accelerator," Bayerd said angrily.

"When the time comes, if you can't give the order..." Mendoza replied, and then didn't finish the statement.

"Oh, go to Hell, all of you!" Bayerd turned away from the man.

CHAPTER SIX

HE FELT the door of the Schrenk cubicle slide close behind him and he leaned back, feeling its magnaluminum solidity through the cloth of his tunic. He felt emotionally drained, as though he had been laughing or crying for hours. A part of him churned with rage at Mendoza's betrayal.

He seated himself in the webbing of the Schrenk suit and buckled the mesh about his legs. The chest harness felt cold and constricting as he moved the face piece toward him.

He felt tension stealing over him, the thin quivering of thighs and the tightness of jaw muscles. If he could just hold off until the mess was finished. He freed his hand and fumbled for the medicine in his pocket, thinking of how they symbolized the thin distance between him and the end—not only of his personal existence, but in a larger sense the end of the existence of this entity he had created out of his life and his brain and his body.

He thrust his left arm into the glove, activated the controls for the robot atop the lookout point, and thrust his head into the face piece. The image of the two cathode tubes reflected in the angled mirrors of the face piece lightened for a second, flared and...

AND HE WAS looking out over the deserted rock, seeing the dead control consoles, the empty robot bodies standing apart where they had been thoughtlessly abandoned. He made walking motions in the harness and moved to the console he had occupied just before the transmission. He activated the metering circuits and checked the board. One meter registering grid potentials on the self-contained amplifier flicked, but the rest were dead. He touched the remote-register and a dim picture flickered on the tube, transmitted from the face of the capsule, buried in the rock.

He saw the loose locking screws and the fatal setting on the face of the capsule. There could be no doubt about it; the settings were quite different than the ones he had placed on the capsule the day before. Norman Bayerd tried to think back. Could he have possibly made a mistake, changed one of the settings while he was adjusting the automatic timing device? No, to make such an error, he would have to have changed three settings from those the Earthside computers at Pelembang had given them. The change was deliberate. No doubt of it.

Then the thought hit him. Whoever had changed the settings might conceivably have trapped himself without knowing it. He stooped and slid back the panel in the base of the console. Inside, a series of tape coils recorded the readings of the meters above from moment to moment. Normally they were erased after every twenty-four hours unless they were needed to compute some slight adjustment of the beam inherently undetectable by the beam's own mechanisms.

HE EXTRACTED the two tapes that recorded deflection and elevation of the transmitted beam and laid them on the surface of the console. After a moment of searching, he found the spot on one where the capsule setting had been changed, and then he found the similar change on the other spool. He noted the time on each and rewound the tapes. Then he found a small wrench in a nearby kit and carefully unseated the oscilloscope from the upper right-hand corner of the console panel. He wedged the two spools into the space beside the tapering tube and reseated it. Then he threaded two new spools onto the recording devices. Now, he thought, should anyone else have the same idea, they'd think the spools had been erased.

Then he rose and walked to the edge of the precipice. Below, he could see the capsule installation, its ceramic shield peeled away like the husk of a walnut. There were two Schrenk robots on the near side, struggling with a heavy mass, which he finally identified as a generator for a monatomic hydrogen-cutting torch.

"Bayerd here," he said. "How much progress you making?"

"Trubner, here," the voice came back. "The other generator broke down. We had to bring this one up from the mining installations."

"Hold it a minute," Bayerd said. He withdrew from the face piece and for a moment the confusion of the transition startled him. He touched the switch that activated the robot unit on the plain and suddenly, as he returned to the face piece, he was standing a hundred yards from the group with the generator. He walked over and said,

"Here, I'll handle the rear."

"THANKS," replied a voice that he identified as Muletti's. He had a mental image of the small wiry Italian, his normally curly black hair dipped short in a matted crew cut. Carefully he moved the generator toward the capsule shield and then slowly set it on the rock.

"I'll get it hooked up," Muletti volunteered.

"Good," Bayerd said, turning to look out over the plain. The accelerator installations still glowed with the bright radiance of infrared near the smelters. The scene reminded him of something out of a surrealist painting, with the inverted highlights seemingly twisting the familiar shapes into alien forms. Strange to think that this great thing of metals and energies might soon end.

It would be so easy, though, he thought. There were three cargo ships based to the south near the ore pits. One need only man a ship, take it up, and crash-dive it into the installation. No necessity of using explosives. Only...

That would be killing the artery. And the man piloting the ship would die a kind of death, though vicariously.

If it had to be done, Bayerd promised himself, it would be done at his hand. He would ride the ship down, die flaming in the wreckage, and walk the Black Field Station afterward to go at last back to Terra to die another kind of death.

WHEN TRUBNER responded over the new channel, Bayerd said, "How soon after I gave the order did you seat the capsule?"

"Three...four minutes, I suppose."

"Did you log it on your tape?"

"Yes," Trubner said.

"Check it, will you?"

Trubner's robot became immobile. Bayerd waited impatiently for seconds, then turned to watch Muletti lowering the generator through the shielding into the capsule pit. They had improvised a second winch to replace the one damaged by the arcing, welding the drum to the interior metal frame of the shield.

"Who's down below?" Bayerd asked.

"Sanchez, Chang, and Girard," Muletti said.

"How are they coming?"

"Very hard working. The metal spattered, however, so that it's somewhat porous and we occasionally cut into a series of vapor pockets, which helps."

"Good," Bayerd said as Trubner's body came erect.

"The time was 9:02," Trubner said.

"Are you sure? I have to have this pinpointed."

"Yes. I was recording from the command net. I dictated the time as I started to lower the capsule. It checks with the time index on the tape."

"That would mean about 9:01 for your time of arrival at the capsule site itself."

"I should think so."

"THANKS," Bayerd said. As Trubner returned to work, Bayerd deactivated the body and he was again in the station, leaning tiredly into the Schrenk harness. He freed himself and debated his next move. The obvious one was to check the tapes on each Schrenk unit. Find the one showing a break in control a minute or so before 9:01."

Overhead, an intercom speaker crackled and Elliott's voice said, "Norm, can you come up to Commo? I've got your shipping information."

He made his way up to Commo to find Elliott and Patel seated at the transceiver. Elliott sprang to his feet and held out a pad. "There's the story," he said.

Bayerd scanned the sheet, noting orbital figures, velocities. "Never mind. You've screened these already. What can we use?"

"Here," Elliott said, "we've made a sketch." He unfolded a sheet of five-foot square graph paper and fastened the sheet to the bulkhead with gummed tape. He had sketched in the orbits of the Earth and the planets past her out to Pluto. The distances were not to scale. Bayerd saw the trans-Jovian distances being much foreshortened. Beside each orbital circle, Elliott had noted figures in hours and minutes, denoting— Bayerd decided—the anticipated progress of the beam front.

"This is all approximate," Elliott said. "You'll notice that Terra is 'zero' and 'Pluto' is 20 hours. The beam front is approximately at this point." He touched a spot just outside of the orbit of Uranus and made a small "x" with his pencil, labeling it *"11 Hours."*

"All right," Bayerd said, "give me the ships."

"FIVE OF various size including the *Ingrid*, a cruiser assigned to the Norwegian Astronomical Society, and a 'drifter', the *SAU-62*, carrying air to the Callisto Experimental Ecological Station. All in this general sector." He pointed at the area past Jupiter and near Saturn. At this point he penciled the inscription: *"Approx. 4 Hours."*

"Then," Elliott said, consulting the sheet, "there's another drifter, the *CX-248*, here just above the asteroid belt. Cargo is an orbital radar lens for the radio telescope the Council is building in the Trojans—you know, one of those big inflatable polyparalene balloons plated with a layer of sodium metal. There are also four plasma drive ships and one chemical ballistic freighter in the same region. It's only an hour and forty minutes to 'zero' at that point though."

Bayerd looked at the sketch. The drifter near Saturn might be promising. Drifters were huge cargo vessels operating on a direct caesium ion drive. They were capable of an acceleration of perhaps one thousandth of a gravity. The trip to Saturn, if he recalled correctly, took almost seven months with a hundred days or so of acceleration and an equal period for deceleration. That meant that the drifter was barely moving at this point so close to its destination.

HE CHECKED the sheet for the data on the second drifter above the asteroid belt. The ship, he saw, had been out of Terra orbit sixty-seven days and now had a velocity of 200 miles per hour. That was not exceptionally high, he realized, but the fragile construction of the vessels, which were never meant to withstand strong acceleration, made maneuvering the things a touchy proposition.

"Patel," Bayerd asked, "what about the exhaust trick?"

"I ran the calculations on it," Patel said. "The theory is pretty, of course. You can build up quite a few statcoulombs on the particle cloud, but they're moving pretty fast at that temperature, and the particles are all charged alike which means they repel each other. A ten-mile cross-section might give you the three-tenths of a second deflection you need at Saturn's orbit—but you couldn't hold the cloud together even if you had the fuel for the density I calculated. No good, I'm afraid."

"It was a wild idea, anyway."

"If we can set up an electrostatic point source close enough to the beam path, we might deflect it," Patel said. "It would deform the plasmoids, but the later impulse might be sufficient to deflect the beam enough."

"All right—we'll play both our cards. Let's see if we can move the *SAU-62* into the beam path with the ships in the area and build up a skin charge using its motors and those of the other ships in the area. We can cut out the charge dissipators and throw out every bit of ionizable mass. That should build up a pretty good charge."

"What about the drifter in the asteroid belt?"

"The *CX-248?* We'll do the same with it. We'll have to have close observations on the path of the beam. Can that Norwegian ship give it to us?"

"Wait," Patel said, "that second drifter with the radar lens— why not unship it and inflate it in space? With so much of a metallic surface, we could accumulate an enormous charge."

"It won't work," Elliott said.

"We've got to try."

"That's not what I mean. Look, drifters are fairly fragile. They're not intended for high accelerations. The *CX-248* might take one 'g' but not much more without breaking up. At one 'g' deceleration, it will take ten hours to decelerate the *CX-248* and we don't have that long!"

Bayerd rubbed his hand tiredly across his eyes and said, "Then we'll just have to do without it."

"No," Patel said, "it's the polyparalene lens we want. We can decelerate the ship, even if it does buckle. Just so long as the lens is intact."

"All right," Bayerd said.

"How much time does the first group have?"

"Six and a half hours. Nine and a half for the second."

He moved past the two men and said, "Raise Luna Station and give me a line to the president of the Council. We'll need his weight behind us before we can start tearing up somebody else's property.

As Elliott began to call Luna Station, Norman Bayerd was thinking of what he had discovered at the accelerator site. Then he remembered the conversation with Muletti. He had, he realized, forgotten to change back to the command net after talking with Trubner. Yet Muletti had answered him immediately when he spoke.

Why, Bayerd wondered, had the man been eavesdropping on his conversation with Trubner?

CHAPTER SEVEN

"THIS DAMNED business of waiting," Elliott said, his voice husky with fatigue. "You feel so completely helpless."

"There's nothing we can do now but wait," Bayerd replied.

"Look," Elliott said, "You look bushed. Why don't you grab some sleep?"

Bayerd shook his head. "No, I want to check with Chang's group." He started for the door and then turned. "Do me a favor and keep your eye on Patel, will you?"

"You think he's the one?"

"I wish I knew. This whole business is completely insane. I don't know who to trust."

All the way down to the Schrenk cubicles, Norman Bayerd could feel the growing tenseness of his body. He was afraid as he had not been in years. He remembered the last time it had hit him—the horrible tensing of the muscles, the uncontrollable desire to scream, and the complete inability to…

"Take it easy," the doctors had told him. "Don't fatigue yourself, keep up the medication, and there's no reason why you should ever worry about an attack again. We've gone pretty far in treating this sort of thing."

As though this were a nice simple recipe, he thought, that one could follow at one's ease. Well, they'd never found out about his illness, the ones who might have taken him away from the project. But carrying this seed in your body, waiting for another descent into darkness. It was like carrying death as a sable shadow on the rim of your consciousness for the rest of your years.

HE THOUGHT of Elliott's advice, but he knew he could not rest—not as long as the man who had tampered with the Artery was free and undiscovered. Who was it? Trubner? Muletti? Or even Elliott? No, he couldn't believe that. Elliott was devoted to the project. It was more than a mere job to him. Why, he remembered when Elliott had first been assigned to his staff.

When Elliott had joined the beam project, fifteen years earlier, Bayerd had said, "Operating the Artery will be like standing back a hundred yards and stoking a furnace by throwing capped blocks of TNT at the open door. As long as your aim is good, the TNT lands inside and burns quietly. But if you miss, chances are the block will land on its fulminate cap. Now, that won't do a great deal of damage, but suppose the furnace supplies the only heat there is in one of the polar cities and suppose there's a tank of chlorine stored in the same room. Now, if you miss the door and the TNT explodes, the tank goes up, too—and you poison the whole area, perhaps the whole city. But you've got to keep the fire going, or the whole city freezes.

"So," Elliott had said, "you keep the game going because the city can't survive otherwise…and you pray your aim is good."

"Which is why you're part of the project."

"Because I'm to be trusted with TNT?"

"No," Bayerd had said, "because we think your aim is good."

AND so far, Bayerd thought, so far their aim had been good. When they first built the Artery, he had held doubts, secret doubts he would never have admitted. How do you concede a possibility to an antagonist without his seizing it, emphasizing it in terms of black or white, beating it out of shape with endless argument until a possibility became a probability and then a certainty? That's what would have happened with the Artery had Norman Bayerd agreed that the possibility of misdirection, of loss of control, existed at all.

He remembered the bitter exchanges in the newspapers, the parade of innuendo with a single fact overriding all others…the growing power-starvation of the world. The opposition had centered around Patel, the young physicist with visions of new power sources, of eventually doing what two generations had already failed to do: harness the hydrogen fusion reaction for power. Young, starry-eyed, all of them, conveniently forgetting the disastrous explosion that had leveled the British Experimental Station on the Isle of Man in the first instant of operation, vaporizing the tons of rock and dirt and scattering radioactive ash abroad on the winds. After that one, there had to be an end. Not even the need for power could justify the danger of annihilating the whole race.

PECULIARLY enough, the arguments of both sides hinged on the Black Field effect—that strange, accidental by-product of binding energy research that promised up to twenty percent conversion of matter in the fission reaction by its ability to contain the incredible forces of even an atomic explosion. Actually, "contain" wasn't the proper term. The Black Field partitioned energy within its influence in a most complex fashion. Particles with a given kinetic energy within the field crossed its boundaries and emerged with that energy much reduced. This was controllable. The density of the field would yield reductions of energy from eighty to almost 100 percent. Coincidentally, a certain number of particles in any group disappeared utterly. Statistically, the mass loss could be related to the reciprocal of the energy loss. The effect was essentially linear.

A German physicist by the name of Kulz found that reversing the polarity of the field under certain conditions resulted in a failure to contain the energy of the nuclear reaction. Had he not communicated his intended experiment to a colleague in Pakistan, no one would have known what happened. One thing developed from the disastrous experiment. Even if you calculated the energy release from total conversion of the contained mass, you came out with less energy than actually released. Something for nothing. Energy out of nowhere. Perpetual motion.

Only it wasn't so.

A TEAM financed by the World Council finally came up with a theory that fit the facts. There was—incredibly—complete conversion within the normally operating field, or very nearly complete conversion of mass into energy. Not just binding energy, the inconsequential residue of splitting into simpler atoms, but complete annihilation of matter.

The initial stage was simple fission, but the Black Field's energy partitioning effect came into operation. A small portion of the enclosed matter gained the major portion of energy within the field, and achieved velocities exceeding that of light in fractions of a microsecond. The stuff disappeared, but not before shedding a phantom particle: a positron where an electron had been; an anti-proton where a proton had been; a gamma-neutron where an ordinary neutron had been. The anti-particles destroyed more of the contained matter, producing more energy, more particles accelerating to the speed of light and disappearing. The creation of the phantom particles? All a matter of topology. Where were the accelerated particles going?

Imagine another…call it dimension, universe, continuum, what you will. Whatever it was, it was smaller than this one of ours, smaller not in terms of dimensions, for that concept had no meaning. Smaller, say, in terms of the amount of available free energy it could contain. A young universe, perhaps, a continuum with a point-for-point congruency with the real universe—if you accepted the postulated geometry for this other place—with an inverse entropy, so far as we were concerned.

The available free energy of that micro-universe could increase; that's what was happening to the partitioned energy. The particles, traveling faster than light, were carrying it elsewhere and dropping back into the real continuum turned inside out, the way you turn a glove inside out. The available free energy of that micro-universe was greater than that of ours for a given…could you say…volume of space. There was an energy incline. If you reversed the field as the unfortunate German had, well…

UNDERSTAND, though, you weren't creating energy. You had already, through a decade of experimenting, poured energy into this other place and the reversal of the field merely released it. Just a matter of two continuua seeking equilibrium. (Perhaps, as someone pointed out, the very operation of the first Black Field had created this other place. No matter. It was there, and the effect could be used.)

The Black Field offered two possibilities. Controlled fusion or the Artery. A long-term gamble with the certain price of failure a collapsing technology—if you were willing to invest the money and the massive labor of building the Artery. The deposits of U-235, as the hydride, had been discovered on Pluto; but it wasn't commercially feasible to bring the metal back by ship. The fleet of freighters needed alone would have severely taxed the metal resources of three worlds—not to mention that the energy requirements for such a commercial flight were such that you'd be lucky to achieve a ten percent payload.

GAMBLE on the development of controlled fusion? With the world starving for power; with space flight itself hanging in the balance; with the populations of one quarter of the world on a minimum subsistence diet after the past two decades' debauch of using Terra's fissionable resources at a drunken rate? The nice thing about the Artery was that there was a near-inexhaustible supply of power to run the accelerator and the other equipment right on the site. Why worry about how much U-235 you consumed, just so long as you didn't have to burn the stuff in a ship?

End result? Hearings following hearings, Bayerd leading them along, explaining, cajoling, meeting the attacks of the Patel faction, seeing always the massive vision of a band of metal stretching from far Pluto to the Earth, pumping in new life. Patel had called the concept a "Goldberg". The solution Bayerd was proposing, he said, was so complex that the expenditure of effort in another direction could find a simpler solution. Only he wasn't sure of just what that solution would be.

Norman Bayerd had seen a great deal of Patel during that period. At first they had been friendly rivals, sane men who had disagreed. Only Patel's people had gone on to attempt to discredit Bayerd. Bayerd's own backers in the Council had rushed to the attack, and the whole affair had been pretty nasty.

What really hurt, of course, was that during the summer when he was in Toronto testifying before the special commission of the World Resources Board, he had brought Diane with him as his secretary. Bayerd should have realized that something was going on, but he had been too busy, putting his final testimony into shape. That she should have found something in Patel to attract her was unthinkable; she knew how he felt about the man at that time. Actually, Bayerd had fallen into the habit of thinking of Patel as being his own age, forgetting that the man was actually only in his mid-twenties.

He still remembered the anguish he felt when she came to him and said that she and Patel were planning to be married. She was the only person Norman Bayerd had any real feeling for since his wife's death, and in many ways she was the living embodiment of his wife as he remembered her—young, vibrant, alert with a ready sense of humor, flavored with a bit of sugar and a dash of vinegar.

BAYERD moved into one of the vacant Schrenk cubicles and he stood, staring into the half-gloom of the room, remembering her face with the skin so smooth that it had an almost transparent paleness. And that little swine, Patel, who had never intended any real interest in the girl. It was his way of striking back after Bayerd had crushed him and almost ruined him professionally.

The cubicle he was in, he saw, was the one assigned to Gilchrist. He found the monitoring tapes with their time codes and carefully ran the last one back to the hour of transmission, searching for the telltale hiatus in the impulse that would indicate a shift to another Schrenk robot. He searched on either side of the spot that marked *9:00* but failed to find any indication of a jump. As nearly as he could determine, the councilman had occupied the robot on the Needle for the entire period after the tour that Elliott had shepherded through the plain installations.

He moved from the room and entered the next one. In quick succession he checked the cubicles belonging to Mendoza, Beckworth (who had not used his in days, since he had no direct concern with operations), and finally Elliott's.

He paused outside of the vacant cubicle assigned to Patel. All at once he knew that he would find the solution here. It had to be here. Who else had a better motive for destroying him? He felt the rage buried within him beginning to stir again.

And he remembered that Patel had not been on the Needle when he had returned. Patel had been wandering somewhere below, completely out of sight of the members of the Needle group, out of sight of the crew below on the plain. How simple, when he saw Bayerd's robot go lax, to switch to the abandoned body, make the changes in the capsule in seconds, and leave?

HE PUSHED open the door, feeling his heart pounding at what he knew must be here. The room was clothed in darkness, except for a glow-panel on the ceiling, shedding a residual light. He moved to the monitor unit, found the tape and began to rewind it to the spot that had recorded the instant when the hate and resentment of years had proved too much, when Patel with a quick movement of a switch had usurped the body by the capsule and condemned millions to disaster...to death.

In the dim light he inspected the tape. It was there! The tiny hiatus where the Schrenk unit had been switched to another robot body. And the time was *9:00*.

For a second, he felt somehow depressed; the reaction was completely anticlimactic. This was the evidence he had been seeking. Yes, the index along the edge clearly established the time. The taped record would show which robot on Pluto he had activated. Bayerd need only run the tape back on the reel and play back the coded data. He leaned forward to inspect the soundtrack running parallel to the data track, wondering what sounds Patel must have unconsciously voiced in that instant of betrayal. In the next instant intense pain lanced through his temples.

It felt as if someone had hit him with a steel bar. There was a suffocating something over his mouth, cutting off air. Swirls of color raced before his eyes as his body tensed. He felt his muscles snapping with the effort, trying to fight upward to consciousness.

He felt something crushing his lips inward, smothering him and he tasted the warm taste of blood before he fell into the smothering darkness...

CHAPTER EIGHT

HE WAS wrapped in pale light while a part of him stood apart and watched the endless drifting of his body. There was something at the farthest range of Norman Bayerd's vision, separated from his living self by great distance, by light years even, that was approaching him with fantastic speed.

It would be only a matter of minutes...seconds...days... years...time until it were upon him and all thinking, all feeling would cease.

Drifting in an eternity of soft light and warmth with the touch of chill on his back. Soft light and formlessness. And he knew that he could not leave in this manner with no form, no substance on which he might pin some memory of his past existence.

Drifting, he searched the light in which he moved and saw that he was enclosed in a fragile sphere whose boundaries were sharp and well-defined...that beyond this sphere of light, the endless black, flecked with bright stars, stretched to infinity and there was nothing that would carry him outward from his sphere of radiance to those other far spheres of light. There was only hereness and nowness and that soon to be dissolved... By something moving toward him with incredible speed, something cold and stifling and smothering and...

SOMEWHERE dimly he heard a voice and he felt something drawing him upward. Bayerd fought against the pull, seeking only to drift silently in his tiny universe of light for the thing rushing down upon him. He looked far out and then he saw it.

Like a great sable curtain sweeping through space, blotting out the stars. A vast mass of utter lightlessness that swallowed his universe. But there was a speck of light that grew in a long parabola racing across his pool of brightness, and he knew that it was a thing upon which he might fasten and which would bear him ever outward to those distant universes before the endless black curtain would enfold him in its stifling substance.

He sent his consciousness outward in all directions, seeking for something. For a stone, a twig, a shard of metal with which he could mark the place where he had been...where in the night that would quickly fall, someone finding it might know that he had been there and had afterwards gone hence...

But there was the pull, something binding him to the spot and pulling him upward...upward into greater light.

Into brilliance and...

"Norm," someone said. "Norm, what's happened?"

189

And there was a warm arm supporting him, buoying him up and away from the bright radiance, away from the onsweeping blackness to...

Light as his lids faltered open.

THE ROOM was a mass of shifting shadows. He felt a deep throbbing pain behind his eyes and the blood pulsing frantically in his temples. There was a tight, burning sensation in the pit of his stomach and his muscles felt lax and drained of energy. He struggled into a sitting position as Elliott said, "Are you all right?"

He shook his head, trying to speak, but his throat was tight and his mouth dry. For seconds he couldn't manage a sound. He wet his lips and swallowed. He felt the astringent taste of blood in his mouth and his exploring tongue told him that in his struggles he must have lacerated his own cheek lining with his teeth.

"I think so," he said at last. "It all happened so fast."

He tried to get to his feet and fell back against the metal bulkhead. For an instant, sharp pain shot through his temples. His exploring hand found a throbbing area at the back of his head.

"You were gone almost two hours," Elliott said quietly. "I began to wonder and came down to find you."

"Where's Patel?" Bayerd asked.

"Up in Commo. He's been handling the message traffic on the operations we set up."

"Has he been there all, the time?"

"Why, yes," Elliott said. Then his brow wrinkled in thought and he said, "That is, I suppose so. I've been busy on the metering bridge. He's been in Commo every time I came down, though. Why? You don't think...?"

"I don't know what to think," Bayerd said, getting unsteadily to his feet with Elliott's help. "I know one thing though."

He made his way unsteadily to the monitoring tape unit and removed the spool.

"Hit the lights, will you?" he said.

Elliott touched the induction plate by the door and the walls and ceiling glowed a soft radiance. Carefully, Bayerd rolled the tape from one spool to the other, searching again for the significant area of the tape. After a few minutes he realized that something was wrong. The break was there, but the time code was not the same. The break was now coded at 9:05.

"This isn't the same tape," he said. "Someone's switched it for the original."

"What's so important about the tape?" Elliott asked.

Bayerd told him. Elliott whistled. "Are you sure?"

"Damn it, of course I'm sure. I was hunting for just such evidence when I started checking the monitor tapes. It isn't likely that I would make a mistake."

"But this means that Patel was the one who changed the capsule settings."

"It looks that way."

"I find that a little hard to believe."

"Don't be a fool," Bayerd said impatiently. "It's hard to believe about anyone, but Patel is one of the most likely. Only I can't prove it now."

He passed a hand over his eyes. The hand, he noticed, was shaking, the tips of the fingers vibrating with tiny tremors. His jaw muscles ached as though he had been holding his teeth clenched for a long time.

"You'd better get Doc Beckworth to check you over," Elliott said, reaching out a hand to steady him. "Give me the tape. I might he able to find something in the coded data."

"You're welcome to it." Bayerd said. "It's probably pretty crude. He didn't have time to do a good job of faking."

"Let's go," Elliott said.

"All right—but the story is that I fell and banged my head. No one's to know about this for the present."

Elliott shrugged. "Any way you want it."

THEY FOUND Beckworth in the Dispensary down the corridor from the Commo room.

"What happened to you?" he demanded as Bayerd seated himself.

"Never mind. I fell over my own feet. Just patch up this bump and take a look at the cut inside my mouth." He turned to Elliott and said, "Go on to Commo and see if you can help Patel. You might look into that other matter as soon as you find time."

"Right," Elliott said, checking his watch.

"How much time?"

"Less than two hours to first contact."

After Elliott left, Beckworth examined the wound on Bayerd's scalp, carefully clipping away a small circle of hair with a pair of surgical scissors.

"That's a nasty bump," he said. "Looks like somebody clouted you one."

"Maybe someone did," Bayerd said wryly. "Ouch, take it easy, will you." He felt moistness as Beckworth followed the antiseptic with a thin layer of topical antibiotic ointment over the wound. He sealed the wound with a thin sheet of porous protein film that would eventually be absorbed into the open tissue and touched the button that rotated Bayerd's chair backwards.

"Open your mouth," he said. He took a small pencil light from an instrument tray and examined the wound on the inside of Bayerd's right cheek.

"How the blazes did you do this?"

"I told you, I slipped and fell."

"You've chewed a hunk of flesh the size of a dime out of the lining," Beckworth said, "The edge of the tongue is lacerated, too. Could give you a nasty infection."

He eyed Bayerd speculatively. "You didn't do that in a single fall. Want to tell me about it?"

"Damn it, Doc," Bayerd said, "it's none of your business. Get the damage patched up and don't ask so many questions."

"And you can go to blazes, too," Beckworth muttered under his breath as he secured a swab from a sterilizer. After he painted the interior wound and affixed two tiny plastic clamps with a forceps, he handed Bayerd two yellow capsules and a glass of water. "Tetracycline," he said. "We'll try to keep the bugs away from that fevered brain."

"Thanks," Bayerd said tiredly, "Look, I'm sorry about snapping your head off. I've been working under a lot of tension."

"Are you sure that's all?" Beckworth asked.

"What other explanation should there be?"

"Wait a while. There are a few checks I'd like to run through."

"Save it," Bayerd said. "I haven't got the time."

"You'd better take the time," Beckworth said. "From the looks of you, if you don't, we'll be taking you back Earthside on a stretcher."

At the door to the dispensary he said, "I'm sending you back anyway by the first shuttle after this mess is cleaned up. I want a complete check-up on you and this is one time I'm going to get my way."

"Your privilege," Bayerd said.

HE LEFT Beckworth, and went down the corridor to Commo. Elliott was working in a corner of the room with a tape data processor. When Bayerd entered, he removed the button earphone and touched the cut-off switch at the base of the mechanism. The jagged patterns on the scanning screen dissolved into a point of blue light that died. Patel was seated at the Commo desk, speaking quietly with Mendoza and Gilchrist. He looked up as Norman Bayerd entered and said, "We were wondering what happened to you."

"How are the two intercept groups coming?" Bayerd asked, ignoring the statement.

"The *Ingrid* has a pick-up mounted to give us a picture of the operations," Patel said. He touched a plate before him on the desk and the wall screen flickered. The image of the drifter, the *SAU-62*, slowly formed. It was a sphere of two hundred feet diameter with a thick tubular leg, and two smaller open girder frames extending rearward to support the broad radiating units that contained the thrust surfaces from which the accelerated anions of the drive were expelled.

FOUR SMALLER points had clustered about the *SAU-62*, which was drifting slowly away from the screen. The ships were all of the corvette class, Bayerd saw.

"It's a touchy job," Patel said. "The drifter shape is a clumsy one to handle, and they don't dare try for more than half a gee acceleration."

"Can they get into position in time?"

"I think so, but then they've got to build up the skin charge. We'll position the corvettes nose-to-nose in a cross to balance their thrusts, cut out their charge dissipaters, and build up a skin charge on each ship by throwing out as much ionizable mass as fast as possible. Then we'll bleed the charge away through a cable to the inner surface of the *SAU-62's* hull. The charge will migrate to the outside surface immediately, of course, which will allow us to build up quite a charge density without worrying about electrostatic repulsion too much."

"What about beam data?"

"The *Ingrid* will be standing off with a bank of ultra-violet sensitive 'strob' units. She should catch the beam angle with an error of perhaps five per cent. Certainly no more."

"What about the group at the belt? The *CX-248?*"

"I can't get a picture on them yet," Patel said. "The captain of the Cruiser *Orion* is handling that end. They're decelerating the *CX-248* but she's buckling badly."

"Let's hope they get that polyparalene bag out intact. Can you give me the details on the charge density they can develop with that thing?"

"I'll check on it," Patel said.

ELLIOTT had approached them and he leaned over now and said, "Norm, the news is out Earthside."

"What do you mean?"

"We've just received a telecast. There's rioting in New Delhi, Stuttgart, and Boston."

"I radioed back," Gilchrist said belligerently. "No reason to hide the fact. If I hadn't, you wouldn't have taken any measures to minimize the disaster."

"Councilman," Norman Bayerd said slowly, "it's difficult for me to tell you just how many varieties of a blow-hard idiot you are. There's absolutely nothing that can minimize the potential disaster in the short time we have, and your little political maneuver has probably cost thousand of lives just from the resulting panic."

"I don't take that sort of talk from anyone," Gilchrist snapped.

"You'll take it from me, mister. I'm damned tired of having you underfoot." He turned to Elliott and said, "All right, we'll be very proper now and declare this a military emergency. Elliott, escort Councilman Gilchrist down to his quarters under arrest."

"By God, that's just about enough," Gilchrist roared.

"It is indeed," Bayerd said.

"Now get below quietly or..."

Mendoza placed a hand on Gilchrist's shoulder. "Let's go," he said softly. Gilchrist glared at Bayerd and then bowed slightly, his face twisted in a crooked smile.

"In a textbook situation," he said, "the little martinets always win. This isn't the end of it though." He withdrew with Mendoza as Elliott said, "He did that deliberately."

"Of course. He wants a panic to dramatize the issue in the Council." Bayerd turned to Patel. "Why didn't you stop that idiot?"

"I'm sorry," Patel said. "He must have got to the radio while I was away from Commo."

Bayerd drew Elliott aside as Beckworth entered and walked over to Patel. "Check that tape thoroughly," he told Elliott, "and get at the message tapes here in Commo."

"Why?" Elliott asked. "The message has gone out already."

"Yes, and it was sent while Patel was away from Commo. If we can get a time on the message, and it coincides with the time I tripped over my feet downstairs, well..."

Elliott nodded in understanding.

"Right now," Bayerd said, "I want to check on the work at the capsule."

"Anything else," Elliott asked, looking at Beckworth and Patel. Beckworth was handing Patel a message flimsy and explaining something to him in low tones.

"No," Bayerd said, watching the other two men. He wondered what Beckworth was sending—probably in med administration code, and he couldn't find out by checking the tapes later. He had a strong suspicion of what the message was about. Why, he thought, didn't the meddling fool leave things alone?

ON THE way down to "S" level, Bayerd moved with a feeling of numbness and fatigue weighting his body. He was going to have to grab some rest shortly, he knew. He was pressing himself close to the limit of his endurance. As he entered his cubicle, he thought: *Please, God, just let me finish this last piece of work. Just this last watch and then it doesn't matter what happens.*

He thought of the vast chaos sweeping whole continents. Of the cities crumbling under the shock wave—the vast, unheard sound toppling bridges, shattering the steel and concrete of buildings and the screams of the millions who would die in the short instant the beam penetrated the atmosphere and shed its energy in the fantastic compression wave that would grow from the livid wound in the air.

He pressed the thought down with quick panic and lowered himself into the Schrenk harness. He sat for long seconds, trying to gain control of his body, which was suddenly wracked, with a thousand small quiverings of fear.

At last he activated the unit and made the movements that hurled him in an instant across over five light hours to stand on that dark Plutonian plain.

HE HAD lost all track of time in the subdued frenzy of the work about the capsule site when Elliott's voice cut into his consciousness with: "Norm, fifteen minutes."

"Right," he said. He gave a few last-minute instructions to Chang, who was down in the pit, and then turned away. For an instant he stared at the Needle, thrusting up from the pool of shadow that was the fissure circling the outcropping. It seemed almost as if the lookout point was floating on a sea of blackness, with the stars blazing intensely about it. He had not realized until this instant how completely isolated, physically and symbolically, the Needle was from the immediacy of the Artery and its installations on the plain.

He withdrew to the Schrenk cubicle in the Black Field Station and made his way up to Commo. Patel met him at the door and said, "They're cutting it awfully close. They've got barely ten minutes to bring skin charge up to strength."

Bayerd brushed past Elliott and Mendoza who were silently staring at the screen. The huge drifter took up a quarter of the image the *Ingrid* was transmitting. The four corvettes were grouped in a tight cluster, their exhausts flaming green and blue, while at some distance a faint gleaming haze expanded like a cloud of fog. The haze, he decided, was colloidal aluminum from the drive and the ships had cut off their water injection so that the metal was being ejected in its elemental form.

"Three minutes," Mendoza said, consulting the wall chronometer.

Norman Bayerd held his breath and then let it out explosively. How long would it take to build up the skin charge? Would it be enough? Just a tiny deflection at this distance, that was all they needed.

In the screen one of the corvette motors flared brightly and in the next instant died.

"What's happening," Elliott said.

"The thrust is unbalanced," Bayerd said as the mass of ships began to move slowly towing the drifter with them. The four corvettes, now with a slight side velocity, began to move out of the screen. In the next moment, the *Ingrid* changed her orientation, bringing the group of ships back into the center of the screen.

"Five seconds," Elliott said.

"They've got to get back in position."

"They've moved in closer to predicted path," Patel said. "Perhaps it is not…"

He did not finish the statement. The beam passed at that point. No one in the room saw it, of course, but the effect of its passage was obvious.

The drifter bloomed in a fraction of a second into an expanding flower of brilliance, engulfing the lesser ships as it soared to an intensity the pickup could not register. An instant later, the pickup ceased to exist as the *Ingrid* was engulfed by the shell of hot gases.

The screen went blank.

"MERCIFUL saints—what happened?" Mendoza asked.

"The ship's pile?" Elliott ventured.

"No," Patel said. "It was something we did not consider. The ship's cargo was air for the Callisto Experimental Station. Oxygen, nitrogen, helium, hydrogen—the normal spectrum of gases. The heat from the beam…"

"A carbon-nitrogen reaction," Bayerd gasped.

"Yes, it appears so."

"But," Elliott said, "that means the same thing will happen if the beam touches the Earth's atmosphere."

"I'm afraid you're right," Bayerd said sickly.

CHAPTER NINE

"WHAT HAPPENED out there?" Mendoza demanded.

"The motor of one of the corvettes failed," Elliott said. "Don't ask me why, but the resulting imbalance started the whole group drifting into the path of the beam."

"How much chance do we have now of stopping the beam?"

"Councilman," Bayerd said, "our only hope now is the CX-248 and its group of ships near the asteroid belt."

"We'll need a greater deflection," Patel said. "Perhaps a quarter of a mile might do it if they build up a high enough charge."

"Well, if our beam data is correct," Bayerd said, "we can get that close."

"I dislike saying this," Mendoza said, "but even if you do deflect the beam, there's still the problem on Pluto. I think the time has come for some drastic action there."

"What about it, Norm?" Patel asked. "Do you think they stand a chance of getting down to the capsule before transmission time?"

"I don't know. They're trying, but the work is slow."

"I think we should try explosives," Mendoza said.

"No, we can't risk damaging the accelerator. We've been all over this before."

"Nevertheless," Patel said slowly, "it doesn't look as if Chang's group is making any appreciable progress."

"IF THE accelerator is destroyed," Bayerd said tiredly, "it's doubtful that we can hold out long enough to build another one."

"I'm afraid it's the only solution," Elliott said.

"I hate to say it, but there is now no other choice." Mendoza turned to Elliott. "You'd better give the order."

"Now just a minute," Bayerd put in. "This is my command and I'll give any orders that have to be given."

"This is on my own responsibility," Mendoza said.

"I'm not in the habit of shifting responsibility to anyone else when it belongs to me," Bayerd said. "All right, this seems to be the general opinion and I frankly can't argue against it." He turned to Elliott. "Give the order he said." He turned on his heel and walked from the room.

He felt as if he were living a dream. His head ached from the scalp wound, and his exploring tongue found the inside of his cheek raw and tender to the touch. The weight of the last few hours pressed heavily on him and he knew now that he could not go on without some rest.

There wasn't much he could do, Norman Bayerd thought as he entered his small sleeping chamber on "R" level. He lay down on the web hammock, drew the counter webbing over him, and secured it to insure that, in this low weight area, a chance movement would not throw him out of bed while he slept. Then he lay for a long time, staring into the darkness and savoring the cool breeze that blew over his face from the air-conditioning duct above his head.

WHAT DIFFERENCE did it make, he thought, if Patel had been the one who changed the capsule settings? It was too late now for recriminations, too late for accusations or revenge or...

No. Patel had tried to destroy the Artery, rob him of the product of his life, destroy the place he had built for himself in the advance of man to the stars.

Only Patel had said that Bayerd had pressed mankind into a straitjacket with the Artery; that humanity had entered upon a period of stasis, of arrested development simply because it took every bit of its energy to survive at the present level.

Never get beyond this system, never go to the stars? He couldn't believe it. The drive was too strong.

Only what had been done in that direction in ten years? Had there been any major advances toward a stellar drive? There had been a thousand and one refinements of existing technique, but the significant breakthrough...

That wasn't right. The Artery represented the life of Earth. Without it she would never have come the distance she had. Nothing...disgrace, death...nothing could stop him before he proved that to Patel. Least of all death, he thought. .

He remembered that it was the summer after the hearings, after Patel and Diane...

Don't think about that...hateful...tragic betrayal...

HE HAD GONE back to the empty house in the mountains just above Colorado Springs, back to the silent green hills and the bite of cool morning air. He had taken to riding in the morning and evening, taking his path up the side of Pike's Peak along some of the old train railways and abandoned roadways. The old concrete roads were crumbling, and footing upon them sometimes uncertain. The decayed roadbed had given way under his mare and the poor animal had fallen to its death.

Bayerd had been more fortunate. A washout had indented the side of the slope perhaps ten feet down, and his body had lodged in the space behind a boulder. He had been unconscious for at least an hour. He remembered waking in the late morning sun with dried blood matting his scalp and caking on the side of his face. Somehow, he'd made it back to one of the traveled roads where a passing driver had found him and taken him down into the valley to a hospital.

Why couldn't it have been a quick death? he thought. Better than this waiting, this secret knowledge of the seeds of death lodged within him…better to…

No, every hour, every tiny instant was important to secure this thing he had built from the assaults of people like Patel. What had Patel said on the Needle those long hours ago, something about the Artery and pyramids?

Well, the Artery was a monument that the ancient pharaohs might well envy in place of their useless masses of ritual stone.

I met a traveler from an antique land who said…

What was that? Shelly? Patel had asked him if he knew *Ozymandias*. *"My name is Ozymandias, king of kings…"* Small, egotistic man who thought of the world as that tiny speck of sand about a muddy river and died, thinking that the stars were bits of fire set in a bowl over his head if he bothered to think about them at all. *"Look on my works, ye Mighty, and despair. Round the decay of that colossal wreck, boundless and bare…"*

That was the whole clue to Patel's thinking. Destroy the Artery because the Artery was the symbol of his life, how he had risen above the little Indian, and…

"Norm!" Someone was shaking him, and Bayerd opened his eyes to find that Patel had switched on the lights. He was staring at the glowing ceiling, trying to orient himself. Then he checked his watch.

"Why didn't you call me earlier."

"You needed the sleep," Patel said. "The *Orion* just radioed in. They've finished their installation."

He pulled himself from the hammock and they went up to the Commo room. "How's charge build-up?" he asked.

"They're still building," Patel said. "They're twenty percent above what we calculated we needed."

"How much time?"

"Two minutes," Elliott said.

"The *Orion's* equipped with a 'strob' pick-up," Patel said, "They've modified it to give us an azimuth reading on the beam after deflection if the thing triggers properly."

"Thirty seconds," Elliot said.

"Now we can only pray," Mendoza said from his seat in the corner of the room.

Elliot began to speak into the microphone before him as a dim image from the *Orion* built up on the screen. It was apparent that the *Orion* was part of the group of ships building up the charge on the inflated lens, for only the sterns of two of the ships showed in the screen at close range. The huge curve of the plastic sphere covered half of the screen, its metallic-plated sides gleaming in crescent. They had inflated the sphere and then cut a hole in its side to position the cable. The sphere once inflated, of course, had maintained its shape.

"Five seconds!" Elliott said.

Bayerd realized that he was not breathing and forced himself to inhale. *Pray God this will end it,* he thought.

"Zero," Elliott said with a sigh.

"Get their readings," Bayerd said. The overhead speaker crackled suddenly as Elliott cut it in for them to hear.

"B. F. Station," a voice said, "this is the *Orion*."

"B. F. Station to *Orion*. Did you get a reading?"

"We got one all right."

"How much deflection?"

"We couldn't measure it."

"What do you mean? What's the accuracy of your sighting?"

"You don't get me," the voice said. "We clocked the beam right on schedule. The only trouble was that it passed five miles outside of the volume you calculated for it."

Bayerd walked over and grabbed the microphone. "What's that again?"

The intercom on the far side of the desk was buzzing insistently. "Patel," Bayerd said, "get that thing."

"You were way off, mister," the *Orion* voice said.

"This is Commander Bayerd. Explain yourself."

"Norm," Patel was saying.

"Shut up," Bayerd snapped. "It's Gilchrist," Patel insisted. "He's on "S" level…down by the Schrenk cubicles."

"I said," the *Orion's* man repeated, "You were way off. We didn't jog that beam a whisker."

"Gilchrist says Chang's team has collapsed the capsule tube. The capsule is buried under a ton of rock."

"What difference does it make now?" Bayerd said, sinking to a chair.

"You don't understand. Gilchrist has barricaded himself on "S" level. He's warning us not to come down."

"What's got into him," Mendoza demanded.

"He's given the men orders to blow up the accelerator," Patel said.

CHAPTER TEN

"WHAT HAPPENED?" Mendoza demanded. "I thought you had the beam path pinned down?"

"We did," Bayerd said.

"Where did we make the mistake?" Patel asked softly.

"That doesn't matter. There must be some way of stopping the beam," Mendoza said.

"And stopping that idiot Gilchrist from wrecking the accelerator," Bayerd snapped. "I'm going down there and try to reason with him."

"Wait a minute," Patel said suddenly, "we must have had the path of the beam calculated fairly well or it would never have struck the *SAU-62*. The small distance she traveled was just enough to bring her into the path."

"That was apparent enough," Bayerd said. Then he slapped his fist into the palm of the other hand and said excitedly, "The explosion! We weren't expecting that."

"I don't see..." Patel began.

"Radiant energy. Lots of it."

"The light pressure," Patel said.

"Of course. The radiant energy of the explosion overtook the beam in a fraction of a microsecond. The light pressure was enough to distort the bean course slightly."

"But not enough."

PATEL SEATED himself at the desk and began to calculate, occasionally referring to the sheaf of flimsies with the Earthside computer data. After a few moments, he looked up.

"This might do it. If we try for a hundred-kilometer displacement of the beam above the Earth's atmosphere, we're probably safe. So..." he touched the last sheet of his calculations, "if we touch off a reaction at say the distance of the Black Field Station...a million miles from Terra, we need a deflection about twenty seconds to each plasmoid segment of beam."

He continued to write rapidly and finally leaned back. "Under those conditions," he said, "it figures out to a hundred and twenty kilos of U-235 twenty per cent conversion."

"Listen," Bayerd told Elliott, "get Luna Station and get a ship—any ship loaded with enough fissionables. They can load a Black Field and set it up on the way out. Better make it two hundred kilos just to be safe."

"Can you do it in an hour and a half?" Mendoza asked.

"We can try," Patel said.

"Just pray Luna can give us what we want," Bayerd said. "Now I've got to stop that idiot Gilchrist."

"I'm coming with you," Mendoza said.

They emerged from the personnel tube into the corridor leading toward the Schrenk cubicles. The pressure hatch, sealing the compartment from the rest of the station was partly closed, blocking their view of the passage.

THEY WERE within twenty feet of the hatch when Gilchrist's voice said, "Don't come any closer. I have a gun and I'll use it if you try to force your way in."

"Come out of there," Bayerd said. "We've got to talk."

"You think I'm a fool? You do your talking from there."

"You've got to call off the men," Bayerd said. "If you destroy the accelerator, we'll never be able to rebuild it."

"Don't you think I know that? But the consequences of destroying the Artery are a hell of a lot more attractive than the consequences of that transmission starting again."

"Wait," Mendoza said slowly, "what about the lens station?"

"Lens stations?" Bayerd asked.

"Yes, the orbital magnetic lens that warps the beam above Pluto?"

"No chance," Bayerd said. "They're self-powered and keyed by c-cube radio to the control capsule. We can't change its position and we can't get a Schrenk body near one to turn off the field. Same problem as with the accelerator. The magnetic fields are too dense."

"There's another way," Mendoza said. "You can replace a lens station a lot easier than the Artery."

"Ram one with a ship?"

"Of course. Then the beam will head into space. It doesn't make any difference if every bit of the reserve metal within the accelerator area goes out. It won't strike anything."

"All right," Bayerd said. "Gilchrist, I'll make a deal with you. Let us through to Chang and I'll take one of the lens stations out of action. We can't let them touch the accelerator."

FOR LONG moments, there was silence. Finally, the hatch door moved aside and Gilchrist stepped out. "You'll have to get out there immediately," he said. "They've already fueled one of the old supply ships. They're going to ram the accelerator with it."

"Thanks a lot, Councilman," Bayerd said savagely, stepping in and hitting the man with all of his strength. Gilchrist slid to the floor without a sound. Bayerd reached down, fumbled with the man's tunic until he found the revolver, which he placed in a pocket of his tunic.

"Why did you do that?" Mendoza demanded.

"He had it coming. Now don't bother me."

In scarcely a minute he was in the Schrenk harness and on Pluto. He made his way across the plain at a low run toward the field where the ships were berthed. He could see the men gathered around one of the ships as he approached. They were finishing the fueling, he saw. Two of the men whirled to face him as he came abreast of them.

"It's Bayerd," he said.

"Don't try to stop us, Commander," Trubner said. "This is the only solution left to us."

"I'm not trying to stop you," he said. "I'm just offering another target."

He explained the plan and Sanchez said, "All right, we'll try it. Chang was taking the ship out."

"That's right," Chang said.

"I'll take over that end," Bayerd said.

"No," Chang said, "I would rather..."

"That's an order," Bayerd said. "This is something that I have to do. I won't have anyone else touching the Artery."

"Of course," Chang said softly.

MINUTES later, Pluto was a fast-receding speck of light in the ship's view plate. Norman Bayerd was crowding the ship to the limit of its nine gravities acceleration but the Schrenk body gave no sensation of weight. Hurriedly he checked the time. An hour and ten minutes left.

He switched the view plate to the forward pickup and saw at a distance the points of light that were the lens stations, revolving ceaselessly around a common center. Carefully he corrected his course and locked the controls. Then he waited, checking the collision course at intervals.

He knew when the magnetic field from the stations began to build up. The legs of the robot became imbued with a life of their own. They quivered and one lashed out against the bulkhead. He was losing his balance, falling...and in the next instant all sight and sound faded and he was an ordinary flesh-and-blood man, embraced in a tight womb of blackness. He waited for long moments for control to return. All at once he was again in the Schrenk body.

He was wallowing in space, his metal body turning slowly like some dancer in a dream ballet. Around him the debris of the ship moved in complex patterns, colliding and bouncing away, still sharing his velocity and path. He thrashed his arms about, trying to stabilize his motion. In one slow turn he saw the lens.

The station he had destroyed was flaring brightly as its power piles erupted. It was falling into the center of the lens, he saw, and in the next turn he saw that the other stations were moving.

In the instant before he cut control of the body, he realized what he had done. The lens stations were falling in on each other, destroying each other as the equilibrium of their system was destroyed.

He was sick with the sight as he pulled from the restraining harness. Mendoza was waiting outside the cubicle and he pushed past him without speaking.

IN THE COMMO room he sank into a chair and lowered his body until his head was between his legs, trying to fight off the sudden wave of dizziness.

"Norm," Beckworth said, "are you all right?"

"I'll be okay in a minute," he said.

"We're finished anyway," Elliott said quietly.

"Leave him alone for a minute," Beckworth said.

"What do you mean, we're finished?" Bayerd demanded, raising his head.

"He means there's not a ship within flight distance," Mendoza said.

"It was a pretty Idea," Elliott said, "but we'll never get to see if it works."

Norman Bayerd shook his head, feeling a sudden roar in his ears.

"Unless..." he heard Patel say.

"Unless what?" Elliott said.

"If we can reverse the polarity of the Black Field."

"Here? This station?"

"It's the only solution left."

BAYERD pushed Beckworth away and rose unsteadily to his feet. "That's what you've wanted all along," he said. "You've rigged this whole thing to destroy the Artery."

"You act as if I were responsible for this situation," Patel said.

"Norm, you'd better sit down," Beckworth said, placing a restraining hand on his shoulder. Bayerd shook it off savagely.

"Keep away from me," he said hoarsely. "Don't think I haven't found out what you've done," he yelled at Patel. "I've found out the whole rotten mess."

"Stop it," Elliott said. "You don't know what you're saying."

"Don't I? I have all the evidence I need. Patel was the one who changed the capsule settings. The monitoring tapes would have proven that, but he got those when he found me in his cubicle checking on him."

"Patel wasn't the one who attacked you," Elliott said.

"Norm," Beckworth said, "there's something…"

"Shut up, all of you," he shouted.

"You didn't find any incriminating tape in Patel's cubicle," Elliott persisted. Bayerd scarcely heard him in the sudden overwhelming hate that seemed to shake his body.

"You've tried to destroy the Artery and me since we first met," he shouted. "Now your underhanded trick has turned on you." He pulled the coded message flimsy from his pocket. "The whole pattern gets pretty clear, this message to one of your plants on my crew…your sabotaging of the capsule…"

PATEL rose slowly and took the flimsy from Bayerd's hand. He glanced at it and looked up. "This isn't mine," he said. "You, of all people, should know who this one was sent to."

"And you know there's no evidence on that monitoring tape from Patel's cubicle," Elliott said. "It's the original tape. He couldn't have faked it in that detail."

Bayerd felt the blood roaring in his ears. The room was suddenly dark with shadows crouching in every corner.

"This is the administrative code the computer sections use," Patel was saying. "Only top brass has the code and you're the only top brass here."

"No," Bayerd said. "It's all a part of the plot. Destroy the Artery. Discredit me."

"I didn't stop with Patel's tape," Elliott said. "I checked the one from your cubicle. You were still in control of the robot at the capsule site up until the moment the crew arrived to seat the capsule."

The room was awash with blackness. A horrible quivering had seized the muscles of his thighs.

"And there was nothing wrong with the calibration of your instruments on the console at the Needle," Elliott was saying.

"Damn it, cut it out," Bayerd yelled.

"It was Bayerd," Elliott said. "He was the one who received the code message. He was the one who changed the vernier settings on the capsule at the last moment."

ALL SUPPORT seemed to disappear from Norman's Bayerd's body. He was falling. He felt the hard floor strike him and nausea washed over him as his body jerked convulsively. From far above hands reached down to him and an echoing voice that might have been Beckworth's said, "Get me a pencil from the desk. Quick! Pry open his jaws before he does any damage to his tongue."

CHAPTER ELEVEN

FROM A GREAT distance, Norman Bayerd heard Elliott say, "My gawd, what brought it on?"

"Originally? A riding accident. I sent for his medical records after I treated his scalp wound. I suspected something like this from the lacerated tongue and cheek lining. There was no mention of epilepsy in the medical records, of course, but one of the encephalograph runs looked significant."

"And the change in the beam setting, all of the other things…"

"*Petit mal,* I suppose. It can pass unnoticed as only a slight lapse of memory. The psychological reasons for doing what he did are another matter. You'll have to look elsewhere for the motivation for that.

"Perhaps the code message is the clue?"

"There has to be a reason. The Artery is his whole life."

Yes, Bayerd thought, wading through darkness, *my whole life.* There was nothing that could force him to damage the Artery. It was the single thing he must leave behind after…

And then the memory came back.

The weeks of work over the new idea, the sudden realization that what he had found spelled the death of the Artery. How had he forgotten… The feeling of loss when he realized that it had all been for nothing...the sacrifice, the work. That the Artery was a useless toy, a vast clumsy makeshift answer, when the simpler solution had been before them all the time...

Who wouldn't have fled from the knowledge that his life had been useless?

ONLY... ONLY there was always a part of a man that demanded that he act in truth and honesty...and if he did not, that inner self would find a way...

He opened his eyes and sat up. He was in the dispensary, he saw, and Elliott and Beckworth had withdrawn somewhat from his bed. He saw that they hadn't removed his clothing.

"How long have I been out," he demanded?

"Fifteen minutes," Beckworth said, moving toward him. "Now lie down until it's time."

"Time for what?"

"We're evacuating the station in another ten minutes or so. Patel is going to reverse the Black Field. He has the engineering crew below making the modifications now."

Bayerd threw back the sheet they had draped over him and dropped to the floor.

"Get back in bed," Beckworth said.

"I've got to see Patel."

"No, absolutely not. You can't stop him anyway."

"No," Bayerd said, "I don't want to stop him."

"You're in no condition..."

"Please, Doc. This is important."

HE PUSHED past the medic and into the corridor. As he made his way to the metering bridge, he felt a kind of nervous strength flowing into his muscles. He found Patel on the bridge in the midst of confusion.

Patel had unbolted several of the control panels on the bridge consoles, ripping wire from the back and inserting hasty cross connections. He looked up as Bayerd entered and said, "Norm...get below. There's not much time."

"How are you going to keep the five stations phased until the last moment?" Bayerd demanded.

"It'll be done."

"How?"

"Manually. How else?"

"I thought so. Now, listen closely. You were right about the code message. It was from the computer section at Pelembang. I had it coded for the simple reason that I didn't want anyone at the station to know what I was working on."

"It makes no difference now."

"Yes it does," Bayerd said. "The problem had to do with the basic nature of the Black Field. The idea came to me and I was checking on whether it was workable."

"What problem?"

"THE SOLUTION was there all the time," Bayerd said. "We had the reverse field effect, releasing all that energy. We knew all about the micro-continuum the physicists had postulated, and how the energy that came from the reversed field was the energy that had been poured earlier into the micro-continuum. Don't you see? The micro-universe had a point-for-point congruency with our own universe. You can put energy into it and later take that energy out...*and you don't have to perform the operation at the same point.*"

Patel was suddenly laughing, his small frame shaking with mirth. "It was there all along," he said. "We've never needed the Artery."

"No," Bayerd said. "We can generate the power right on Pluto, shunt it via the Black Field into the micro-continuum, and draw on that power any place in the system."

"No—any place in the universe."

"Now," Bayerd said, "we've got the problem of the beam. Are you through up here?"

"Yes," Patel said. "The fields will have to be balanced manually on all of the stations in the Black Field up to the moment of reversal. I've wired the circuits into the controls in one of the Schrenk cubicles so we can use the c-cube transmitter on "S" level."

He looked at Bayerd and said, "*My* cubicle, Norm."

"No, this is my job."

"You've got your hands full, converting to the new system."

"That's a young man's job," Bayerd said, stepping close to him.

"Get out of here," Patel said. "There's only a few minutes." He turned and began to activate the board before him. As soon as the board was operating, Norman Bayerd reached into his pocket and found the revolver he had taken from Gilchrist. He reversed it and brought it down on Patel's head. He collapsed silently.

HE GRABBED the man by the shoulders and dragged him toward the hatch in the floor of the bridge. He was about to enter the hatch and pull Patel after him when he heard a noise below.

"Norm," he heard Beckworth yell, "come on. We've got to get away from the station within the next five minutes."

"Here," he yelled through the hatch and started to lower Patel's body. He felt Beckworth relieve him of the weight and he stuck his head through the opening.

"Get him to the lifeshuttle," he said. "This is my party." Before Beckworth could answer, he closed the hatch. Then he went to the console and finished the check that Patel had started. After a moment, a light glowed on a far panel and he knew that the shuttle with the men had left the station.

He flicked the switch that cut in the transmitter relay on the bridge and said, "This is Bayerd, calling the shuttle."

The speaker crackled and Patel's voice said, "Norm, why did you do it?"

"Sorry about the bump on the head," Bayerd said. "It's better this way though. Now give me the details on this setup just to make sure I've figured it out correctly."

AFTER PATEL finished speaking, Bayerd said, "All right. So we need some light. So we'll now burn the place down." He laughed half hysterically.

Then he said, "You'll be getting out of this system now, going to the stars."

"That's what we wanted all along."

"Now go home and have some more kids," Bayerd said. "Only don't name any of them after me. Name a planet for me."

And he cut the transmission. At five minutes to calculated contact time with the beam, he abandoned the bridge and hurried down to the Schrenk cubicle that Patel had modified. He laced himself into the harness and made the changes on the improvised board at its side, which initiated the changing polarity and the building instability of the Black Field. Then, as the bridge chronometer signaled two minutes to the board, he threw in the automatic system, keyed to the "strob" units on the skin of the station.

"There," he said at fifty seconds before zero, "the rest is up to you."

He pushed his head into the Schrenk face piece. "Look on my works, ye Mighty, and despair," he whispered, keying the unit.

FOR AN INSTANT he was in the body on far Pluto, poised on the edge of the Needle, looking down the precipice into the chasm far below.

He would fall into the great fissure, he saw, fall like a stone into the far depths at the instant the Artery ceased to exist.

Which was as it should be—the final irony.

He thought of the Artery, its vain glory, and those ancient kings of Egypt whose time-dusted eyes had looked upon their magnificent tombs.

Then he quickly switched to the body beyond the Plutonian Magnetic Lens, still holding static control of the body on Pluto.

He was surrounded with the debris of the wrecked ship but he was still moving at an incredible velocity. The last flare of energy from the colliding lens stations must have accelerated him, he thought.

It was then that he realized he was probably moving at a velocity greater than the escape velocity of the system.

That he was moving out to the stars.

While the Artery would signal his going in a blaze of light.

"A damned magnificent tomb," he shouted.

And the cold Plutonian rock of the Needle with that one fraction of his consciousness, and the other part of him that was moving out to the stars... All this dissolved in fire as the thing that was Norman Bayerd's life spark expanded in a wave of radiance until it seemed to encompass the universe in searing light and ceased to be.

THE END

If you've enjoyed this book, you will not want to miss these terrific titles…

ARMCHAIR SCI-FI & HORROR DOUBLE NOVELS, $12.95 each

D-31 **A HOAX IN TIME** by Keith Laumer
  INSIDE EARTH by Poul Anderson

D-32 **TERROR STATION** by Dwight V. Swain
  THE WEAPON FROM ETERNITY by Dwight V. Swain

D-33 **THE SHIP FROM INFINITY** by Edmond Hamilton
  TAKEOFF by C. M. Kornbluth

D-34 **THE METAL DOOM** by David H. Keller
  TWELVE TIMES ZERO by Howard Browne

D-35 **HUNTERS OUT OF SPACE** by Joseph Kelleam
  INVASION FROM THE DEEP by Paul W. Fairman,

D-36 **THE BEES OF DEATH** by Robert Moore Williams
  A PLAGUE OF PYTHONS by Frederick Pohl

D-37 **THE LORDS OF QUARMALL** by Fritz Leiber and Harry Fischer
  BEACON TO ELSEWHERE by James H. Schmitz

D-38 **BEYOND PLUTO** by John S. Campbell
  ARTERY OF FIRE by Thomas N. Scortia

D-39 **SPECIAL DELIVERY** by Kris Neville
  NO TIME FOR TOFFEE by Charles F. Meyers

D-40 **JUNGLE IN THE SKY** by Milton Lesser
  RECALLED TO LIFE by Robert Silverberg

ARMCHAIR SCIENCE FICTION CLASSICS, $12.95 each

C-10 **MARS IS MY DESTINATION**
  by Frank Belknap Long

C-11 **SPACE PLAGUE**
  by George O. Smith

C-12 **SO SHALL YE REAP**
  by Rog Phillips

ARMCHAIR SCI-FI & HORROR GEMS SERIES, $12.95 each

G-3 **SCIENCE FICTION GEMS, Vol. Two**
  James Blish and others

G-4 **HORROR GEMS, Vol. Two**
  Joseph Payne Brennan and others